UNBALANCED

ALSO BY D.P. LYLE

The Jake Longly Series

Deep Six

A-List

Sunshine State

Rigged

The O C

Cultured

The Cain/Harper Series

Skin in the Game

Prior Bad Acts

Tallyman

The Dub Walker Series

Stress Fracture

Hot Lights, Cold Steel

Run to Ground

The Samantha Cody Series

Original Sin

Devil's Playground

Double Blind

The Royal Pains
Media Tie-In Series

Royal Pains: First, Do No Harm

Royal Pains: Sick Rich

Nonfiction

Murder and Mayhem

Forensics for Dummies

Forensics and Fiction

*Howdunit: Forensics;
A Guide for Writers*

More Forensics and Fiction

*ABA Fundamentals:
Forensic Science*

Anthologies

Thrillers: 100 Must-Reads
(contributor); *Jules Verne,
Mysterious*

Island Thriller 3: Love Is Murder
(contributor); *Even Steven;*

For the Sake of the Game
(contributor); *Bottom Line*

UNBALANCED

A JAKE LONGLY THRILLER

D. P. LYLE

OCEANVIEW PUBLISHING

SARASOTA, FLORIDA

ISBN 978-1-60809-554-4

Published in the United States of America by Oceanview Publishing

Sarasota, Florida

www.oceanviewpub.com

10 9 8 7 6 5 4 3 2 1

ACKNOWLEDGMENTS

To my wonderful agent Kimberley Cameron of Kimberley Cameron & Associates for her always steady guidance, sound advice, unwavering dedication, and friendship. KC, you're the best.

To Bob and Pat Gussin, Lee Randall, Faith Matson, Tracy Sheehan, and the great folks at Oceanview whose dedication, professionalism, hard work, and creativity made this book better in so many ways.

To the fans who have allowed Jake Longly and crew into their lives and supported their adventures. You are the reason we writers write.

To Nan for everything.

CHAPTER 1

MY NAME IS JAKE LONGLY, it's Monday, and I'm bored. Not a common affliction for me. Not that I have a bunch of stuff to do, or need to engage in any specific activities, keep to some schedule, or even strain my brain with creative thinking. In fact, the opposite is true. On a typical day, I have little or nothing on my plate. As Nicole and Pancake are quick to point out. They're jealous that I have such an uncluttered mind. Regardless, doing nothing suits me, and I do nothing well. How could that be boring?

Back when I played Major League Baseball, fully scheduled days became the norm. During the season anyway. Which seemed to last forever. Not as long as the NBA, where they take a twenty-minute break before cranking up the next year, but the baseball season lingered long after my interest waned. I mean 162 games? Who came up with that number? Exhausting. Don't get me started on doubleheaders. Particularly, if I wasn't pitching either game. All day sitting in a hot bullpen with a bunch of dudes telling stupid jokes and embellished sexual escapades that recycled week after week. Worst of all, there was no place to stretch out and take a nap. Before fifty thousand fans. Not a good "team" image. I'd much rather be on the mound firing fastballs. That focuses your attention.

Back then, finding time to do nothing was no small task. Games, practice, meetings, press obligations, long flights, hotel ins and outs, dinners, drinking, and of course chasing the young female baseball groupies that collected in each city's popular bars filled every day. I get a headache thinking about it. How did I do that? I was younger and didn't know better, I guess. Now I do.

I own Captain Rocky's, a bar/restaurant on the sand in Gulf Shores, Alabama. A place I bought with the ridiculous money the Texas Rangers paid me to throw a baseball. I was a pitcher, and not bad at it. When you're a professional athlete, the team pays for everything so the funds that flow from your contract are cake icing. Unless you piss it away, as many of my teammates did, you ended up with a pile of cash. Like I did. So, I bought Captain Rocky's from Rocky Mason, its original owner.

Most people believe that running a restaurant is a twenty-four-seven endeavor, and that's true. Not in my case. More like zero-zero-zero. Carla Martinez, my manager, did all the work, which meant I had little to do. Except hang out at Captain Rocky's with Nicole and Pancake.

Their absence now the cause of my boredom.

Today I was on my own, so I passed the afternoon napping in a beach chair beneath a yellow Captain Rocky's umbrella. Perfect. For a couple of hours anyway. Then I became antsy, and bored.

That word again.

Pancake, my best friend since childhood, worked for my father, Ray, at Longly Investigations, a P.I. outfit Ray runs from his home not far down the beach. Pancake thrived on work. He enjoyed it much more than downtime, which he avoided. A mystery to me.

Nicole, my girlfriend, also wasn't around. Last night we stayed at my home rather than at her Uncle Charles' mansion out on The

Point. My place is nice; Uncle Charles' is insanely better. Like every other home out on Perdido Beach's Peppermill Road. This morning we slept in before hopping into Nicole's Mercedes SL and rolling over to one of our favorite beachfront cafes for an early lunch. Nicole then headed for her place to do some work. Another unpleasant word.

Nicole writes screenplays and has had a mega-hit movie titled MURDERWOOD and a couple of smaller film festival productions. She was working on a new project and had a Zoom meeting with a team of producers at Regency Global Productions, or RGP. Uncle Charles' company. He of the Ultra A-list with a shelf full of Oscars and Emmys.

She had asked if I wanted to go with her and hang out on the beach there, but I told her I needed to stop by Captain Rocky's.

"Why?" she asked.

"I own it," I said. "I have responsibilities."

She laughed as she pulled to a stop in front of my beachfront house. "Pancake must be coming by."

"No. He and Ray are into some case, and it's been giving Pancake fits. Some financial thing."

"That embezzlement deal they're working on?" she asked.

"That's the one. Pancake said it has umpteen moving parts."

"Umpteen? That's a lot."

"His new favorite word. He's used it umpteen times lately."

"Get out, Jake. I have work to do."

I climbed out. "I'll meet you at Captain Rocky's after your meetings are done."

"In time for happy hour."

She roared away. I climbed in my vintage Mustang and pointed it toward Captain Rocky's.

That was four hours ago. Long enough for boredom to creep in and bivouac.

I slipped on my shirt, snatched up my towel and sandals, headed across the soft, warm sand, and climbed the stairs to Captain Rocky's expansive and crowded deck. A good thing. Meant I could pay the rent.

On the way to my always-reserved corner table, I stopped and chatted with a few folks and waved to a couple of others. That little bit of schmoozing completed my work for the day.

Carla flopped in the chair across from me. "Poor baby."

"How so?" I asked.

"No one to play with." She shrugged. "It's what happens when everyone has a job and you don't."

"Sure I do. Didn't you see me stop and chat with the customers?"

She raised an eyebrow. "You must be exhausted."

"I am."

"I told Libby to bring you a margarita."

Libby Sagstrom, a newer hire, had been doing a great job. The customers loved her. So did Pancake since she brought him food without him having to order. She knew what he was hungry for, which in fact was a hefty amount of anything and everything, and had it in front of him almost as quickly as he could settle in his chair. A win-win.

"You're a stellar human," I said. "So is Libby."

Libby appeared. She placed a massive schooner of frozen green margarita in front of me. "Here you go, boss man." She smiled.

"Do you think that's enough?" I asked.

She shrugged. "Maybe. If not, there's more where that came from."

"You're a peach," I said.

"Better than a lemon." She gave a little wave and walked away.

"I have a pile of invoices and purchase orders," Carla said. "Want to look them over?"

"Probably not."

"Didn't think so. That's why I didn't bring them."

"You're a smart woman."

Carla glanced past me toward the entrance. "Speaking of smart women. Here comes your girlfriend."

"Which one?"

"Yeah, right."

I looked that way. Nicole wore black cargo shorts, which accentuated her long perfect legs, a tangerine cropped tee shirt that exposed her also perfect midsection, and a black baseball cap. She stopped and chatted with three guys, some of our regulars, laughed, and walked toward us. She was good at schmoozing too.

Carla stood. "He's all yours. I did as much as I could."

Nicole ruffled my hair. "My problem child." She indicated my drink as she sat. "I see you're off and running."

"Carla and Libby forced it on me."

"I'm sure." She tilted the long straw her way and took a couple of sips. "Good."

"You can finish it. Or get your own."

"I'd better eat something first."

Thirty minutes later we had finished some fish tacos and drained the schooner.

"Where's Pancake?" Nicole asked.

"Since it's near feeding time, I suspect he'll be along any minute."

Her cell chimed. She snatched it from the tabletop. "Speak of the devil." She waved the screen toward me, revealing the big red-head's smiling face. She brought the phone to her ear. "What's up?" She listened for a full minute. "We can do that."

We can? Several responses came to mind. I was too busy. I wanted another margarita. My stomach hurt and I didn't want to go to school today. A waste of breath, so I remained silent.

Nicole listened for another half a minute and then said, "We're on it."

Those three words—or is it four?—three-and-a-half?—are the bane of my existence. Whenever they fell from her perfect mouth, what followed was never good.

She ended the call. "Pancake needs us to do something for him."

And so it begins. Again.

CHAPTER 2

"WHERE ARE WE GOING?" I asked.

"It's nothing big, so relax," Nicole said.

She maneuvered her SL through the traffic along Perdido Beach Boulevard toward Orange Beach. A short drive from Captain Rocky's. It was nearing six thirty and the shadows of the high-rise condos that dotted the beachside lay long across the roadway.

"Where have I heard that before?" I asked. "Everything with Ray and Pancake is easy until it implodes."

With the SL's top down, the warm wind whipped around us. Nicole snugged her cap while wiggling past a delivery truck. "We're picking up some papers from an office near here."

"Pancake couldn't do that?"

She glanced at me. "He's busy. We're not."

"Yeah, but he gets paid for doing this stuff."

"What else did you have on your dance card today?"

"I own a business. I have duties and obligations."

She laughed again. "No, you don't."

"Maybe I needed another margarita."

"After the gallon you just knocked back, taking a break might do you good. Your liver will appreciate it for sure. This'll only take a few minutes."

"Bet it doesn't," I said.

"All we're doing is grabbing a stack of documents and taking them to Captain Rocky's. Pancake will meet us there."

"Now it all makes sense," I said.

"It does?"

"Pancake sends us on the mission so he can get to the menu quicker."

"He's a growing boy."

"He hit his limit long ago. If he grows any more, he'll wobble the planet out of orbit and we're doomed. A fiery death spiral into the sun."

"You're an idiot. You know that?"

"It's been said." I glanced at her. "By you. Just yesterday."

"Believe it." She slowed. "Here's our destination."

She waited for a break in traffic and then turned left into a parking lot that fronted a single-story tan building with a dark brown roof. A sign over the entry door read, "Orange Coast Realty." The small paved parking lot, lined with palm trees, held only a single vehicle, a white Cadillac Escalade.

"Is this for that embezzlement case?" I asked.

"Exactly. We're to see Carl Davis, one of the owners. He's accused his business partner, Mitch something, of skimming funds from the company accounts."

"I hate it when that happens."

"So does Carl Davis."

The SL's tires chirped as she jerked to a stop several slots away from the Escalade. "Wait here. I'll grab the papers."

"I'll go with you. I've spent too much time on my butt today and need to stretch my legs."

I climbed out of the car and scanned the area. A couple of hundred feet to my right, a business of some sort faced Perdido Beach Boulevard, and behind it a cluster of houses tucked into the sandy and scrub brush dunes. To my left, an open lot of more sand and brush, centered by a weather-chewed concrete pad. An abandoned construction project. I knew that beyond the real estate office were more dunes and then a spit of water known as Bayou Saint John. Its opposite shore lined with south-facing homes, most with docks and boats. None small or cheap.

The heat evaporated once inside the office; the AC cranked to arctic levels. Somewhere between refreshing and uncomfortable. The empty reception area, everyone gone home for the day, was so quiet that I could hear my sandals scrapping across the carpet.

"Mr. Davis?" Nicole called out.

No response.

We followed a hallway toward the back of the building, Nicole again calling Davis' name, getting no response. Three open doors revealed dark offices, while a single closed door sported a WC sign. Light spilled through a cracked open door at the end of the hallway. A door sign read "Carl Davis." Inside the large well-lit office, a comfy-looking leather office chair sat behind a desk topped with a computer and several folders and stacks of papers, but no Carl Davis.

"Hmm," Nicole said. "Maybe he's in the bathroom."

I moved further into the room. A shoe and a pant leg extended from behind the desk. I walked that way. A man lay on his back near the chair. He wore tan slacks and a navy blue polo shirt and appeared as if sleeping. Except for his pale gray skin and the dark hole near the center of his forehead.

"He isn't," I said.

"Oh my god," Nicole said, stepping up behind me.

I knelt and reached for his wrist. Not cold but cool, no pulse. No surprise there.

"Is he alive?" she asked.

I stood. "No. Call 911. I'll call Pancake."

"Let's get out of here first. The killer might still be here."

I needed no convincing. Once out in the parking lot, we each made our calls.

"They're on the way," Nicole said.

"Ray and Pancake too."

"What do you think?" she asked.

"I think someone had issues with Mr. Davis. If that's him."

"It's his office."

"Doesn't mean it's him."

"I suppose." She leaned against the front fender of her car and stared at the asphalt. "Do you think this has to do with the case Ray and Pancake are working?"

"That'd be a good bet." I shrugged. "Don't things like this always lead back to Ray?"

A black-and-white Orange Beach PD SUV rolled into the lot and parked at an angle. Two uniformed officers stepped out. The driver appeared young, mid-twenties, Hispanic, fit, with buzzed, dark brown hair. His partner was older, fortyish, with light brown hair and a well-trimmed mustache. Neither smiled, neither approached, remaining near their vehicle. The driver's hand rested on the butt of his service weapon at his right hip.

"I'm Officer Ed Moran," the older one said. "This is Officer Carlos Rivera. You the ones that made the call?" he asked.

"Yes," Nicole said.

"Dispatch said there's a body." Moran scanned the lot.

"Inside," I said.

"Anyone else inside?" Rivera asked.

"Not that we saw," I said. "But we didn't search the place. Once we found him, we hustled outside."

"Good move," Moran said. "Wait here."

The pair approached the door. Each pulled a weapon. Rivera pushed the door open. "Orange Beach PD," he shouted. "If you're in here, make yourself known."

No response. They disappeared inside, the door closing behind them.

"I'd feel better if Ray and Pancake were here," Nicole said.

"They will be."

"I hope Pancake's driving. Ray drives like an old lady."

"Says speed racer."

Nicole shrugged. "Is what it is."

"I just hope they don't arrest us."

"Why would they?"

"Whoever finds the body is automatically a suspect."

She gave me a headshake. "You watch too many of those cop shows."

The door opened and two officers walked toward us, a brown wallet in Rivera's hand, Moran's cell to one ear.

"Orange Coast Realty," Moran said. "One victim. Deceased. Looks like a single gunshot." He listened. "Okay. We'll mobilize the crime scene guys."

While Rivera made the call, Moran began the questions.

"You do business with Mr. Davis?"

"No. We stopped by to pick up some papers and found him."

"Papers?"

"My father, Ray Longly, asked us to pick up some documents for a case he's working on?"

Rivera had been eyeing both of us as he made the call, but now he focused on me, one eyebrow elevated. Uh-oh. What was that about? What did the person on the other end of the line say? Guilty feelings are funny. Not funny in a ha-ha way. More odd and uncomfortable. That look, the raised eyebrow, sent an electric current up my spine. I could see Nicole and me cuffed, doing the perp walk. Like on TV. I ran through everything we had done since we arrived. We were in the same room as a murder victim, dropping hairs and fibers and god knows what else. Our fingerprints would be on the door handle. Where else? I couldn't remember. As if that weren't enough to convict, I had touched the dead guy. They'd get my DNA, and I'd be cooked. No doubt. I wondered if Nicole would visit me up at Holman Prison. Maybe I did watch too many cop shows.

Officer Moran reeled in my imagination when he asked, "Ray Longly, the P.I.?"

"That's him," I said.

"What kind of case?"

"Something to do with this realty company is all we know."

Rivera slipped his phone in his pocket. "Lieutenant Peters is on the way." Then to me. "Are you Jake Longly?"

"I am."

"I thought I recognized you." A half smile. "I'm a big baseball fan. I remember you."

My heart rate dropped. I wasn't going to jail after all. Well, maybe not. Rivera's look was simply recognition after I mentioned Ray.

"Baseball?" Moran said.

"Jake here was a pitcher for the Texas Rangers," Rivera said. "A good one."

"*Was* being the operative word," I said.

Moran didn't seem impressed. For sure not interested in small talk. "So you came by to get some papers for your father, the P.I., and found the victim?"

"That's right."

"But you know nothing about it?"

"It was a favor for Ray," Nicole said. "I sometimes work for him."

"Doing what?"

"Whatever he needs."

Moran considered that. "You see anyone else around here?"

I shook my head. "No."

"Okay. Lieutenant Peters will have more questions, so hang tight. We need to secure the scene."

We watched as they began to unroll and hang the crime scene tape.

"I told you," I said.

"Told me what?" Nicole asked.

"That this would be neither quick nor easy. That anything Ray touches goes to hell in a hurry."

CHAPTER 3

A BLACK UNMARKED Ford Taurus sedan turned into the lot, followed by a black-and-white patrol unit. A woman exited the plain wrapper. Five-five, trim, light brown hair pulled into a short ponytail. She wore jeans, a tucked white shirt, and a navy blue jacket. She eyed us as she approached Officers Moran and Rivera, who had just finished hanging the crime scene tape and now stood near the office entrance. The two officers from the black-and-white joined the huddle. Moran did most of the talking, too far away for me to hear his words, but the woman looked our way a few times. She gave a final nod and headed toward us.

"I'm Detective Brooke Peters," she said, hooking one thumb in her belt.

"Jake Longly," I said. "This is Nicole Jamison."

"You found the body?"

"We did," I said.

"You were here to pick up some papers for Ray Longly?"

"Yes."

She nodded.

"Do you know Ray?" I asked.

"Only by reputation." She shrugged. "People say he's a stand-up guy."

"He is," Nicole said. "He and Pancake both."

"Pancake?"

"His partner. His name's Tommy, but everyone calls him Pancake."

I could see that Pancake's name intrigued Peters—it did everyone. She probably had a few questions but apparently decided to let it slide for now. She said, "Tell me the story."

I did. How we got a call from Pancake and he asked us to stop by here to grab some papers. The front door unlocked, the inside empty, and no one answered when we called out. How we saw light at the end of the hallway and walked that way, calling Carl Davis' name, getting no response. How we found him on the floor. A gunshot to his forehead.

She glanced toward the entry door, back to me. "Did you see anyone else?"

I shook my head.

"No other vehicles nearby?"

"Only that one," I said, pointing to the white Escalade parked in a slot near the front door, facing a sign that read, "Carl Davis." The adjacent slip had a similar sign that read, "Mitchell Littlefield."

Peters nodded. "Rivera ran the plates. It belongs to Carl Davis. One of the owners."

"He's the dead guy?" I asked.

"According to the ID in his wallet."

I stared at her, but said nothing.

"Did you know him?" Peters asked.

"No. Until an hour ago, I'd never even heard of this business."

She digested that for a few seconds. "These papers? What were they?"

"I don't know. Ray and Pancake are on the way, and they can tell you more."

"Did you disturb or touch anything in the scene?"

"The front door handle." I glanced at Nicole. "And I touched the man."

"Oh? Why?"

"To make sure he was dead." I sighed. "I know better, but we needed to know whether to call the medics or you guys. He was cold and had no pulse."

"That's when we came back outside and called," Nicole said.

"Okay. Wait here. I need to take a look."

She disappeared inside along with Moran, while Rivera and the other two officers loitered near the two cruisers. Their heads turned in unison as Pancake's black Chevy Dual-cab rolled into the lot and stopped near us. The massive vehicle rocked as Pancake and Ray stepped out.

"What's going on?" Ray asked.

I ran through the story again.

"You sure the victim is Carl Davis?"

"That's what Detective Peters said."

"He was shot?" Pancake asked.

"Looked that way to me. Center of his forehead."

I saw movement at the entrance and then Peters exited the building and walked toward us.

"Ray Longly?" she asked.

"That's me," Ray said. "This is Pancake."

"I'm Detective Brooke Peters." Peters eyed Pancake. Not easy since Pancake's six-five had a good foot on her. "I understand you knew Mr. Davis."

"He was a client," Ray said.

"What was the nature of your work for him?"

"I can't say," Ray said. "There's a privilege involved."

"Your client is deceased," Peters said. "I'm not sure that privilege still exists."

Ray nodded. "You're certain the victim is Davis?"

"His office, his driver's license in his pocket, on the floor next to his desk." She shrugged. "Yeah, I'm pretty sure."

"But not one hundred percent."

"The ME will make it official when he arrives, if that's what you're asking."

"Or I can ID him," Ray said.

She hesitated a beat, then said, "Follow me. Don't touch anything."

"I know my way around a crime scene."

"I figured, but had to say it."

Off they went.

"You guys okay?" Pancake asked.

"Another day with Ray," I said.

Pancake grunted.

"He can turn a simple errand into a cluster . . . well, you know."

"Yeah, don't use the F word around me," Nicole said. "Because I'm very fucking sensitive and might get my feelings hurt."

Okay, okay, I got the point.

"Ray didn't do this," Pancake said.

"Yet this kind of stuff follows him around."

"Nature of the business," Pancake said. "Besides, how do you know the chaos isn't following me and not Ray?"

He had a point.

Everyone was making points today.

Pancake smiled. "Or maybe it's you that attracts the weirdness."

I started to say that I had spent the day stretched out on the beach, not bothering anyone, not making any waves, and then had a relaxing margarita with Nicole when he sent us on this errand. But why bother? I let his assessment lie there.

Ray and Peters returned.

"It's him, isn't it?" Nicole asked.

Ray nodded. "No doubt."

"So?" Peters said.

"Carl Davis hired us a couple of days ago. Friday, to be exact. To look into some financial irregularities at the company. Orange Coast Realty." He waved a hand toward the building. "We found that a significant amount of money had evaporated."

"How significant?" Peters asked.

Ray nodded to Pancake.

"Three hundred and eighty thousand so far," Pancake said.

"Evaporated as in embezzled?"

"Looks that way. Everything I found points toward his partner, Mitchell Littlefield."

The dude with the other marked parking space. I knew that embezzling could lead to murder when the scheme fell apart. Was that what this was? Littlefield learned he had been exposed and decided to take care of Davis? How that would solve his problem escaped me but then a lot of things do. Or so I've been told.

"You uncovered all this since Friday?" Peters asked. "Over the weekend?"

"It's what we do," Pancake said.

Translation: It's what Pancake does. He can get into places and effortlessly hoover up information faster than anyone I've ever known. No sweat. I get exhausted thinking about it.

"You sure about all this?" Peters asked.

Pancake gave her one of those mischievous Pancake smiles. "I can go through everything with you."

Was that a glint in the eyes of the good detective?

"You can bet on it."

"Whenever you want."

"Tomorrow," Peters said. "Right now, I need to finish processing the crime scene and make the death notification."

"He has a daughter," Pancake said. "Savannah. She and her fiancé, dude named Dustin Hobson, live with Mr. Davis. Out on Ono Island."

"Anything about them I should know?"

Pancake shook his head. "We only know their names and living situation. We've never met them. As far as I know, they weren't aware of our involvement. Carl Davis wanted it kept under cover until we finished our investigation."

"Interesting," Peters said. "So, he didn't want to alert his partner that he was snooping around for dirt on him?"

"Exactly," Ray replied. "At first, he didn't understand what he had. Just bookkeeping discrepancies. Once things started drifting in Littlefield's direction, he didn't want him to know what he was doing or what he had discovered. He hired us for a fresh set of eyes and to continue exploring the discrepancies. He felt it was best if he kept it more or less arm's length."

"Makes sense. Is there a Mrs. Davis in the picture?"

"Passed a few years ago," Ray said. "We can give you Davis' address."

"Thanks. That'd help."

"You going to talk with Littlefield, the partner?" Pancake asked.

"You bet."

"Are you going to confront him about the embezzling?" Ray asked.

Peters considered that for a beat. "Not yet. Not until I see everything you have and get a firmer grasp on it all."

"I think that'd be the smart move," Ray said. "Keep him calm and cooperative."

"I'll track him down after I speak with the daughter."

"We have his address too," Pancake said.

Peters smiled. "You're a fountain of useful information."

Pancake matched her smile. "One of my many talents."

The big guy had a way.

CHAPTER 4

ONO ISLAND IS NOT for those with thin wallets. The fatter the better. A million bucks won't get you much. Five and a half miles long, exclusively residential with only 800 homes, and divorced from Baldwin County governance, it's a private enclave that residents jealously guard.

Bound to the north by Bayou Saint John and to the south by Old River, it lies east of Orange Beach and extends more into Florida than Alabama, requiring the state dividing line to make a swoop around its eastern end before bending back west and dropping south to the Gulf of Mexico just west of the famous Flora-Bama bar. A rowdy place for locals and tourists who love live music and alcohol. Ono Island residents can enjoy, or be annoyed by, the music on any given night. Particularly during summer when tourists swell the population of the entire Gulf Coast to the bursting point.

Back in the early 1800s, President James Monroe seized Ono Island and other lands from the Spanish, who owned what ultimately became Florida, by declaring the land part of the Louisiana Purchase. Take that. The resulting line divided the U.S. from the Spanish Territory, and later Alabama from Florida. So, Alabama got Ono Island and Florida got the remainder of the panhandle.

The island has a single connection to civilization, Ono Island Way, a bridge near its western end that extends from Highway 182 on Perdido Key to Ono Boulevard, the island's main east–west artery.

Detective Brooke Peters, left hand shielding her eyes from the lowering sun, rolled over the bridge. She turned right, the sunlight now painting her rear window a bright orange. She had left Moran and Rivera to handle the crime scene crew and the ME's folks. Stuff she found tedious. She only cared about their results, not how they teased it out.

She felt anxious and needed to move. The embezzlement angle amped her up like a double espresso. It put a twist on Carl Davis' death. No evidence of a break-in or a robbery and Davis shot in the face meant he likely knew his killer. The missing money dropped Mitchell Littlefield right into her crosshairs. She was already chewing on how she would approach him, what questions she'd ask.

But first things first. Notify the daughter and see what info she could share. The one thing she knew for sure is that she wouldn't bring up the missing funds. Unless the daughter did. Did the daughter know what her father suspected? Had he confided in her? According to Ray Longly and his partner, Pancake— what's up with that?—Davis wanted to keep everything on the down-low. Did that include his daughter?

She found the Davis home near the middle of the island. Large and expensive, with a generous circular drive lined by palm trees. She rang the bell. An attractive young woman greeted her and introduced herself as Savannah Davis. When Peters said she needed to chat with her, concern settled over Savannah's face. She led Peters into an open-concept living area. A wall of windows faced south, revealing a swimming pool and a flagstone sun deck, palm-lined, with lounge chairs and a table topped by a bright lime-green umbrella. Beyond, a long dock ended at an impressive boathouse.

"What's this about?" Savanah asked.

Before Peters could answer, she saw a young man rise from the pool, grab a towel, and begin drying himself.

Savannah followed her gaze. "That's Dustin. My fiancé. Maybe he should be here."

"That would be good," Peters said.

Savannah walked to the door, opened it, and ushered the man inside. She introduced Peters to Dustin Hobson.

"What's going on?" he asked. The concern on his face matched Savannah's.

"Let's take a seat," Peters said.

Savannah hesitated before moving to the sofa. Dustin indicated his damp bathing trunks and said, "I'll stand." He rested a hand on Savannah's shoulder.

Peters took a chair across from the couple. "There's no easy way to do this. Your father, Carl, was shot and killed in his office."

Savannah recoiled. Her hand flew to her mouth. Her face paled. She wavered on the sofa. Dustin now ignored his wet swim suit, stepped past her, and dropped to the sofa, his arm going around her shoulders, steadying her.

"What?" Dustin said.

"A couple came by to pick up some papers and discovered him in his office."

"Oh god," Savannah said. Her shoulders collapsed forward and her face disappeared into her hands as sobs racked her body. "I don't believe this." Her hands dropped into her lap and she looked at Peters. "Are you sure?"

Peters nodded. "I'm sorry."

"Did the couple do this?"

"We don't think so," Peters said.

"Then who?" Savannah's eyes glistened. She appeared frantic and confused. "Who would kill my father?"

"We don't know, but we're early in our investigation."

"When did this happen?" Dustin asked. "I just left there an hour ago."

"Was he alone after that?"

"Yes. He was when we left."

"We?" Peters asked.

"Me and Mitch. We left together."

"Mitchell Littlefield?" Peters asked.

Savannah nodded. "He's Dad's partner in the real estate business."

Well, well. Money missing, Carl Davis dead, his partner one of the last people to see him alive. Motive and opportunity. The means, the gun, was an easy one. Guns along the Gulf Coast came and went, and moved around with alarming frequency. Hell, she knew dozens of places she could buy one, no questions asked.

"Carl still had work to do," Dustin said. "He said he'd be along in an hour. Before dinnertime."

"What did you do after you left?" Peters asked.

"Let's see. I called Savannah to see if she needed anything from the store. I swung by and picked up milk and hamburger meat to grill tonight. I came home and then swam my laps."

"You do that every day?"

Dustin nodded. "Most days, yes."

"Mr. Littlefield left at the same time you did?" Peters asked.

"He pulled out of the lot right in front of me."

"You don't think Mitch had anything to do with this, do you?" Savannah asked.

"Do you?"

"No. No way."

"You agree with that, Dustin?"

"Yes. Of course. Carl and Mitch are best friends. They've been in business together for years."

"They go back to their college days," Savannah said.

"How long have you worked at the agency?" Peters asked Dustin.

He glanced at Savannah. "A year?"

She nodded her agreement.

"We graduated from Vandy last year and then moved here."

"We live with Dad right now," Savannah said. She choked back a sob. "Or did."

"He's been great to us," Dustin said. "We're getting married in a few months and we've been saving for our own house. He's let us stay here in the meantime."

A weak smile cracked Savannah's tear-streaked face. "He likes us here. Ever since Mom passed, he's been by himself. Having us around has been good for him."

"A win-win," Peters said. Then to Dustin she asked, "Any issues at work? Problems with employees or his partner?"

Dustin shook his head. "None. We're busy, do a lot of deals, but it's really a small business. Only a dozen agents."

"So it's a happy family?"

"The office is pretty drama free. I can't imagine any of the employees are involved."

"What about other people?" Peters asked. "Any issues with anyone? A disgruntled client or former employee?"

"Not that I can think of," Dustin said.

"What about someone in his social circle?"

Savannah considered that, gave a slow headshake. "No. No one. Dad got along with everybody."

"Not everyone, it seems," Peters said.

"Did someone break in?" Savannah asked. "Something like that?"

"Doesn't look that way. The office was open, he was at his desk."

Savannah massaged her temples. "This is a freaking nightmare." She looked at Dustin. "I don't know what to do. I mean, what do I do?"

Dustin tugged her tightly against him. "We'll be okay. Let's take it one step at a time." He looked at Peters. "Is there anything we need to do?"

"Not right now. The coroner is of course involved, and once he completes his work, you can arrange the funeral."

"How long will that be?" Savannah asked.

"A day or two at the most."

"I don't believe this." Savannah fought back tears. "None of this makes any sense."

"These things never do," Peters said. "But we'll do everything we can to discover who's responsible."

Savannah took a deep ragged breath and let it out slowly. Her lips trembled as she spoke. "Do you have any idea who might've done this?"

"Like I said, we're just getting started so we have no real suspects. But we will."

Savannah looked at Dustin. "This isn't real, is it?"

Dustin squeezed her shoulder. "Unfortunately, it is."

"Who would do this to Dad?"

Dustin shook his head. "I have no idea." He glanced at Peters. "The front door was unlocked when Mitch and I left, but that's not unusual."

"Any other entrances?" Peters asked.

"There's a back door. It's locked because no one ever uses it. There's nothing but sand and scrub brush behind the building. A couple of the employees go out there to smoke. It's not allowed in the office. But they're pretty good about locking it when they come back inside."

"Pretty good?" Peters asked.

"Yeah," Dustin said. "They've failed to do so at times." Then he seemed to think of something. "There're security cameras. Two of them. They face the parking lot and the front entrance."

Peters had seen them while at the scene. She nodded. "That could help."

"You're thinking some stranger came in and did this?" Savannah asked.

Peters shrugged. "It's a possibility."

"There're several houses nearby," Dustin said. "There's also a construction site just west of the office. There hasn't been anyone there and as far as I can tell no work has been going on for at least six months."

"We'll check it out." Peters stood. "I'm sorry for your loss. Thanks for talking with me under the circumstances."

"Of course," Savannah said.

"I'll leave you two alone," Peters said. "I'm sure I'll have more questions as we move along with our investigation. If you think of anything, no matter how insignificant it might seem, call me." She placed a card on the coffee table. "Anytime. Day or night."

CHAPTER 5

I NEEDED A DRINK. Actually lots of drinks. The image of Carl
Davis on the floor, cold and dusky, a black hole in his forehead,
refused to fade. I'm not sure why it nagged me. I'd seen dead guys
before. Part of bouncing in and out of Ray's world. But Davis was
different. He seemed a normal, everyday guy, working late, taking
care of business, and then bang, gone. Looked that way to me. I
saw no evidence of a struggle, or a knock-down, drag-out fight, or
even a burglary. Rather, Carl sat at his desk and someone pumped
a round into his head.

The old cliché about life being short and unpredictable came to
mind. As well as Pancake's common adage: eat dessert first
because you never know what comes next. God forbid Pancake
missed dessert. Talk about grumpy.

I needed to unwind and unsee the entire scene. An impossible
task, so a little medicinal help might be in order. Plus, a bit of
Nicole. That usually cleared the clutter from my brain.

"Are you okay?" Nicole asked.

"Yeah. Why do you ask?"

"You're quiet. That's not like you."

"I am?"

"You are."

"Just thinking about what we stumbled across."

"That's what I mean. What's going on?"

After we left the realty office, the crime scene, we drove to Nicole's place.

Ray and Pancake, after agreeing to meet with Detective Peters in the morning, returned to Ray's house to organize the info they had on Carl Davis. We had stripped down to nothing, grabbed a bottle of tequila, and hopped in the hot tub. We watched the western sky darken from blue to a deep indigo. A cooling breeze rose from the Gulf. Nicole nestled against me, a leg flopped over one of mine. She felt warm. Didn't she always?

I didn't respond to her question, so she said, "Talk to me."

I knocked back my third tequila. "Carl Davis. Seeing him on the floor, dead as hell. It doesn't seem fair."

"Are murders ever?"

"No. But he was a normal guy, going about normal business, and someone executed him."

"Sure looked that way."

"Not like the other corpses Ray's left in his wake. Not a criminal, or a murderer, or a stalker, or an organized crime thug. Ray's usual debris."

She laughed. "*Debris*? That's an odd way of putting it."

"It fits."

"It does." She grabbed the tequila bottle and poured each of us another shot. "You're quite the poet."

"I must've missed the rhyme."

"Not all poetry rhymes."

My fourth shot went down easy. "Neither does life sometimes."

She gulped her shot, set the glass aside, and straddled my lap. "Worry about that later. Right now, let's enjoy life."

Great idea. We splashed the water for a while, then staggered inside and rumpled the sheets. Now I stretched out on the bed, recovering, Nicole nestled in the crook of my arm.

"Feel better?" she asked.

"Much."

The master bedroom French doors stood open and the cool breeze intensified. I tugged the comforter over us. Nicole settled more deeply against me. We lay in silence for several minutes.

"You know Ray and Pancake will dig into this," Nicole said.

"Of course they will."

"Even though their client is dead, and I guess they have no real standing any longer, Pancake won't let this go."

"No, he won't." I gave a soft laugh. "I feel sorry for Detective Peters."

"My impression is that she can take care of herself."

"But can she take care of Pancake?"

"You sensed that, too," Nicole said.

"I did."

"The boy has a way." She kissed my chest. "So do you."

"Flattery will get you everywhere."

"I know. But then, you're easy."

Hard to argue with that. Particularly with Nicole's naked body plastered to mine.

"We'll end up getting dragged into it," I said.

She raised her head and looked at me. "Are you okay with that?"

"This time, I think I am."

"Well, look at you. The big bad P.I."

"That's me. Longly, Jake Longly. P.I. extraordinaire."

"I wouldn't go that far." She laid her head on my chest. "But I'm glad you're onboard this time."

Onboard? The *Titanic* came to mind. Every time I got dragged into Ray's circus, I kicked and complained and moaned, but this was different. I wanted, really wanted, to find out who killed Carl Davis. I don't know why. Hell, I didn't even know him. Had never heard of him until a few hours ago. Had never seen him until he lay before me on the floor of his office. Dead as dead can be.

Why? Who? Part of me wanted to quash that curiosity, but the bigger part had to know.

What the hell was wrong with me?

CHAPTER 6

MITCHELL LITTLEFIELD'S HOUSE occupied a corner lot in an upscale Orange Beach neighborhood. A short, wiry man with shaggy gray-touched light brown hair and a clean-shaven face answered Brooke Peters' knock. He wore baggy gray shorts, an oversized blue tee shirt, and an annoyed expression. He held a glass of amber liquid and ice cubes. Bourbon or scotch most likely.

"Mr. Mitchell Littlefield?" she asked.

"Yeah."

"Sorry to bother you at this hour, sir. I'm Detective Brooke Peters, Orange Beach Police Department."

"Detective?"

She held up her gold shield. "Can I speak with you?"

"What's this about?"

"A few questions. It should only take a few minutes."

Or longer, depending on his answers.

He hesitated and then, "Sure. Come in." He stepped back and ushered her through the doorway.

The interior AC cool, neat, and well appointed. The entry foyer led into an open high-ceilinged living room. He sat in a chair at one end of a low coffee table, where he placed his drink, the ice tinkling against its side. She caught a whiff. Scotch. She tugged her small notebook from her pocket and sat on the sofa.

"What can I do for you, Detective?" he asked.

"You're co-owner of Orange Coast Realty? Right?"

"That's correct."

"Along with Carl Davis?"

"That's also correct."

Confusion and concern spread across his face. Did he fear that his embezzling had been discovered? Or was it something else? Like him shooting Carl Davis in the face?

"I'm afraid I have some bad news," Peters said.

His eyes narrowed, his shoulders elevated, but he said nothing.

"Mr. Davis was murdered."

Littlefield visibly recoiled with a sharp intake of air. "What? When?"

His shock seemed sincere. A true reaction, or did he know this was coming and prepare for it?

"He was found around six thirty," Peters said.

His eyes widened, his forehead creased, and his jaw slackened. "I don't understand. I just saw him at what? Five thirty?"

"At the office?"

He nodded. "Yes. He was at his desk."

"Which is where he was found. On the floor beside it. He'd been shot."

"Jesus." He stared at the floor, his face now a couple of shades paler. His gaze rose back to Peters. "Who did this?"

"We don't know. Tell me about when you last saw him."

"He often works late. I collected several documents from him. A commercial property we're brokering. I was reading through them when you knocked."

That explained the annoyance. Maybe the scotch, too.

"Did he seem normal? Everything routine?"

"Yes."

Peters scratched a note. "Besides the property, did you talk about anything else?"

He gave that a few seconds thought. "No. Dustin came in and . . ." His eyebrows elevated. "Savannah? Does she know?"

Peters nodded. "I just left their house. I talked with her and Dustin."

"Oh god. She must be devastated." Now his shoulders sagged as if drained of all the strength. "She and Carl were so close. She was his only child and he worshipped her. And her him. Even more so since his wife, Martha, passed a few years ago."

"She was shocked and saddened," Peters said. "But overall, she handled it well. For now anyway."

"I need to call her."

"Just a few more questions."

"Of course."

"So, Dustin came in the office. What happened then?"

"He had a stack of papers for Carl. Like me, he was heading home so we left together."

That jibed with what Dustin had said.

"Did you see anyone else around?" Peters asked. "Anything odd or out of place?"

"No. All the office staff had already left. Only Carl's SUV was in the parking lot. Everything was quiet. Normal."

"You and Dustin left together," Peters said. Not really a question.

"That's right. He pulled out of the lot right behind me."

Exactly as Dustin had said. Corroboration or conspiracy? Did they innocently end their day, head home, and leave Carl to the mercy of the killer? Or were they in on it and now delivered their mutual scripted alibi? She possessed no way of knowing if either, or neither, of those scenarios was true, but nothing was off the table.

"How's the business doing?" Peters asked. "Any financial or other issues?"

His forehead creases flashed deeper, then relaxed. He shook his head. "We're doing great. In fact, exceptionally so."

"Any employee or client issues?"

"Not that I know." He appeared thoughtful, gave a slow nod. "We did fire a salesman a few months ago. Actually, it's been a year now. Time flies, I guess. He wasn't performing well and had issues with a couple of clients. Or them with him would be more accurate."

"What sort of issues?" Peters asked.

"If you wanted to be kind, I guess you'd say he was overly zealous. Pushy and demanding. Intolerant. Made some potential buyers uncomfortable." He opened his palms. "He could be surly and impatient. We don't do things that way. No hard sales. We prefer a low-key approach."

"A company policy?"

"You could say that. It's not specifically written down, but everyone knows that's the way they must conduct themselves."

"But this guy didn't?"

"I'm afraid not. We talked to him a few times. Both me and Carl. But I guess he wasn't capable of altering his stripes. So, we let him go."

"What's his name?"

"Gary Wayne Frawley."

Peters scribbled the name in her notebook. "Do you know where he is?"

"I heard he got a job with an agency in Fort Walton Beach. Uh . . . uh . . ." He snapped his fingers. "Seaside. Seaside Realty."

Peters added that to her note. "Anyone with a beef with Mister Davis?"

"Not that I know. Or can even imagine. Carl's a good guy." He sighed. "We've been friends since college. Started the company together. A long time ago."

"You two still get along?" She smiled to soften the question, but not too much.

"We've never had issues. Mainly because our visions for the company were in lockstep."

Except for the possible embezzling thing, Peters thought. But broaching that subject would wait until she had more information. Which hopefully Ray Longly could supply. Any confrontation right now would put Littlefield on alert, make him defensive, maybe shut him down completely. Evidence came from questions and answers and she wanted him talking. Casual like.

"So, to be clear, you last saw Carl when you and Dustin left the office together, you saw or felt nothing out of place, and you have no idea who could've done this?"

He nodded. "That's correct. Maybe with the exception of Gary Wayne. But to be honest, I don't see him doing this. He might've been irritating but I never saw any real aggression from him. Nothing threatening or anything like that."

"Not even when he was fired?"

"He wasn't happy. No doubt about that. But he seemed more depressed than angry. Even despondent. As if disappointed in himself."

"Anyone else you can think of?"

Littlefield gave that a moment. "Not right now. But then my brain isn't working very well at the moment. I still can't believe this."

"Understandable."

"Let me give that some thought. I'll let you know if I think of anyone."

"That'd be good," Peters said. "One more thing. I saw a pair of security cams out front. Do they work?"

"They do."

"Are those the only two on the property?"

"Yeah. There's not much behind us. Just some scrub brush and sand dunes."

"I'll need a copy of today's video."

"No problem. I'll get someone to do that in the morning."

"The back door?" Peters asked. "Is it always locked?"

"Usually."

"What does that mean?"

"A couple of our employees smoke. They go out back for a cigarette break. So it's often open during the day. The last person to leave is supposed to lock it." He shrugged. "It doesn't always happen though."

Her survey of the scene revealed no evidence of forced entry. No jimmied door or broken windows. "Do you have keys for that door? Do the employees?"

"They do exist, but to be honest, I don't know where they are. Probably in some drawer or filing cabinet. No one comes and goes that way, except the smokers, and at night it's locked from inside so we never really need a key."

That made sense. Unless someone wanted to sneak back in and avoid the front cameras. Someone who had access, knew where the key was kept, and knew that Carl Davis would be there alone. Or someone, like the man before her, unlocked the door before he left. And circled back.

Was Mitchell Littlefield the killer? Was what Ray Longly and his partner, Pancake, said about the missing money true? A motive, no doubt about that. Guns are easy to come by, and he would know how to get in and out without being seen. Through the door he unlocked before he left. The problem, of course, isn't what you know, or suspect, it's what you can prove. How could she put him at the scene with a gun in his hand?

What happened to the gun? Where was it? Surely, he wasn't stupid enough to keep it. She damn sure didn't have enough evidence to garner a search warrant for his home so if he stashed it here somewhere she had no way of knowing. If he dumped it, which anyone with a brain would've done, plenty of options existed. Dumpsters and the plethora of swampland and lakes in the area. Not to mention the Gulf of Mexico.

After offering her condolences, giving Littlefield her card, and telling him she'd call if she had more questions, Peters left him standing on his front porch. As she climbed into her car, Littlefield disappeared inside, pulling his front door closed. She sat for a couple of minutes, running through her conversations with Savannah and Dustin, and Mitchell Littlefield. Everything lined up. No red flags. Except for the embezzlement angle. Which was huge and would need to be addressed sooner rather than later. After she gathered more evidence. And then there was Gary

Wayne Frawley. Maybe Littlefield was correct and he was simply depressed, despondent, and disappointed. But those emotions can swirl into a soup of anger. And revenge.

She cranked up her car and gave Littlefield's home a final look before pulling from the circular drive. Was the entire Gary Wayne story a deflection? A head fake? Get her looking elsewhere and not at the guy stealing from the company? Not like she hadn't seen that before. Criminals often drop little crumbs in an attempt to direct the flow of the investigation in any direction away from them.

She always found the beginnings of an investigation frustrating. When you didn't know all the potential players and hadn't yet teased out the dynamics among them. Who was who and who had the strongest motive? Who had the opportunity and the balls to commit the crime? Shooting someone in the face was no easy task. Not like TV.

Did Mitchell Littlefield have the huevos to look his partner and friend in the eye and shoot him? Three hundred and eighty thousand dollars was a lot of hand-steadying motivation.

CHAPTER 7

I AWAKENED TO DARKNESS, only to find my head burrowed beneath my pillow. I tossed it aside. Dawn fell through the window. I rolled over. No Nicole. Then I heard the shower running. What time was it?

As I attempted to slide out of bed, I found the sheet wound around one leg. More evidence of a fitful night's sleep, underscored by the tequila-induced fuzziness in my head. The image of Carl Davis had invaded my dreams several times, precluding any chance of reaching a restful REM zone.

Pancake's fault. Had he run his own errands, Nicole and I wouldn't be in the middle of this. I would be rested and ready to go. Go do what, I wasn't sure, but likely it wouldn't include a dead guy. More like coffee and burritos at Captain Rocky's. Relaxed and civilized. My kind of morning.

But now? This ordeal was just beginning. Nicole, and inexplicably me to a lesser extent, had her teeth in this, like a dog with a new chew toy. She wouldn't let go. Not in her nature. Something Ray and Pancake knew how to feed. I think they wound her up just to annoy me.

I wanted to burrow back under the covers and let it evaporate. A pipe dream so I unwound my leg and sat up. The shower fell silent. I lifted my jeans from the floor and slipped them on. A steam cloud followed Nicole from the bathroom. She wore black thong panties and nothing else. Coffee and burritos could wait.

"You're up early," I said.

"It's six. That's not early."

"Oh. It feels more like midnight."

"That's because you wrestled your pillow all night. Not to mention I had to fight you for the covers."

"Sorry."

"No problem. I kicked you a couple of times, which settled things down. For a while anyway."

"No wonder I'm sore and achy."

"Poor baby." She ruffled my hair. "Jump in the shower and get ready."

"For what?"

She gave me the look that said I should know something. I wasn't sure what. In fact, I didn't have a clue. My brain stumbled through bits and pieces of last night, mostly disjointed and indistinct images. If I did, or ever had, possessed that bit of whatever knowledge Nicole referred to, I filed it somewhere I couldn't access.

Nicole apparently sensed my struggles. "We're seeing Ray and Pancake at seven. Detective Peters wants to talk to us."

"*Us* as in Ray and Pancake, or as in me and you?"

"All that."

"Why?"

"Let's see. Ray and Pancake are investigating the embezzlement and we found the body."

Oh, yeah. Did we ever. It made sense that Peters had more questions for us. Cops are that way. They want to hear the same story over and over and repeat the same questions to see if anything changes. Pancake explained it once. The truth is easy to remember, but making crap up takes effort and the so-called facts are harder to keep straight. As he put it, it was like juggling bowling balls with butter on your fingers.

He of the food metaphors.

The fact that Detective Peters wanted to talk with us wasn't a surprise, but it wasn't something I looked forward to. The prospect made me search my mental files, the same jumbled ones as before, for what we had told her yesterday. If we stumbled on any detail, I was sure we'd be under hot lights, fielding questions like a pepper game.

Me, of the baseball metaphors.

After a quick shower, we headed out. Nicole did well driving until the traffic congealed along West Beach Boulevard. She fidgeted, tapped the steering wheel with her fingers, cranked her neck one way and then the other, looking for a chance to pass, either left or right. A road shoulder merely an extra passing lane to her.

"In a hurry?" I asked.

She glanced at me. "How many times have you ridden with me?"

I knew better than to answer.

"I'm always in a hurry," she continued.

"Stop and smell the roses."

"The only aroma I detect is exhaust fumes."

Which was true. The top of her Mercedes SL was down and two vehicles ahead a pickup needed a valve job, evidenced by the blue-gray cloud billowing from its exhaust pipe. If a breeze existed or if we weren't in stop-and-go, five-miles-an-hour traffic, the fumes might not have amped up my hangover headache.

Despite becoming woozy from the fumes, we made it to Captain Rocky's where we grabbed a bag of breakfast burritos and made it to Ray's right at 7:00 a.m. Detective Brooke Peters' unmarked black Ford Taurus sedan joined Ray's 1966 black Camaro SS and Pancake's black dual-cab Chevy pickup. Nicole's white SL broke the color theme.

Ray's deck table overlooked the Gulf and offered plenty of room for the five of us. After accepting one of the burritos and taking a bite, saying they were good, Peters didn't waste time. First order of business a recap of what Nicole and I had seen yesterday. Turned out to be less stressful than I imagined. The retelling of our story satisfied her so I guessed we made no glaring errors. At least she didn't pull her weapon and tell us we had the right to remain silent. Ray added that he had asked us to pick up some papers but that we didn't know anything about the case or exactly what the papers were.

"Sorry you had to see Mr. Davis," Peters said.

"Jake had a rough night," Nicole said. "For some reason, it bothered him."

"And you?" Peters asked Nicole.

"I'm tougher than he is." She laughed.

"True that," Pancake added, speaking around the remnants of his second burrito.

Peters smiled, then looked at Ray. "Tell me how you became involved with Carl Davis and this suspected embezzlement."

"He contacted us last Friday," Ray said. "A guy we did some work for a couple of years back referred us to him. That case involved financial shenanigans at an investment firm. Davis explained he had discovered several accounting irregularities he didn't understand, but it looked like money was missing or being diverted or something of that nature. He admitted he wasn't a numbers guy. He said at Orange Coast Realty, he handled most of the day-to-day and the hiring and firing and the marketing while Mitchell Littlefield handled the financials. For the most part anyway."

"Which means Littlefield could've manipulated the books," Peters said. Not a question.

"Exactly," Pancake said. "Carl said they started the business a couple of decades ago. They'd been friends since college and set up shop right after graduation. They worked hard and built the company into one of the most successful along the coast."

"He told us they, he and Littlefield, had never had issues," Ray said. "When he discovered the numbers weren't adding up, his initial concern was that an employee had been siphoning off money, but when we pressed him, he admitted no one had access to the cash. Only he and Littlefield."

"He wasn't thrilled with the prospect that his partner was taking advantage," Pancake said. "In fact, he seemed to be personally injured." Pancake opened his palms. "He hoped we'd find nothing and that he was mistaken."

Peters raised an eyebrow. "But you found something?"

Pancake nodded. "Not one hundred percent sure yet. The papers Carl collected for us might've nailed things down, but right now it's just suspicious."

"We need those documents," Ray said.

"Unfortunately, they're evidence in a homicide," Peters said.

"Since you have both the originals and the duplicates, giving us the copies wouldn't contaminate the evidence," Ray said.

Peters considered that. "Maybe so, but that would take time to sort out."

"With those copies, we might be able to help you here," Pancake said.

Peters raised an eyebrow.

"I know you have financial crime folks, but we have a head start." Now Pancake's eyebrow elevated. "And we won't cost you time and money."

"I'm sure you have limited staff and funds," Ray added. "If we can finish our investigation and wrap it in a bow for you, wouldn't that help?"

"It would. So long as it remains admissible."

"No problem," Pancake said. "We deal with evidence rules all the time."

"I understand," Peters said. "In an ideal world, I agree with you and would welcome any help. Hell, I would've brought them with me today. But, in the end, it's my boss's call. He'll have to okay it. He's not one to bend the rules, so he might not." She smiled. "I'll broach the subject with him."

"Here's my concern," Ray said. "I think you'd like to keep Littlefield in the dark about you knowing the embezzlement angle. At least until you have all the evidence. Keeps him from destroying evidence, and lawyering up."

"That's crossed my mind."

"The sooner we analyze those documents," Pancake said, "the less time he'll have to do either."

"I assume you're thinking Littlefield is the prime suspect," Nicole said.

Peters nodded. "Motive, means, and opportunity."

"Wouldn't that mean he knew Carl Davis was on to his embezzlement scheme? That being a motive for Carl Davis' murder."

"To cover his crimes," I added. "So, wouldn't he already be destroying evidence?"

"If he's smart," Peters said. "We took the relevant files from Davis' office, so if Littlefield has copies, shredding or burning them or whatever wouldn't help. It would, in fact, be a strong indication of guilt."

"But we don't know he's guilty," Pancake said. "Of any of it. Not the theft and not the murder."

"No argument there," Peters said.

"We can help," Ray said. "With the financial angle. If your people go through the files and see that the ones intended for us aren't originals, then releasing the duplicates to us would preserve the evidence. We could press on and perhaps give you the information you need."

Peters considered that.

"There might be another way," I said.

Peters looked at me. "How?"

"Savannah. Carl Davis' daughter. Won't she inherit half the company now?"

"Maybe," Peters said.

"We haven't looked into it yet," Pancake said. "Inheritance wasn't an issue until yesterday."

"The corporate docs will be part of my subpoena," Peters said. "As will Carl Davis' will."

"Work on your subpoena," Ray said. "But before you pull the trigger on it, let us talk with Savannah and tell her what we know and what we think she should do. See how she wishes to proceed. She might give us, both of us, what we need without going through the court."

"This is no longer a financial case," Peters said. "It's a homicide investigation."

Pancake smiled. "The two are married to one another, aren't they?"

Peters' gaze never left the big guy. I caught the look. No doubt she was intrigued.

"We aren't interested in stepping on your toes," Ray said, "but since her father hired us, we're obligated to let her know what we've uncovered."

"She could pass that on to Littlefield if you do."

Ray shrugged. "She could, but we'll impress on her the need for discretion here."

"She didn't know her father hired us," Pancake said. "Part of the deal. Everything done off the record." He unwrapped a third burrito and took a bite. "I agree with Ray. Carl's death might terminate our agreement, but we're obligated to tell her everything we unearthed. Who knows, she might hire us to continue our investigation."

"And make my life miserable?" Peters said. A half smile lifted one corner of her mouth.

Pancake tilted the burrito toward her. "We'll do our best not to bump up against you."

Interesting word choice. Punctuated by the lingering gaze between the two. Pancake the dog.

CHAPTER 8

NICOLE AND I followed Pancake's pickup to an impressive Ono Island address. Multimillions worth of impressiveness. Two-stories, modern, lots of glass, and a generous circular drive. Half a dozen steps led to the double entry doors.

The woman who answered Ray's knock was on a good day a very attractive brunette with bright green eyes. This wasn't one of those days. She looked worn and fractured, with dull, red, and swollen eyes and disheveled hair. She wore a gray, oversized Black Rifle Coffee Company hoodie. I knew from Pancake's research she was Savannah Davis and that she was twenty-three. She appeared older, but the murder of your father will do that.

"Savannah Davis?" Ray asked.

Her gaze traveled to me, Nicole, then Pancake. She didn't step back, but her weight shifted that way. "Who are you?"

"I'm Ray Longly. I want to talk to you about your father."

"What about him?"

"Can we come in?"

She hesitated, indecision in her eyes. I got it. Why would she let strangers into her home? Less than twenty-four hours after her father's murder by someone as yet unknown? A personal tragedy that infused her entire being. I imagined a dark room and a huge pillow to hug and cry into were at the top of her wish list.

"Honey, who is it?" The male voice came from behind her.

"I don't know."

A young man appeared, moved in front of Savannah in a protective posture. "Can I help you?"

"You must be Dustin," Ray said.

"And you are?"

"Ray Longly. Private investigator. Carl Davis hired us."

"What?" Savannah asked. "Why would he do that?"

"Maybe we can sit down, and I'll explain everything."

"Will this take long?" Dustin glanced at his watch. "I need to get to the office. We open up in a half hour and things are going to be chaotic."

I could see it. Employees coming in, expecting a normal day, and wham, they're hit with Carl's murder. In his office, in that very building. Like a sharp slap to the face. Confusion and anxiety and fear front and center. Were they safe? Were their jobs safe? What happens now?

"Only a few minutes," Ray said.

Dustin hesitated, then nodded. "Sure."

We gathered in the living room. Twenty-foot south-facing windows exposed a pool, an expansive deck, and a wooden dock with a boathouse that jutted into Old River. The morning sun gilded a half dozen palm trees.

"First," Ray said. "I'm sorry for your loss."

Savannah nodded as her fingers wound into a knot.

"Your father was a good man. I liked him."

"You knew him?" she asked.

"Briefly. Enough to know what kind of person he was."

"You're a private investigator?" Savannah asked.

"I am." Ray waved a hand. "We are. Your father hired us a few days ago to investigate some troubling financial matters for him."

Dustin's expression changed. If not more tense, at least concerned. "What matters?" he asked.

"It's delicate," Ray said. "Before I get into it, you need to understand that this conversation can't leave this room. Not yet."

Tears welled in Savannah's eyes. "You're scaring me. I don't understand any of this."

Dustin wrapped a protective arm around her. "So, you're the one," he said to Ray.

That surprised me. Apparently, Ray and Pancake too.

"You knew?" Ray asked.

"A little."

"Will someone talk to me?" Savannah asked. "Tell me what the hell is going on." A tear escaped, slid down her cheek. She wiped it away with the back of one hand.

Pancake leaned forward, elbows on his knees. "Just so you know, Brooke Peters, the detective in charge of the investigation, the one that came by and talked with you last night, knows we're here. So, we aren't talking out of school."

Now Savannah swiped the back of her hand across her nose, sniffed. "So what's so secret?"

"No one else can know what we're going to tell you," Pancake said. "I think you'll understand once we bring you up to date."

Savannah straightened her shoulders, sniffed again. "Okay."

"Your father believed that someone was embezzling from the company. He hired us to find out who and how."

Savannah's head swiveled right and left, her gaze catching each of us, not locking on anyone before returning to Pancake. "What? Who?"

"Everything we've uncovered so far points to Mitchell Littlefield," Ray answered.

Savannah recoiled. "Mitch? No way."

"Honey, let them finish," Dustin said.

She leaned away from him, looked in his eyes. "You knew about this?"

He nodded. "Not the details, but yes."

"Why didn't you tell me?"

"Carl swore me to secrecy. He didn't want you to worry about it. He didn't want anyone else knowing what he suspected. Not until he was sure."

"How long have you known?"

"Three days," Dustin said. "Well, four now. Carl called me into his office, told me what he suspected, and that he'd hired someone." He glanced toward us. "He didn't say who." Back to Savannah. "All he told me was that it appeared that money was missing and that he'd hired someone outside to look into it."

"He told you this?" Savannah said. "That Mitch was stealing from him?"

"He suspected Mitch, but didn't really know. He hoped not, but I felt he knew it had to be." Dustin now looked at us. "The way things work at the agency is that Carl handled the business and marketing and client information while Mitch handled most of the financial side. Carl liked people more than he liked numbers. My college degree was in accounting and then I got an MBA. That, plus Savannah and I getting married was the reason he confided in me."

"How long have you worked there?" I asked.

"A year. I've known Carl for three years." He glanced at Savannah. "We met in college. Dated for a couple of years. That's when I met Carl. Savannah finished her undergrad degree at the same time I finished my MBA. We moved in with Carl, and I began working for him then."

"We're getting married in a few months," Savannah said.

Dustin offered her a smile. "We are. When Carl called me in and told me of his suspicions, he said that with my financial background, he was going to turn much of this over to me. Once you guys had finished your work and he knew what was what and who was who." He shrugged. "I guess he wanted to know who he could trust first."

"So, if Littlefield was guilty," I said, "and prosecuted, you'd be ready to take his place?"

"Carl and I never talked about that, but he, Mitch too, for that matter, involved me more and more in the financial side of things." He shook his head. "I have to say, I can't picture Mitch doing this. Not to Carl. They were close."

Savannah nodded. "Like brothers."

"Money makes people do crazy things," I said.

Savannah stared at each of us. "Are you saying Mitch killed my father? Is that what this is about?"

"Look," Ray said, "we don't know if any of this is true. The embezzlement or whether Mitch was involved in Carl's death or not. But I think you can appreciate the need to keep this low key for the time being."

"What do we do now?" Savannah asked.

"Deal with your loss," Nicole said. "Grieve and recover."

Tears filled Savannah's eyes. "I don't see how right now."

Nicole stood and moved to sit next to the shaken young woman. She took Savannah's hands in hers. "It won't be easy, but you will. The cliché is that time heals all wounds. It's a cliché because clichés are true."

Savannah exhaled a long breath. "It just hurts so much."

Nicole squeezed her hands. "If you need anything, even if it's just to talk, or cry on someone's shoulder, call me."

"That's so kind of you."

"It is," Dustin said. He looked at Savannah. "I hate it, but I must get to the office. So many things to do, clients to take care of. But I'm uncomfortable leaving you alone."

Savannah swiped her eyes again. "You go ahead. I'll be fine."

"Before you go," Ray said. "I want to underline the importance of keeping our involvement and the embezzlement issue to yourselves."

Savannah and Dustin nodded in unison.

"Detective Peters will include that in her investigation, of course. It goes to motive. We'll work with her on what we already know. But, given the circumstances, our relationship with your father has ended. I felt obligated to tell you what we had uncovered. You need to know that all our discovery will be handed to the police."

"That makes sense," Savannah said. "But I have a question."

"Fire away."

"Can I hire you to continue doing what you're doing?"

Ray nodded. "You could."

"If my father trusted you, so do I. There can't be too many people looking into who murdered my father."

"We appreciate the vote of confidence," Pancake said. "But piggybacking on what Ray said, as far as anyone else knows, we're looking into the murder. Nothing more. No hint that we're also following a money trail."

"So Mitch won't get spooked?" Dustin asked.

"Exactly," Ray said.

CHAPTER 9

SEASIDE REALTY WAS the end unit of a strip mall just north of Highway 98, which Fort Walton Beach tagged the Miracle Strip Parkway—cute. Next door a Mexican restaurant and down the way a dry cleaner, an office supply store, and a women's boutique, the window manikins suggesting it sold swim and beach wear. The lot only half filled, so Brooke Peters found a slot near the front door. Rich aromas from the restaurant greeted her as she stepped from her car. Had she not had that burrito earlier at Ray Longly's place, she might've veered that way.

Inside, a reception counter to her left, a waiting area to her right. The decor, cheaper and less plush than that at Carl Davis' Orange Coast Reality, but not outdated or tired.

"How can I help you?" the young woman seated behind the counter asked, her smile genuine.

"I'm looking for Gary Wayne Frawley."

"Do you have an appointment?"

"Sort of," Peters said. She extended her shield. "I'm Detective Peters. Orange Beach Police Department."

The girl's smile collapsed.

"Relax," Peters said. "I just need to ask him a few questions."

Recovering, somewhat, the young lady picked up her phone, punched a couple of numbers, waited, then said, "Gary Wayne, there's a detective here to see you." A pause. "I don't know." Another pause. "Okay." She hung up. Her smile returned, more forced than genuine this time. "Down the hall. Third office on the left."

Frawley stood as she entered. He had a couple of inches on her five-five and a good eighty pounds more bulk. They shook hands and he sat. A concerned—or was it fearful?—expression took a foothold on his round face, one that his uncomfortable smile couldn't hide. He wore a plaid shirt, blues, greens, and browns. His longish brown hair needed combing, washing too. His face showed a scattering of acne scars, many covered by his wedge-shaped sideburns.

"I'm Detective Peters, Orange Beach Police Department."

Frawley said nothing; didn't ask her to sit.

She did anyway, in the straight-back wooden chair that faced him.

"Let me guess," he said. "This concerns Carl Davis."

Not what she expected. "So you've heard about his death?"

"Everyone has."

"How'd you learn of it?"

"When I came in this morning, everyone was buzzing." He folded his hands on his desktop. "Carl Davis is a heavyweight in real estate along the coast. It's big news."

"I understand you worked for him."

"I did, and he fired me. Rather, Mitch did. But nothing happened around the office without Carl's approval." He stared at her. "I assume that's why you're here."

"Why did he fire you?"

"A bunch of bullshit."

"Want to explain?"

"They said I wasn't good with customers. Didn't fit their cor-porate image. Bullshit." He waved a hand. "I'm doing okay around here."

"Did you have specific issues with any of the clients?"

A smirk broke across his face. "A couple. What I call time wast-ers. Lots of showings, questions, contingencies, and, in the end, not interested in buying." He forked his unkempt hair back. Didn't help. "I think it came down to one old blue-hair. A demand-ing and whiney old lady. I suggested she go somewhere else."

Peters got the picture. She would've fired this arrogant prick too.

"So customer service wasn't your forte?"

His eyes narrowed. His jaw flexed. He checked himself and his smile returned. This one gravitating toward smug condescension. "I guess I don't appreciate people wasting my time."

Which Peters took as an implication that she was doing exactly that. Fuck him. "What do you know about his murder?"

"Nothing. He was shot in his office. Sometime last night. That's it."

"Any idea who might've done it?"

He shook his head. "None."

"Not you?"

He gave a soft laugh. "Why would I? I have nothing to do with Carl Davis anymore."

"I understand you were angry when you got fired."

"Of course I was. You would've been too. It was a bunch of trumped-up bullshit."

He liked that word. Probably viewed the entire world as BS. Everyone and everything. Did he see so much BS in Carl Davis that he killed him? She possessed little doubt that Frawley was unhappy and angry and didn't play well with most people. But was he a stone-cold killer? Could he look someone in the eye and pull the trigger? He seemed soft, but how much did it take to discharge a firearm?

"Where were you last night?" she asked

"And so it begins?"

"What's that?"

"The interrogation. At least you didn't bring the hot lights and the rubber hose."

She wished she had.

"We're talking with many people," Peters said. "Those who knew Carl, worked for him, had issues with him. Or who he fired." She waved a hand. "This is part of that."

"So this is a friendly chat?" Another smirk.

Was he trying to piss her off or was he inherently a dick? She smiled. "I hope so."

He gave a disgusted shake of his head. "You realize they fired me over a year ago? Don't you think if I was going to do something stupid, I would've done it back then?"

"Did you? Do something stupid?"

"No. And I don't like you suggesting otherwise."

"I'm not suggesting. I'm asking."

"Sounds accusatory to me."

She shrugged. "Sorry you feel that way." No, she wasn't. "But again, where were you last night?"

"What time are we talking about?"

"Let's say between five and seven."

"With a friend."

"What friend?"

"I'd rather not say."

She could play the game. "I'd rather you did."

"Do I need an attorney?"

"Do you?"

He hesitated. She feared he'd invoke his rights, which would put her out the door with nothing to take away. Nothing concrete anyway.

"No," he said. "I've got nothing to hide."

"Except the name of your friend?"

"It's delicate."

Bingo. A lover. One with entanglements.

"Most secret liaisons are," Peters said. "But this one's important."

He rubbed his nose with the heel of one hand as if stifling a sneeze. "I don't see how."

"Right now, you're a suspect." He started to speak, but she held up a palm to silence him. "You and Carl Davis had issues. He fired you. You were angry. Sometimes anger festers and then erupts." She cocked her head. "I've worked murders with less motivation. Where we are isn't all that far from Carl Davis' office. You know the place, the layout, where he would be, when he would be alone."

"That's bullshit."

She sensed angry heat rising in him. Good. Say something stupid, you smug prick.

"Motive, means, and opportunity can seem like BS. Until it's not."

He leaned forward, shoulders elevated, elbows on his desk, fists balled. Trying to look imposing. He was too pudgy to pull it off.

She continued. "In these types of investigations, everything and everyone is considered. Suspects come and go. If you want to go, make that happen with a reliable alibi. One that puts you far from the scene at the time of the murder. If you have such a person, now would be the time to play that card."

Grasping the situation, he seemed to deflate.

She ramped up the pressure. "Otherwise, I'll have to keep digging into your life." Another smile. "Like you, I don't like my time wasted and don't enjoy chasing dead ends. I'm sure you don't want me sniffing around your private world either. No telling what might come up. But it's my job and so there you go. If you can eliminate yourself and show me you're clear of this, we can both move on down the road."

He settled back in his chair. She loved this part of any investigation. When the suspect felt cornered, and squirmed, and hemmed and hawed, and found no graceful way out the door.

"I can't," he said.

"So, she's married."

He didn't hide surprise well.

"This isn't my first investigation," Peters said. "I've heard this story more times than I care to remember. The denying, the delaying, the bargaining, but in the end, the alibi comes forward and life goes on. So, cut through the bullshit, as you like to say, and let's get on with it."

"We were together. In a motel. From four until around nine."

"Who and where?"

He sighed. Shook his head. "I have to talk with her first and see if she will do it."

"It you want the heat off your back, convince her to talk with me."

"I had nothing to do with Carl Davis' murder."

"Prove it and we'll both be happy."

CHAPTER 10

I WALKED RAY and Pancake out to Pancake's truck while Nicole remained inside with Savannah, comforting her. We watched as Dustin backed from the garage, gave a brief wave, and drove away.

"That worked out well," Ray said. "Her hiring us keeps us in the game."

"Allows us to keep following the money," Pancake said.

"I thought you said Mitchell Littlefield skimmed it," I said.

"I said it looked that way. No smoking gun yet. There is one, but it'll take a little more time to uncover it. Like where did the money go and how did it get there? Things like that."

No doubt that Pancake, who was like a truffle-seeking boar, would dig it up. Once he locked on to something, get out of the way. He approached work like he did a plate of ribs. Scorched earth, leaving behind only skeletal remains.

"I'm sure Detective Peters will appreciate that." I smiled at him.

He gave me that Pancake flat stare. "She just might."

"While you're doing all these favors for her," Ray said, "charm her into giving up the files we need."

Now Pancake smiled. "Gladly."

"What about us?" I asked.

"Look at you," Pancake said. "Hopping on the team bus for a change."

"I'm not on the team. Or the bus."

"Sounds that way to me."

"I want you and Nicole to help Savannah through this," Ray said. "Help her cope with her loss. Also, see what else she might know about her dad and his partner that might help us. She's known Littlefield her entire life. She might give us something we can use."

"Like what?"

"We won't know until we see it. So, get her talking and listen to everything she says. Even little things can be important."

"Will do," I said.

Which more or less put me on the bus.

I watched them drive away and then went back inside. Nicole and Savannah remained on the sofa where I had left them. Savannah seemed even smaller and more fragile than she had just minutes ago. The weight of her father's death a heavy burden, dragging her shoulders down. Her face pale, drawn, fingers still wound into a knot in her lap.

As I sat, Savannah said, "Yeah, maybe he's been distracted lately. Like something's out of sorts."

"Who?" I asked.

"Her father," Nicole said.

"For the past month, maybe a little longer," Savannah said, "he's been more preoccupied. Not a lot and not something that jumped out. Until now, anyway. Looking back, maybe whatever was bothering him was more intrusive than I noticed."

"Does he get that way often?" I asked.

She gave that a minute, then said, "Sometimes. The trials and tribulations of running a business. Things would come up, things that impacted the agency, and he would fret over them." She glanced out toward the pool and held her gaze as if visualizing something. "Thinking back, this was different. He wasn't so much agitated as he was . . . I'm not sure what the right description would be. Maybe sad, disappointed, depressed." She shook her head. "I can't put my finger on it, only that he was different." She looked at her clasped hands. "I wish I had paid more attention."

"He never said what was bothering him?" Nicole asked.

"No." Another headshake. "Dad never talked about those kinds of things. If something was out of sorts, he fixed it. He never wanted to bother anyone with his issues."

"Did you sense any problems between him and Littlefield?" I asked.

Her gaze dropped to the carpet. "I still can't believe it's true. That Mitch would steal." She sighed. "Or worse, that he killed my father." She looked at me. "But, no, I sensed no issues between them. Of course, Dad would've kept that to himself."

"He felt he could handle everything on his own?" I said.

"He was old school that way."

"Can I ask you something?" Nicole said. "It's a bit sensitive."

"Sure." Concern flashed across Savannah's face.

"Was your father seeing anyone? A girlfriend or something like that?"

"No." She glanced at her folded hands. "Not that I knew." She looked up. "And I think I would." A weak smile appeared. "Part of me wanted him to move on from Mom's death and part of me feared the day he would. I guess I felt it would be a betrayal of my mother."

"It's life," Nicole said.

"I know it's silly. Mom's been gone for two years, and yet, I still miss her every day. I can't seem to shake it. I also know it's not fair to Dad. Wasn't fair. He knew I was hurting and that he could do nothing about it. Though he tried. I think in the end he figured it would simply take time." She sighed. "It has. Two years now." She exhaled through puffed cheeks. "I feel guilty. Like my inability to give up, to forget, to move on, might've prevented him from exploring his own possibilities."

"It's possible he wasn't ready, either."

"I suppose that's true." Her eyes glistened. "I hope that was the reason, and it wasn't my immaturity." She sighed. "Why are you asking this? Did you uncover anything like that?"

"No," Nicole said. "It's the way this all went down. He was shot in his office. After hours. That suggests the killer knew the layout, his routine, and could get close to him. These things are often domestic in nature. A scorned lover is one scenario."

Savannah absorbed that. "I guess it's possible. That could also explain his preoccupation." She looked at me, then Nicole. "But, honestly, I don't know where he'd find the time. His life bounced between work and here."

I refrained from pointing out the obvious—that real estate agents do most of their work outside the office. A *showing* could camouflage a *rendezvous*.

CHAPTER 11

THE TRAFFIC ON the bridge leaving Ono Island thickened to a crawl. Nicole wasn't happy. She muttered things like, "Who taught this idiot to drive?" She indicated a lowered Honda with a loud and raspy exhaust note. "This guy needs a new muffler, and driver's ed."

I chose not to respond. Why spin her up more than she already was? Instead, I called Pancake.

"What's up?" I asked.

"Where are you?"

"Leaving Savannah's and coming your way."

"Abort that mission," Pancake said. "Meet us at Carl Davis' office for a chat with Mitchell Littlefield."

"Why?"

"I'll explain later." He disconnected the call.

"Change of plans," I said. "We're meeting Ray and Pancake at Carl's office. They want to talk with Mitch Littlefield."

"We're invited?" Nicole asked.

"He insisted."

"This will be fun."

Probably not. I wondered if Mitch kept a gun in his office. It would be so Ray if small arms fire entered the picture. Or large arms fire. I could see Mitch barricaded in his office with an AR15 blazing, screaming, "You'll never take me alive."

Okay, so I have a vivid imagination, and watch too many cop shows. But on the other side of the ledger, this is Ray we're talking about.

Reaching the end of the bridge, Nicole whipped onto Perdido Beach Boulevard toward Orange Beach. The lighter traffic still not sparse enough for her.

"This planet has too many people," she said.

"It does," I agreed.

"What is it? Over seven billion now?"

"Something like that," I said.

"Half of them are on this road."

"Not that many."

"This dude in the Honda with the busted muffler is more than enough."

"I don't think it's busted," I said. "I think he bought it that way."

"Where's a rocket launcher when you need one?"

The Honda possessed the audacity to turn in the same direction we did, trapping us behind him. Not for long. Nicole whipped past him on the right, the Mercedes' suspension doing a great job smoothing out the bumpy sand and gravel shoulder. He blasted his horn. Nicole accelerated, and flashed him a wave out the open top.

The traffic thinned, and we made it to Orange Coast Realty without terrorizing anyone else. Nicole swerved into the lot, and, tires chirping, jerked to a stop next to Pancake's truck. Ray and Pancake climbed out. We did too.

"What's the plan, boss?" Nicole asked Ray.

When Nicole said things like, "What's the plan?" or "We're on it," or anything that ended with "boss," nothing amusing followed. History had a troubling way of repeating.

"A chat with Mitchell Littlefield," Ray said.

"All of us?" I asked. "Won't that make him feel ganged up on and defensive?"

"That's the plan," Pancake said. "Let him know we're sniffing around. Apply a little pressure. Stress makes folks say stupid stuff."

Well, I tried. The hope was that pointing out that all of us might not be the best plan and that Nicole and I could be elsewhere might get us out of this powwow and off to someplace fun. Like Captain Rocky's, or Nicole's place, or anywhere away from Ray's shadow.

"So he's not expecting us?" Nicole asked.

"Nope," Pancake said. "We wanted to catch him cold. A heads-up would give him time to think about things and create some clever answers."

I guessed that if you wanted to tilt someone off balance, that made sense. Unless it backfired. Littlefield might feel threatened and refuse to talk. But then, such a refusal might suggest he had something to hide, which would be an answer of sorts.

"I'm curious how he'll react to us," Ray said. "If he's the bad guy here, if he killed Carl, he'd expect police involvement. Our appearance will be a curveball. Might shake him up. All four of us will show how seriously we're taking this. Crank up the pressure."

I didn't know Mitch Littlefield yet, but part of me felt sorry for him. I wouldn't relish Ray and Pancake in my face. I mean, Ray has that no-nonsense, no-BS, military attitude, and Pancake can block out the sun, literally, making everything seem dark and threatening.

"Remember," Ray continued. "We're looking into the murder and helping the police. Not a word about money."

The receptionist said that Littlefield wasn't in and was at a nearby property with a client. A ray of hope. Maybe Nicole and I could leave. Instead, we walked down to Dustin's office, finding him on the phone. We waited until he finished his call and hung up.

"That was Savannah," he said. "She's not happy that I didn't tell her about Carl's concerns. But I explained it was Carl's wishes and not mine."

"Is she okay with that?" Nicole asked.

"Yeah. She knows, knew, her dad. He did things his way." He looked at Nicole. "Thanks for talking with her. It helped her deal with this."

"I simply offered a shoulder," Nicole said.

"Exactly what she needed." He sighed. "I feel guilty being here and not with her right now. But I have a couple of deals ready to pop and I have to take care of them."

"Life goes on," I said.

That's me, the philosopher. A modern Descartes. Without all the science, math, and geometry stuff.

"Fortunately, it should only take a couple of hours and then I can get back home." Dustin's brow creased. "What brings you by?"

"We wanted to talk to Mitchell, but he's out of the office."

"He had to run over to a commercial property we're selling and go through a few things with the buyer. It's a minor issue and nearby so he should be back in a few minutes."

"I need to remind you," Ray said, "outwardly we're looking into Carl's murder. Not the money."

"I know," Dustin said.

"Do you know if Carl had anything in his office that might help with our investigation?" Ray asked.

"It's possible," Dustin said. "Carl was big on redundancy. He kept both hard copies and digital files of almost everything. But the police loaded a bunch of boxes out of his office and locked down the rest. I'm not sure how much longer that'll be the case, but right now it's a no-go zone."

"Standard procedure," Ray said.

"How are the employees handling this?" I asked.

"They're shaken. Confused. Like the rest of us. Not sure what the future holds or who's in charge. Exactly what you'd expect."

"Who is in charge?" Ray asked. "Officially?"

"I guess Mitch and Savannah now."

"Savannah?" I asked. "Was she part of the partnership agreement?"

Dustin nodded. "I don't know of all the details, but I do know that when Carl retired or passed, his half of the company was to go to her. He and I talked about it several times over the past few months. He was bringing me more and more into the workings of the business. Not just selling, but the nuts and bolts of running the operation. Since Savannah and I are going to get married, he planned that one day I'd take his place and he wanted me prepared." He hesitated, smiled. "That's so Carl. Always prepared."

"A good lesson to learn." Ray glanced at me. "One everyone could use."

Ray missed few opportunities to fling darts in my direction. As misguided as they were. What did I have to prepare for? I spent my days at Captain Rocky's or stretched out on a beach chair in its shadow. The restaurant cranked out a profit without me doing anything. Thanks to Carla. She's the one that needed to be prepared. I only needed a beer and some sunscreen.

"Oh, sorry, Dustin. I thought you were alone."

I turned. A man stood in the doorway. Middle-aged, thin, unkempt brown hair, graying at the temples, gray slacks, and a forest green polo embroidered with a white BMW logo on the left chest.

"Mitch," Dustin said. "Come on in."

So this was Mitch Littlefield. He appeared normal, more like a college professor than a killer or an embezzler. He offered a gracious smile and a firm handshake.

"They're private investigators," Dustin said.

"Oh?"

Concern wrinkled Mitch's forehead. Fear, or guilt? Now he looked more like an embezzler, but still not a murderer. Of course, during my episodic dips into Ray's world, I had encountered several killers who appeared average, vanilla. Even Florida serial killer Billy Wayne Baker carried a benign vibe.

"Savannah Davis hired us to look into her father's murder," Ray said.

"I didn't know," Mitch said.

Ray smiled. "It just happened."

"What about Detective . . ." He struggled to recall her name.

"Peters," I said.

"Yeah. Does she know you're involved?"

"She does," Pancake said.

Not the whole truth and nothing but the truth. Yes, she knew Carl Davis had hired us, and yes, she knew we had talked with

Savannah, but no, she didn't know that Savannah hired us to parallel her investigation. Or that we were here to talk with her prime suspect.

Listen to me. *We?* Ray and Pancake, maybe Nicole, but not *we*.

"She seems tough and by the book," Mitch said. "I'm surprised she's pleased with your involvement."

Pancake smiled. "We charmed her."

"If you have a few minutes, Mr. Littlefield, we'd like to talk with you," Ray said.

Littlefield hesitated, glanced toward the window, then said, "Sure. Let's go down to my office." He offered a smile, somewhere between genuine and forced. "And pease, call me Mitch."

CHAPTER 12

WE LEFT DUSTIN to his work so he could finish up and head home to Savannah and followed Mitchell "Call Me Mitch" Littlefield to his office. Simply decorated with a plain desk and chair, bookshelves, a bank of filing cabinets, and a potted plant in the corner. Mitch settled in his high-backed chair. Ray and Nicole sat in the two chairs that faced him, Pancake standing behind them. I loitered near a generous window. Open vertical blinds revealed the parking lot. An office designed for work, not aesthetics.

"I'd be lying if I didn't say I'm uncomfortable with this," Mitch said. When no one responded, he continued. "No offense, but isn't this a matter better handled by the police?"

"No arguments there," Ray said. "We're not here to interfere, but to help them if we can. Primarily, we want to gather information for Savannah so she can better understand why this happened."

That seemed to calm Mitch somewhat. "I can't imagine what she's going through. I mean, it's hard for me, and for everyone here, but for her, it has to be devastating."

"She's crushed and confused," Nicole said. "Hopefully, we can help her and bring her some relief."

Mitch nodded but said nothing.

"We've talked with Detective Peters," Ray said. "Assured her we'll share anything we find. She seemed comfortable with that."

Mitch digested that. "Savannah doesn't believe the police can adequately investigate this? Is that why she hired you?"

"Not really," Pancake said. "Though we'll share everything we uncover with Detective Peters, we have no illusion it's a two-way street. The police hold things close to the vest, which frustrates family and friends. Private investigators, too. Since we work for Savannah, whatever we discover, we'll pass along and keep her informed as best we can."

"Seems like a bit of a conflict," Mitch said.

"It can be," Ray said. "We've been involved in similar situations. It's not so much a distrust of the police, it's just that they can be closed mouth, for obvious reasons, and the person feels they're being kept in the dark. Or not being told the truth. That's standard procedure with every cop I've ever known. They rarely expose their hand. Which is necessary for many cases, particularly early on when they don't know who all the players are. Who's a witness and who's a suspect." He shrugged. "The family's frustration leads them to hire someone like us. Not only to help with the case, but to keep them up to date."

"I guess that makes sense." Mitch flattened his palms on his desktop. "So, what can I tell you?"

"About Carl Davis," Pancake said. "Your history with him, what kind of guy he was, anything and everything you know."

"That's a lot. Carl and I had a long history. As college freshmen, we were in the same dorm and immediately became friends. We were both in the business school, interested in sales and real estate, and drank the same beer." He offered a weak smile. "Seems like only yesterday, but it was nearly thirty years ago. After graduation, we got our broker's licenses and opened this office. We've been right here since then."

"Looks like the business is doing well," I said.

"Better than Carl and I ever imagined."

"Why do you think that is?"

"Hard work. We both put in long hours. When you own the business, there's no time clock. It sinks or swims on your back."

Funny, but I never felt that kind of pressure. Even back when I bought Captain Rocky's and jumped into the deep end of a business I knew nothing about. It helped that the restaurant was already up and running and all I had to do was write a check and show up. And hire someone who knew how to run a restaurant. That would be Carla Martinez. She's been my manager from day one and without her Captain Rocky's would have sunk into the sand long ago. I wanted to own a restaurant and bar; I just didn't want to "own" one. I wanted to hang out, drink whiskey, chat with people, and pick up women. Captain Rocky's served all those needs and required me to do very little else. Thank you, Carla. I couldn't relate to what Mitch said, but I had seen it with Ray. When he left the military and opened his agency, he worked very long hours. Mom and I wouldn't see him for days sometimes.

I prefer my life. Gives me time to do other things. Like come and go as I please, avoid anything that resembles work, and hang out with Nicole. Pretty good deal. Of course, this free time often led me into Ray's world.

"How does the business work?" Ray asked. "Division of work, responsibilities, finances, those kinds of things."

"Always fifty-fifty. Even when we took out the original start-up loan, we were co-signers. We did that with everything. Early on, we fell into a new sixty-unit condo project here in Orange Beach. We knew the developer from school, and he hired us to handle the sales. They sold themselves, and within six months we were not only solvent but profitable. Since then, we've continued to grow. As for the division of labor, Carl and I had no formal agreement. We drifted to our areas of interest. His in sales and people and mine more in finances and office management. We were lucky it worked out that way."

"Sometimes no plan is the best plan," Ray said.

See? I told you. Planning took energy and stress and work. Better to sit back and see what happens. Of course, Ray didn't mean that. He was building rapport. Drawing Mitch in. Ray planned everything. Always.

"I never thought of it that way, but I agree," Mitch said. "We meshed in that regard."

"Any issues between you two? Friction or anything?"

Mitch hesitated. His eyes narrowed. "No. Like I said, we meshed. Carl and I never argued, never even had cross words." He sighed. "I wish me and my ex-wife could've said the same."

"After you paid off that initial loan," Pancake said, "the cash flow was good?"

"Very."

"What about employee problems?" I asked. "Any issues?"

"A few. Like every business. But for us, those have been rare. I told Detective Peters about one. A guy named Gary Wayne Frawley. He didn't fit in. We run a very low-key and friendly ship here but he was aggressive and impatient. Turned off several clients. Some Carl and I smoothed over and kept their business, but a few bolted and went elsewhere. In the end, we fired him. That was a year ago."

"Do you know where he is now?" Pancake asked.

"I believe he went over to Seaside in Fort Walton Beach. I've heard nothing else about him."

"Is he the type that might want revenge?" I asked.

"For sure, he was angry. Stormed out the door, threatened to sue us, but in the end it was all blather and bluster. Nothing ever came of it and we never heard from him again."

"But is he capable of some act of revenge?" I asked again.

"Initially, we worried about that, but as the months went by, we decided he had blown off the steam and moved on."

"Anyone else that raises concern?" Pancake asked.

"Hmm." Mitch glanced past me toward the window. "Maybe." He gave a half nod. "A guy named Everett Lowe. He owned a company that made plastic containers. He had a commercial building, a simple block and metal structure here in Orange Beach, where he did his manufacturing. Anyway, he was retiring and wanted to sell the building. We brokered it and found him a buyer. At a good price. Some guy who wanted to begin a plumbing business. Maybe six months later, a group from up north, near Pittsburgh, was looking into this area to expand their business. They were in residential and commercial construction. With the way things are growing around here, they wanted in the market. Anyway, they had done their own research and wanted to buy the plumbing business out. They came to us and we did that deal too."

"So, what was the problem?" I asked.

"Money." He sighed. "Isn't it always?"

Says the embezzler, I thought.

"The Pittsburgh outfit bought the property for twice what the plumber had paid Lowe. When he found out, he had a fit. He came to the office angry and flushed and threatened to sue us.

Which he did. Accused us of fraud, saying that we knew the property was worth more. Even that we were in cahoots with the buyer to defraud him. There was no evidence of any such thing and the judge tossed the case. When we brokered the Lowe deal, we knew nothing of the Pittsburgh outfit. It was simply that property values had risen. Plus, the Pittsburgh group needed the property quickly, so they waved around wads of money. They didn't want to haggle, so they overpaid." He shrugged. "Which was fine with us."

"When was this?" Ray asked.

"A year and a half ago."

"Any issues with him since then?" Pancake asked.

Mitch shook his head. "He finally realized that we'd done nothing wrong and that he'd gotten a good deal."

"Do you know where we can find him?" Pancake asked.

"Sure. I have his information. Unless he's moved, he lives nearby."

CHAPTER 13

"I'M HUNGRY," PANCAKE said.

"You're always hungry," Ray replied.

"I interrogate better when my stomach isn't grumbling."

"When doesn't it?"

"When I'm sleeping. Come on, it'll only take a minute. Just a couple of tacos."

Ray relented, as Pancake knew he would. They entered Carmen's Taqueria, a Mexican restaurant next door to Seaside Realty, where Gary Wayne Frawley worked. As with Mitch Littlefield, they hadn't arranged an appointment, so they could catch Frawley flat and not give him time to refuse to meet, or create a story. When they arrived and parked in the lot out front, Ray had called and asked for Frawley, and when the receptionist put him on hold to connect the call, Ray hung up, saying, "He's there."

Which to Pancake meant they had time for a bite.

The tacos were great. Ray even had one, Pancake three. Took all of five minutes.

Pancake wiped his chin with a napkin, tossing it onto the plastic tray. "Okay, I'm good now."

The helpful receptionist didn't bother asking who they were or what they wanted, more interested in texting on her phone, and directed them toward Frawley's office with a wave of her hand. They found Frawley behind his desk, pen in hand, scratching notes on a piece of paper. He looked up.

"How can I help you?" Frawley asked with a friendly real estate agent smile.

"We want to chat with you about Carl Davis," Ray said.

Frawley clicked his pen, underlining the annoyance that creased his face. "Jesus Christ, do you guys fly in squadrons?"

"Pardon?" Ray said.

"You cops."

"We ain't cops," Pancake said.

"Then who are you?"

"Private investigators."

"That's worse. Why don't you go bother someone else?"

"It'll only take a couple of minutes," Ray said.

"I already told everything to that detective. I forget her name."

"Peters," Pancake said.

He shrugged. "Whatever."

"If you'd answer a few questions, it might help Carl Davis' daughter cope with this," Ray said.

"Savannah?"

"You know her?" Pancake asked.

"Of course. I worked there for over a year. She would come in from time to time. Unlike her father, she was nice."

"Yes, she is," Ray said. "She's our client. I'm sure she'd appreciate your cooperation."

Frawley relented. Sort of. "Okay. I'll tell you what I told Detective Peters. I don't know shit about Carl's murder. I didn't know it happened until the next day. You, her, everything is all a bunch of bullshit."

"Since you were there for over a year, and know the folks who worked at the agency, are you aware of any issues Carl had with anyone?" Pancake asked.

"You mean besides me? And that was a bunch of trumped-up bullshit. I never did half the things they said I did."

"What did you do?" Pancake asked.

"Nothing. A couple of clients didn't like me. That's the truth of it. I did nothing wrong." He dropped the pen onto the desktop. "I bet you've had people who don't like you either. Not that you did anything wrong, just that they didn't feel all warm and fuzzy about you."

Pancake nodded. "That's true."

"That's what happened. They created a pile of bullshit out of it and dropped it on my head."

"So you were angry with Carl Davis?" Ray asked.

"See? There you go. Just like Detective Peters. Let me make this clear for you. I didn't do it."

Pancake raised a hand. "Relax. We're not saying you did."

"Sounds that way to me."

"Did Carl have issues with anyone else in the office? Or any clients?"

"Not that I know." He glanced toward the window, sighed. "Truth is, despite what he did to me, I thought he was a decent guy." He looked back at Pancake. "As far as I could tell, everyone liked him."

"Any issues with his partner? Mitchell Littlefield?"

His eyes narrowed. "You don't think Mitch did this, do you?"

"Do you?" Ray asked.

Frawley hesitated. "No. They seemed tight. I think they'd known each other for years." He gave a headshake. "I'd be surprised if he was involved."

That fit what everyone else had said. But then none of them knew about the embezzling thing. Or did they? Of course, if Mitch was guilty, he would know, and Carl knew from his investigating the bogus numbers. But was anyone else aware of it? If so, would that make a difference? Would it motivate someone to kill Carl Davis? Pancake didn't see how that made sense. What would the payoff be? Unless, maybe, someone felt that if money was being siphoned off, their paycheck would be smaller than it should be. Pancake didn't buy that either. From what he had seen, the contracts were clear. The agency made six percent on each sale and the agent that closed the deal got half of that. That was baked into the deal, so any change in the company's pile of money would have little if any effect on the agents' take-home check. Unless, until, the company wobbled, or went bankrupt. Pancake's research showed the business was not only solvent but was raking in wads of cash.

"During your employment were you aware of any financial issues with the company?" Pancake asked.

"You mean other than needing a truck to haul all the money away?" He actually smiled. "They, Carl and Mitch, knew how to make money. They just weren't big on sharing it with their employees."

"I assume you were all on commission," Ray said. "The sale price of each property you sold dictated your pay. Right?"

"That's true."

"So the overall health of the company, its total cash flow, wouldn't impact your pay?" Pancake said.

"Also true," Frawley said.

"Anyone ever complain about the money situation?" Ray asked.

"Someone might say they needed to make more money. But doesn't everyone everywhere say that?" He cocked his head. "A couple of the employees felt the company had too many agents and that, with fewer, they'd get more listings and make more money."

"Did you agree with that?" Pancake asked.

"It makes sense." He shrugged. "But everyone was busy. Nobody was starving." A half smile. "Besides, there was nothing to do about it. Carl and Mitch made the rules."

"From where you sat, the company seemed sound and the employees more or less happy?" Ray asked.

"I'd say so."

"No hint of financial problems?"

"I wasn't in the know on any of that. I was an agent. I sold houses. That's it. I wasn't involved in any of the business stuff. But it seemed to me the company was flush."

"That seems to be the consensus," Pancake said.

Frawley scratched the back of one hand. "You know, there was one guy. I don't remember his name or the details. He tried to sue Carl and Mitch. Maybe a year and a half ago. I think he accused them of ripping him off. The word I heard was defrauding. It was a commercial property. I worked in the residential side but I heard the office gossip about it."

"Everett Lowe?" Ray asked.

"That might be him. The name sounds familiar."

"Lowe tried to sue but the case got tossed."

"He must be the guy I'm thinking of. See? There's bullshit everywhere."

"So it seems," Pancake said.

"To be clear," Ray said. "You had nothing to do with Carl's murder and you don't know anyone who would have done it?"

"That's right."

"I assume you gave Detective Peters an alibi," Pancake said.

"Yes."

"One that satisfied her?"

A longer hesitation. Frawley's gaze dropped, then bounced back up. "Sort of."

"What does that mean?" Ray asked.

"I have an alibi. An ironclad one, as they say."

"But?"

"It tricky."

"Let me guess," Pancake said. "You were with someone who has entanglements."

Frawley nodded but said nothing.

"Married?"

Another nod. "That's why I couldn't tell Detective Peters who it was."

"You know you'll eventually have to, don't you?" Ray asked.

Frawley smirked. "You sound like her."

"Because it's true. You had issues with Carl Davis. You know his habits and the layout of the office. That makes you a suspect until you're not. Which means she'll be on top of you until you can convince her you couldn't have done it." Ray shrugged. "Thus, your secret lady will have to come forward."

"Not going to happen."

"My impression," Pancake said, "is that Peters isn't the kind to ignore loose ends. You're one of those right now. She'll keep digging into your life, your friends, your activities, your bank accounts, and social media posts. Everything is fair game in a homicide investigation. That's how it works."

"What about my rights? What about my privacy?"

"Step by step, those will fall away," Ray said. "She'll find something. A small thread. She'll tug on it. That'll loosen up another thread. You get the picture. Soon the whole ball of yarn unravels."

"But I'm innocent," Frawley said.

Pancake grunted. "Like that makes a difference."

"This is bullshit," Frawley said. "She can't do that."

"She can and she will," Ray said. "Any good detective would."

"Unless," Pancake said. "We can intervene."

"What does that mean?"

"Get your lady friend to talk with us. If she corroborates your alibi and if it's solid and can be backed up, we might be able to influence Detective Peters."

"How would you do that?"

"She knows us and trusts us," Pancake said. A bit of a lie, but so what? "If we believe your girlfriend's story, maybe we can convince her that her time could be better spent looking elsewhere."

"You can do that?"

"Maybe," Pancake said. "Don't know until we try. But one thing's a given. Peters'll get to her one way or the other."

Frawley seemed defeated and deflated. "I don't know if she will."

"It's either us or the police," Ray said. "We're a lot nicer."

"And we don't carry handcuffs," Pancake added.

CHAPTER 14

YOU SEE? THIS is how it happens. First, a simple errand to gather information for Pancake and we stumble on a dead guy. Then we have to talk to the police and convince a seasoned detective that we had nothing to do with it. Okay, that wasn't that difficult. And now, Ray had another errand for us. A chat with Everett Lowe. His thinking was that he and Pancake should handle the angry and aggressive Gary Wayne Frawley while Nicole and I talked with the more benign and less suspicious Lowe. See, the hole gets deeper and the spiral steeper. If history teaches anything, this wasn't the end. Not even close. The descent into Ray's world had no bottom.

A lot like an incurable toe fungus.

Everett Lowe lived in a quiet neighborhood in nearby Myrtle Grove. His white clapboard home possessed a large picture window and a small stoop that led to a dark blue front door. A well-maintained front yard completed the picture of the perfect place to retire and kick back. I knocked. No one answered. I knocked again, then heard footsteps approaching. The door swung open.

I knew Everett Lowe was seventy-one. He looked trim and fit, with a shock of white hair and a tan so deep it looked like a walnut stain. Shirtless, he wore a friendly smile, bright orange swim trunks, and a navy blue Atlanta Braves baseball cap, a glass of tea in his hand.

"Sorry. I was out by the pool catching the rays."

"Mr. Lowe?" I asked.

"Yes. And you?"

"I'm Jake Longly. This is Nicole Jamison."

He smiled as his gaze devoured Nicole. She wore white shorts and a lemon-yellow crew-neck shell. Her silky blonde hair, squeegeed into a ponytail, hung over one shoulder. It took him a moment to yank his gaze away and find his voice.

"What can I do for you?" he asked.

"Can we talk?" I said. "We have a few questions."

"About what?" His smile remained, but a hint of concern gathered in his eyes.

"I assume you've heard about Carl Davis."

His concern increased. "What about him?"

"Can we come in?" Nicole asked.

After a brief hesitation, he said, "Sure. Sure. Sorry."

He led us into his home, neat and clean. "Can I get you some sweet tea?"

"We're good," Nicole said.

We passed through the living room and out onto a pool deck, which backed up to a large pond. He offered us seats at a round teak table shaded by a pale blue canvas umbrella.

"What's this about?" he asked.

"Someone murdered Carl Davis yesterday," I said.

His shoulders jerked back and his eyes snapped open. "What?"

"He was shot in his office last night."

"Who? Why?"

"That's what we're trying to figure out," Nicole said.

Lowe's confusion now in full flight. "Who are you?"

"We're private investigators," Nicole said. "Carl's daughter hired us to help find out the who, what, and why of her father's murder."

Lowe seemed to slump in his chair. "I can't believe it."

"Neither can Savannah," I said. "His daughter."

Concern again replaced the shock on his face. "Why are you here?"

"You knew Carl," I said.

"I did."

"You and he had issues."

"So?" His eyes narrowed. "Wait a minute. Are you thinking I had something to do with this?"

"We don't," Nicole said. "I have to admit that we considered that possibility, but after meeting you, seeing your reaction, I don't think so."

"Then you're an excellent judge of people," Lowe said. "I'd never do such a thing."

"Somebody did," I said. "Can you tell us about your connection with Carl? I know you guys had a conflict over property."

"We did. I planned to sue him. My attorney drew up the papers and sent Carl a letter of intent to sue. But when he ran it by a judge he knew, he said there was no case." He took a slug of tea. "I'd come to the same conclusion even before it went that far."

"Why?" I asked.

"I had a plastics company. We made containers, lids, and other molded products. A year and a half ago now, I retired so I sold my facility. A couple of sizable buildings. Nice piece of property. Carl brokered the deal. Sold it to a guy with a plumbing supply business. The price was excellent and the closing smooth and easy. Then six months later, maybe a little longer, the new owner sold it for twice that price. Carl brokered that deal, too. I was angry. Thought maybe Carl had scammed me."

"Understandable," I said.

"It was the fast turnaround that got me. I thought Carl should've known about the other buyer when I was selling." Another sip of tea. "But after looking into it, the new buyer was some outfit from Pennsylvania. Not local and not anyone Carl knew. They needed space to expand down this way and were under a time crunch. They paid top dollar. Actually, they overpaid." He sighed. "In the end, I realized Carl had done nothing wrong, and he'd gotten me a good deal." He smiled. "Now I only have to lie around and play a little golf and tennis."

"How well did you know Carl?" I asked.

"Not very. If it weren't for this deal, I doubt I'd've ever met him."

"Did you meet his partner? Mitchell Littlefield?"

"A couple of times. At their office."

"What'd you think of him?" Nicole asked.

"He was quiet. Didn't have Carl's sense of humor, for sure. Carl could tell a joke and seemed to find everything somewhat funny. Mitch, less so. More serious."

"Did you sense any friction between them?" I asked.

"Are you thinking Mitch did this?"

"We're considering all possibilities."

"You know how these things go," Nicole said. "You start with those closest to the victim."

"I suspect that's a fact. But, no, I saw nothing between them. But like I said, I only saw Mitch Littlefield twice, and then only briefly."

"I assume you can't think of anyone who had issues with Carl or might want to harm him," I said.

"Me? No. But other than this real estate deal, I didn't really know him."

CHAPTER 15

"So, WHAT'VE YOU GOT?" Detective Brooke Peters asked Liam Murphy as she rolled a chair over next to him

"Top of the morning to you, lassie," Liam said.

Officer Liam Murphy's family had indeed come from Ireland, a handful of generations earlier, but he had never been there and for sure wasn't raised there. Which meant he was about as Irish as she was, which wasn't much, if any. Not that she knew anything about her roots, and didn't care. Liam, born and raised in Shreveport, Louisiana, spoke with a syrupy Southern drawl, but he liked to fake the Irish from time to time. Just for fun.

Young, only twenty-four, and very intelligent, Liam had been with the Orange Beach PD for only two years but was by far the most tech-savvy employee they had. A whiz with images and digital data.

"Aye, laddie," Peters said. "What have you for me?" Her fake Irish accent was terrible, but never failed to draw a chuckle from Liam.

He tapped his keyboard and opened a folder titled "Orange Coast Realty Security Cams." Two video files inside. He double-clicked one. A grainy video of the parking lot in front of the company opened.

"This is the camera at the right corner of the building—as you face it. The other file is from the opposite corner. The cameras cover the same ground, just from different angles. This camera is clearer. Less dirt on the lens. As you can see, half a dozen cars are in the front lot. This is four fifty."

He fast-forwarded the video. Comical images of three people, two women and one man, viewed from behind, appeared as they exited the facility. Each climbed into their car and drove from the lot. He returned the video to normal speed.

"The white Escalade belongs to Carl Davis, the black BMW to Mitchell Littlefield, and the small white Lexus SUV to Dustin Hobson. It's eight after five, according to the time stamp, which is accurate."

Peters leaned forward. For a full two minutes, nothing happened, and then Littlefield and Dustin came into view. They stopped near Littlefield's Beemer and chatted for a minute. Casual and relaxed. Then Littlefield climbed into his car, and Dustin his SUV. Dustin followed the BMW to the lot's exit, where both turned right and disappeared from view.

Liam hit fast-forward again. "Nothing happened until six thirty-one." He slowed to normal speed. "Then this."

A white Mercedes convertible turned into the lot and parked near the Escalade. Jake Longly and Nicole Jamison climbed out and headed toward the building. They laughed about something, and Nicole gave Jake a swat on the seat of his jeans. Peters smiled.

"This is the couple, the P.I.s, that discovered Davis' body," she said.

Liam stopped the video. "That's it. The other camera shows the same thing."

"These are the only two, right?"

"Correct. No cameras toward the rear. Nothing back there, anyway. No inside cameras."

"How did the killer get in and out?" Peters asked.

"Not through the front door."

No doubt, the killer knew of the security cameras, how to avoid them, and how to approach and enter the building to avoid detection. Mitchell Littlefield checked every box. So did Dustin Hobson, but the motive needle pointed at Littlefield. Still, a disgruntled employee or client as well as a random dude must be considered. Proving who and how was the problem.

The answer to that? Keep digging. The evidence was out there somewhere. Either she hadn't found it yet, or she had, but didn't possess enough information to make sense of it. That's the way it always was in the beginning. You gather bits and pieces, try to mesh them together, gather more evidence, and ultimately things fit and a picture emerges. Right now, she felt far from that finish line.

CHAPTER 16

NICOLE ZIGGED INTO the Captain Rocky's lot and zagged into my reserved spot near the entry stairs. As we climbed from Nicole's SL, Detective Brooke Peters rolled up in her black Taurus. She slid into a slot next to Pancake's truck. The boy was never late for a meeting, or food.

"Perfect timing," Nicole said.

"I'm meeting Pancake here," Peters said. "He has some financial information for me."

"We have something for you, too."

"What?"

"Let's get inside and we can go from there," I said.

It was just past two in the afternoon, the lunch crowd thinning, the happy hour folks yet to show. Still, the place was busy.

Pancake hunkered at my private deck table, phone to his ear, a plate of nachos before him. He ended his call and stood as we approached. He pulled back the chair next to him for Peters.

"A gentleman," she said.

"That's me." He sat. "I'll even share my nachos with you."

"Thanks. I'm starving."

"You came to the right place. The food here meets every requirement."

"Oh?" Peters asked.

Pancake raised an eyebrow. "Good, and lots of it."

"Not to mention free," I said.

Libby arrived, stopping next to Pancake. She wore tan shorts and a blue Captain Rocky's golf shirt. "Carla told me you guys were on the way. I warned the cooks that Pancake was here." She smiled. "Two of them screamed and ran out the door."

"You're funny," Pancake said.

She smiled. "That's why Jake pays me."

"He don't pay you enough," Pancake said.

"Maybe you can put in a word for me."

"He don't listen either."

"This is Detective Brooke Peters," I said, introducing Libby and Peters.

"Detective?" Libby flattened one hand against her chest. "I didn't do it, wasn't there, and don't know anything about it." She ruffled Pancake's hair. "But I'd bet this guy's involved."

"You're on a roll today," Pancake said.

"It's what I do." Libby tugged a pad and pen from her back pocket. "What can I get you guys?"

"Margaritas," Nicole said. She looked at Peters. "That work for you?"

"Normally, no, but today's been a grind, so why not?"

"The fish tacos are to die for," Nicole added.

Peters slid her menu aside. "Sounds good."

I nodded, indicating I'd have the same.

Libby tapped Pancake's shoulder with the pen she held. "What'll it be today?"

"You decide," Pancake said. "A couple from page one and a couple from page two."

Libby spun away and headed to the kitchen.

"Where's Ray?" Peters asked.

"He's got a barbecue this afternoon. With a bunch of his old military buddies. They do that several times a year."

"Which branch?" Peters asked.

"Mostly the Marines," I said. "But Ray moved on to Special Ops so he spent more time with those guys than he did the Marines."

"What kind of Special Ops?"

"The usual," Pancake said. "Recon, blowing up shit, killing bad guys."

"Really?"

"True that," Pancake said.

"So, what do you have for me?" Peters asked.

Pancake lifted his canvas messenger bag from the floor and flapped it open. He rummaged inside and came out with a gray envelope. "This is what I have so far. When you go through it, you'll see the accounting is unbalanced."

"Meaning?"

"The numbers don't add up. I couldn't account for around three hundred and eighty K."

"That's a big number," Peters said. "How'd he bleed off that much without attracting attention?"

"Maybe he didn't," I said. "Maybe Carl found out, confronted him, and that's the reason he shot him. To conceal his embezzling."

"If he killed Carl, that is," Peters said. "We aren't there yet. But, he's my best bet. But then, I've seen murders to cover lesser crimes."

"What I have here," Pancake said, handing her the envelope, "isn't quite a smoking gun, but there's smoke nonetheless. The docs that Jake and Nicole were picking up were more recent and complete and would've told me more. Carl apparently copied them without Littlefield knowing."

"Or perhaps he did," Peters said. "And that was the final straw."

Pancake shrugged.

"I still don't see how he did this without someone knowing," Peters said. "I mean, this is adult money."

"Mitch Littlefield handled the finances," Pancake said. "He kept the books, did the taxes, made the payroll. In short, the financial business of the company. Carl took his word for everything. Why wouldn't he? They trusted each other and had been friends and partners for decades."

Peters stole another nacho and bit into it. "So Carl Davis was asleep at the wheel? Letting his partner handle the money and him not being curious."

"I think that's a natural selection thing," Pancake said. "Someone gravitates toward the finances, another toward marketing, another toward office management, another toward sales. Over time, each is consumed with what's in their lane and stays there. I think most successful companies work that way. Orange Coast Realty included."

"Still, three hundred and eighty thousand should've attracted someone's attention."

"Are you aware of how big Orange Coast Realty is?" Pancake asked.

Peters shook her head.

"Over three million a year in commissions."

"No way."

"They do both residential and commercial. All along the coast. As far east as Panama City and as far west as Biloxi. So, ten thousand a month getting lost didn't even make a blip. Until someone who can crunch numbers looked."

"You?" Peters asked.

"First, Carl, then me."

"It took him three years. I'd think he would've noticed sooner." Pancake grabbed another chip and popped it in his mouth. "Let me ask you this. If your checkbook was off five dollars, what would you do?"

"Probably nothing. I'd assume the bank was right and that I mis-added or subtracted somewhere."

"But you wouldn't go back and redo all the numbers? Right?"

"Probably not."

"Same thing here. Even if someone sensed things might be off a few bucks, would they go back and recalculate everything? Rows and rows of numbers. That'd take time and effort." Another chip. "These numbers sound big, and they are, but relatively speaking, it's like your checkbook."

Libby approached with margaritas and distributed them. "The food will be up shortly." She wound back through the tables toward the kitchen.

"We talked with Mitch Littlefield and Dustin," I said.

Peters looked at me over the rim of her glass. "What'd you think?"

"Nothing felt off base to me," I said. I glanced at Nicole. She nodded her agreement. "Mitch seemed shaken and shocked. Dustin, too. Like I assumed anyone would be after losing a partner or a future father-in-law."

"I agree," Nicole said.

Peters looked at Pancake.

"I also agree," he said.

"Where did the money go?" Peters asked. "If Littlefield took it, he must've put it somewhere."

"Don't know yet," Pancake said. "Best bet is a secret account somewhere. Probably offshore. I hoped the material Carl had for us would provide a hint where to look."

"Wouldn't it have to be electronic transfers?" Peters asked.

Pancake nodded.

"Aren't those easy to track?"

"Sometimes. But some can be convoluted and clever. I need to get into Orange Coast Realty's accounts. Littlefield's too."

"A subpoena could help," Peters said.

"And alert Littlefield that we're sniffing around. Might spook him and if he knows how to scrub electronic data that would give him time to dust his trail. We need to assume he does."

"Okay, what do you propose?"

Pancake smiled. "I have ways."

"Enlighten me," Peters said.

"Better that you don't know. Plausible deniability."

Libby appeared with three plates of tacos and placed them before each of us. One of my kitchen guys stood behind her, a large tray in his hands. Libby began placing plates before Pancake. With each, Peters' eyes widened further. Onion rings, cheeseburger, large bowl of chili, and a smothered burrito.

"Good lord," Peters said.

"This is nothing," I said. "You should see him when he's hungry."

"I wouldn't want to pay your food bill," she said.

Pancake popped an onion ring in his mouth. "Me either."

"He doesn't pay for any of this," I said.

"Jake likes having him around," Nicole said. "And the best way is to provide food. Like baiting a bear trap."

Peters laughed. "I take it you guys have a history?"

"Since childhood," I said.

"It's nice of you to let him eat here for free."

"I don't have a choice," I said. "He knows where the bodies are buried."

Pancake slid the plate of onion rings toward Peters. "Have some."

She did. "Wow. Perfect."

"I told you the food was good." Pancake took a bite of his cheeseburger. "Ray and I talked with Gary Wayne Frawley."

Peters wiped grease from her fingers with her napkin. "Littlefield told you about him?"

"He did." Another bite of burger. "You talked to him. You know the story."

"How many times did he say 'bullshit'?"

"A bunch. Seemed to be his go-to phrase."

"What was your read on him?" Peters took a bite of her taco.

"Wouldn't count him out." Now Pancake took a spoonful of chili. "He got fired. He was angry. He knows the layout, the schedule, the rhythm of the place."

"And his alibi is a big secret."

"Most people like to keep adultery undercover. I told him that she'd have to come forward if he wanted to be cleared. I also told him that if she talked to us, us not being the police, and if she could alibi him and prove it, that we'd talk to you and you might slide him to the back burner." He glanced at her. "You okay with that?"

"If she can prove he was elsewhere, probably, but if it's just her word, no."

"He's going to ask her, so we'll see."

"Nicole and I talked with a guy you might not know about," I said.

She had taken a bite of her taco, so she held up a finger while she chewed and swallowed. "Who?"

"Guy named Everett Lowe," I said. "A little over a year ago he sold his company."

"He made plastic containers and similar stuff," Nicole added. "He owned a pair of commercial buildings."

"Carl sold them for him," I said, picking up the story. "Six months later, an outfit from Pennsylvania paid twice as much for it. Carl brokered that deal too."

"Oh? Sounds sketchy."

"That's what Lowe thought at first. He hired an attorney and intended to sue, but in the end realized the new buyers overpaid and that Carl did nothing wrong. He backed away."

"You believe him?" Peters asked.

"I do. He felt he got screwed, got mad, prepared to sue, realized that it was simply the vagaries of the market, took his money, and settled down in retirement."

"Give me his info and I'll give him a visit," Peters said.

I smiled. "I expected you would."

"What about you?" Pancake asked. "Anything new on your end?"

"I reviewed the security cams from Orange Coast Realty. They only have two. Both show the front door and the parking lot."

She told us of seeing Mitch and Dustin leaving at the same time, just as they had said, and then Nicole and I arriving. Nothing in between.

"The killer entered from somewhere else then," Nicole said.

"There's a back door," Peters said.

"Unless Mitch and Dustin are in it together," I said.

"Why would you say that?" Nicole asked.

"They left together. They were the last to see Carl alive. Mitch had motive and what if Dustin was involved with him in the thefts?"

"The thefts began long before Dustin joined the company," Pancake said.

"Maybe he learned what Mitch was up to and wormed his way into the deal. His education is in accounting and finance."

"Look at you," Pancake said. "Getting all conspiratorial on us."

"What? You don't think that's possible?"

"Of course I do." Pancake grunted. "I'm just amazed you came up with it."

"My precious, clever little boy," Nicole said. She nudged me with an elbow.

Peters laughed. "I considered that too. More so after seeing the security video."

"And?" I asked.

"It's one of my working theories."

"I still think it was someone else," Pancake said. "And he came through the back door."

"There's sand, scrub brush, and a dirt road behind the building," Peters said. "Doesn't go anywhere, so no one drives there. Hell, most people don't even know it exists. I for sure didn't."

"Have you checked it out?" I asked.

"Not yet. On my list, though."

"Maybe we should check it out," Pancake said. "After dessert."

"Dessert?" Peters said. "After everything you ate?"

Pancake looked at her as if she had no concept of how the world worked.

"Not having dessert is a sin," Pancake said.

Peters laughed. "Well, if we're saving your soul, how could we refuse? What do you suggest?"

"The peach cobbler and the bread pudding are always good," Pancake said. "Oh, and the pecan pie."

Peters thought for a minute. "I'll go with the cobbler. You?"

"I can't decide, so I'll have all three."

Gotta love the big guy.

CHAPTER 17

THE SANDY ROAD, that label being generous, marked the western edge of Orange Coast Realty's property and separated it from a similar sized lot where construction had begun and halted as witnessed by a cracked foundation, hugged by thick weeds. The owners had big dreams but ran out of money. Not an uncommon occurrence.

The road, path, whatever it was, elbowed to the right, paralleled the rear of the realty office, and ended a hundred and fifty feet ahead. Nicole jerked to a stop. We faced a brushy dune. It obscured a small cluster of homes, only the highest points of their roofs visible. Similar dunes flanked us and hid the realty company to the south and the high-dollar waterfront homes to the north. Tucked into this low area, we were hidden from view in almost every direction.

Is this where the killer had parked?

Nicole and I climbed from her SL. Behind us, Peters rolled to a stop and she and Pancake emerged. How did he fit inside a Taurus? At least he didn't have to hang his head out the window like a dog. I'd seen that before. More than once. When we were young and stupid and alcohol clouded—what little judgement we possessed.

"This is cozy," Pancake said.

Peters did a three-sixty. "A perfect hiding spot. Only open to that empty lot behind us."

She ascended the hump that hid the realty office, weaving among the waist-high sea oats. We followed. The rear door, only a hundred feet away, easily reachable. Two windows flanked the entry, each covered by closed curtains.

"You're thinking the killer came this way?" I asked.

Peters shrugged. "It would explain why we saw nothing on the cameras out front."

"That means he knows the area," Nicole said.

"Exactly." Peters gazed north. "I can see the houses across the water." She nodded east. "And those there. But neither are visible from down there where we parked. If the killer parked here, he'd be well hidden."

"Maybe someone saw him coming and going," I said.

"My guys canvassed all those nearby houses, but got nada. No one saw or heard anything. One woman said that at night kids pulled in here to make out and drink and party. Said when they got too loud, she'd come over and run them off. But yesterday, she heard nothing."

Pancake tugged his iPhone from his jeans pocket and snapped several pictures in each direction. "Ray'll want to see this."

"What are you thinking?" I asked.

Pancake pocketed his phone. "The killer knew Carl Davis would be alone. Knew there were no security cams back here. Knew the back door was unlocked. Knew where Carl's office was. He simply parked back here, went inside, pulled the trigger, and retreated. No sweat." He shrugged. "If that's how it went down."

"A big if," Peters said.

"Mitch Littlefield would know all that," I said.

Pancake nodded. "He would. So would everyone else who worked there."

Peters stared at the building. "Okay, let's say it wasn't Mitch. Let's say it was Gary Wayne Frawley, or an employee, or someone with a grudge. The killer could've parked down the street somewhere and waited until Mitch and Dustin drove away, leaving Carl alone. He then pulled in here, popped over this dune, did the deed, and drove away."

"If the back door was unlocked," I said.

"That's true," Peters said. "Who would know that?"

"Anyone who worked here," Nicole said.

Peters kicked at a clump of sand. "Makes for a robust suspect pool."

"What about Dustin Hobson?" I asked. "Like Mitch, he would know every bit of this too."

"He would," Peters said. "But would he kill his future father-in-law? If so, why?"

"Savannah inherits half the business if her father dies," I said.

"And they're getting married soon," Nicole added.

Peters eyed me, then Nicole. "You saying Savannah and Dustin did this? A conspiracy to grab half the company?"

"Just tossing out a possibility," I said.

"My take on Savannah, Dustin too, is that Carl's death shook them. When I made the death notification, they each were genuinely shocked."

"That's my take, too," I said. "But they did have motive. This company's worth a pile of cash."

"Which Savannah could already access," Peters said. "And would inherit in the end."

"That's probably true," Nicole said. "They seem to have it pretty cushy. Living in her father's house, working for his company, no real overhead expenses."

"Didn't Savannah say they lived with Carl to save up and buy their own place?" I asked.

"She did."

"Inheritance is cheaper," Pancake said.

Isn't that the truth. Nice homes in Orange Beach didn't come cheap. The one Carl Davis owned was in the millions. That's a powerful incentive to do something stupid. Still, I didn't see Savannah being involved. Of course, I didn't know her all that well after only a couple of conversations, but my read was that she was jolted by her father's death. Or, she was a very good actress.

"It's a theory that needs pursuing," Peters said. "I have a couple of guys trying to track Mitch's and Dustin's movements between here and home."

"If we had access to their cell phones, we could do that pronto," Pancake said.

"But we don't and right now I see no way to get a warrant for that." She sighed. "Maybe if your embezzlement angle gets legs, we could use that to go after Mitch."

"There might be another way," Pancake said.

"How?" Peters asked.

Pancake smiled, raised an eyebrow.

Peters raised a hand. "No. Don't tell me."

"Wasn't going to. But if I find anything worthwhile, you'll be the next to know."

My cell buzzed. Ray. I answered and walked back down the dune.

"Got a call from Frawley," he said. "His girlfriend will talk to us."

"That's great."

"I want you and Nicole to handle this. Actually Nicole."

"Why?"

"The woman's married. I think she'll be more open if she talks to another woman."

"Makes sense."

"Of course it does. I'll text you the info. Call her. Frawley said she's anxious to get this done."

I glanced back up the slope where Pancake was making some point, Nicole and Peters listening. I turned my back to them and spoke softly. "We're here outside the realty company with Peters. Should I share this with her?"

"Not yet. The woman agreed to do this if she speaks with us alone. If she senses the police are involved, she might balk."

"Couldn't Peters subpoena her or something?"

"A cooperative witness is more forthcoming than a hostile one."

"You got it." I disconnected the call just as Peters, Pancake, and Nicole sidestepped down the slope.

"Everything okay?" Peters asked.

"Yeah. I brought Ray up to date on what we found here."

She nodded. "I'm taking Pancake back to my office so he can decipher these financials for me."

"Lock him up for a couple of days while you have him. It'll save me a ton on my food purchases."

"He's funny," Pancake said. "He really is." He looked at Peters. "Let's go back to Captain Rocky's. We can go over the numbers there." He smiled, glanced at me. "Free food and drink."

"We just ate, what, an hour ago?" Peters said.

"Your point is?" Pancake asked.

CHAPTER 18

THAT'S HOW WE ended up back at Captain Rocky's. A bright yellow umbrella shielded my table from the sun that toasted the sand and the beachgoers.

"We just cleaned up from your last visit," Carla said.

"Love a fresh start," Pancake said.

Carla looked at me. "Where's his leash?"

"He ate it," I said.

Carla propped a fist on one hip. "I want a raise."

"You don't get raises," I said. "You're part owner."

"You are?" Peters asked.

"Jake gave me a percentage for running the place. Which is good since left to his own devices this place would've collapsed into the Gulf by now."

That was true. Carla understood business. I understood, well, very little. Something she often pointed out. Like now.

"This place is a lot of work," I said. "It takes two people."

"One and a half," Carla said. "The half is being generous."

"Poor baby," Nicole said. She ruffled my hair.

Libby walked up. "You're back already?"

"We got hungry," Pancake said.

"Speak for yourself," Peters said. She patted her belly. "My waistline can't afford to hang around with you."

"Your waistline's just fine," he said with a smile.

Only Pancake ordered. His usual, "Surprise me. Whatever you think I might like."

Libby shook her head. "Which is everything."

Libby and Carla walked away.

"Let's go over the materials I gave you earlier," Pancake said to Peters.

Peters had hung her purse over the back of her chair and now swung it into her lap. She pulled out the gray envelope, which she had folded in half to make it fit, and handed it to Pancake.

"These are the balance sheets," Pancake said. "Up to three months ago." He thumbed through the pages, finding the one he wanted, and flattened it against the table. Peters scooted toward him. "Here are the summed expenditures for the month of January. These are the expenses." His finger ran down the page. "The P and L shows a positive of around sixty-five K."

"So they made good money," Peters said.

"They did." He flipped to the next page. "This is an expense breakdown. These"—he pointed to a column of numbers—"are for office expenses, marketing, and the last is miscellaneous expenses. So far, so good. Except they don't match the receipts that Carl gave me. These numbers are inflated."

"By how much?"

"For that month alone, sixty-eight hundred. The other month's balance sheets show similar discrepancies, ranging from around three thousand up to ninety-five hundred."

"Adds up to a pile of money."

Pancake nodded. "The three hundred and eighty thousand I mentioned earlier."

Peters studied the pages. "You're sure about this?"

"Mostly. The materials Carl gathered for us, the documents Jake and Nicole planned to pick up, were more recent and detailed. This is a macro look." He waved a hand. "The others are more micro. If they show what I'm sure they will, you'll have your smoking gun to pursue that angle with Mitch Littlefield."

"But not for Carl's murder, I'm afraid."

Pancake folded the pages and handed them back to Peters. "Not directly. But this goes to motive and might be enough to secure your search warrants. Scratch below the surface of his life. Put him under pressure. If we're lucky, he'll do or say something stupid."

She stuffed the pages back into her purse.

"This is why I need the copies Carl made for us," Pancake said.

"My bosses, and the DA, aren't keen on releasing even duplicates. They're afraid the case will get exposed. But I'm working on it."

"We're experienced in handling sensitive information," Pancake said. "We know the rules."

"But he doesn't know that."

"Want me to sweet-talk him?" Pancake asked with a mischievous smile.

"He doesn't sweet-talk well. Besides, you might scare the hell out of him."

"Would that help?"

"Not in the least."

Food arrived. A tray of fried calamari, and another of loaded potato skins.

"You done good, darling," Pancake said to Libby.

"Don't I always?"

"That you do."

Peters rolled her eyes. "You're amazing."

Pancake bounced an eyebrow. "In every way."

"On that note," I said, "we're out of here. All those numbers gave me a headache."

Nicole stood, tapped my shoulder. "Come on, we have errands to run." She hung her purse over one shoulder. "Then maybe I'll take care of that headache for you."

CHAPTER 19

THE ERRAND WAS a meeting with Gary Wayne Frawley's secret lover. Nicole felt guilty deceiving Brooke Peters, but understood the value of discretion. For now, anyway.

It was midafternoon by the time Nicole rolled her SL into the Pensacola Super Walmart parking lot. Where she and Jake would meet Gary Wayne's married and very reluctant alibi-girlfriend, Megan Varner.

The massive, chaotic lot covered an entire block near where U.S. Highway 98 ended at Florida Highway 295. Cars, minivans, and overstuffed shopping carts somehow avoided mutual contact. It looked like a moving maze. Shopping here was serious business.

Nicole stuck to the perimeter where the anarchy was more subdued.

Yesterday, Megan Varner had answered Nicole's call after a single ring. As if she expected it, but hoped it would never come. Her anxiety flowed over the phone and she almost backed out. Nicole convinced her that chatting with them was a better option than sitting in a police interrogation room. Regardless, somehow, some way, Gary Wayne Frawley's alibi needed confirmation. That was the nonnegotiable part.

Nicole explained that as private investigators, they weren't connected to the police. That Ray Longly had been hired by Carl Davis' daughter to help solve her father's murder. She added that, no, she didn't believe that Gary Wayne was involved, but this was a loose end and cops hated loose ends. Sooner or later they would swoop in and pressure Gary Wayne to the point that Megan would have to step forward in a more public fashion.

A resigned Megan agreed. She chose the Walmart parking lot as the meeting place. Not the one near her home in Fort Walton Beach, but rather here in Pensacola, diminishing the risk of running into someone she knew. Plus the expansive, congested lot offered anonymity.

"See a green Jeep Cherokee?" Nicole asked.

"Nope."

"She said she'd be back here toward this corner." Nicole circled to the area near the adjacent Chick-fil-A. "She should be around here somewhere."

"There," Jake said. He pointed. A green Jeep turned into an empty space near, but not next to, other cars.

Nicole pulled into an adjacent space. "Stay here." She jumped from the car.

Nicole approached the passenger's side, bent, and looked through the open window. "Megan?"

The woman nodded.

Nicole climbed in and closed the door behind her. The vehicle was neat and clean, a child's booster seat in the back. Nicole sensed Megan's skittishness. Her gaze scanned the lot, Nicole, the lot again, everything. White knuckles gripped the steering wheel.

"Thanks for talking with me," Nicole said.

"I almost didn't show." Her eyes glistened.

"Relax. We aren't the bad guys and aren't here to cause you any distress. And hopefully avoid you talking to the police."

"Do you really think you can?"

"Depends on what you have to say and how well it can be proven."

"Proven? Gary Wayne and I are the only ones who know about this. Other than his word and mine, how can we prove it? I don't understand why the police are harassing Gary Wayne? He would never do anything like this."

"It's simple," Nicole said. "Gary Wayne had issues with Carl Davis. Davis fired him, which angered Gary Wayne. Makes him a person of interest."

"That was long ago."

"Sometimes grudges simmer. The police investigate all possibilities, including past employees like Gary Wayne."

"He would never do that. They should look somewhere else." She fought back tears. Not successfully. She swiped her cheeks with the palms of her hands.

"Let's not get ahead of ourselves," Nicole said. "Take a couple of breaths and relax."

Megan tried, her breaths ragged at best.

"How long have you two been seeing each other?" Nicole asked.

"This is so humiliating. I feel like a tramp or a slut or something."

Nicole reached over and laid her hand on Megan's arm. "Not true. This isn't an unusual situation. I'm sure you know that."

"It is for me." She stared through the windshield, saying nothing for a full half a minute. She looked back at Nicole. "I feel so dirty."

"Don't. You care for Gary Wayne, don't you?"

She sniffed. Nodded. "I do."

"Then you'll get through this."

"If my husband finds out, it'll crush him." She took a deep, shuttering breath. "We have a three-year-old. I could lose everything." She sniffed. "I'm ashamed. And scared."

"Look," Nicole said. "I grew up in LA. Beverly Hills, in fact. In the movie industry. Affairs like this were, and still are, the norm. Almost expected."

"Not here. Not for me."

"I understand. Trust me, I'm not judging you. Not in the least. Just tell me everything and we'll leave you alone and you can get back to your life."

"What's left of it."

Nicole sensed the fear and the shame that seeped from every pore of Megan's body. "Nothing will change here. We only want to see if Gary Wayne's alibi checks out. That's it. Nothing more."

"He didn't do it. We were together when it happened."

"That's what we need to know."

Megan released a long sigh, her shoulders relaxed, her grip on the steering wheel eased. "Okay." She stared through the windshield, unfocused, no doubt gathering her thoughts. "We met a year ago at a Chamber of Commerce event. I'm in real estate too. At first, we were friends, but we both knew it was more. Or could be." She watched a woman several slots away toss a plastic bag into the rear seat of her car, climb in, and drive away. "Then one day I stopped by one of his open houses. It was quiet and we talked. We ended up in a bar, had a couple of drinks, and then drove to a motel." She looked at Nicole. "Isn't that awful? I mean just like that and we were . . ." Her voice faded.

"How did you feel about that?" Nicole asked.

"Guilty. I couldn't look my husband in the eye. I couldn't sleep. I told myself it was a one-time mistake. That I'd never do it again." She took a deep breath and exhaled, puffing out her cheeks. "Two weeks later, we were back at the same motel."

"Did you always go to the same place?"

"No. We changed locations." She gave a headshake. "Gary Wayne said it'd be best if we didn't become too familiar to the owner or the employees."

"When would you meet?"

"During the day. Mostly noontime or early afternoon. In real estate sales, much of your time is out of the office. Open houses, seeing clients, examining properties, that sort of thing. It was easy for us to find an hour or two."

"How often did you meet?"

"Two or three times a week."

"The night in question," Nicole said. "Monday. You two were together?"

"Yes."

"What time and where?"

"Later than usual. We met around four thirty at the Sunset Lodge in Navarre." She offered a weak smile. "It's quiet and never crowded and cleaner than most. And it's not in Fort Walton."

Navarre, a small community halfway between Fort Walton and Pensacola, was enough off the beaten path for the couple to feel safe from prying eyes. Well outside their social circles so that stumbling across someone they knew and dealing with awkward explanations for being there would be unlikely.

Megan continued. "We met there more than any other place."

"On Monday, what time did you leave the motel?"

"It was . . ." She hesitated. "Let me check." She lifted her phone from the center console tray and punched it to life. She scrolled. "I called my husband at four twenty-three. I told him I had a client meeting. I was on my way to the motel. I arrived maybe five minutes later. Then I called him at six thirty-six, telling him I was on my way home."

"Did Gary Wayne arrive and leave at the same time?"

"Arriving, yes. Leaving, he stayed behind to make a couple of calls and then he left. So maybe ten minutes after I did."

Which meant that Gary Wayne could not have killed Carl Davis. He was thirty to forty-five minutes away. If Megan and Gary Wayne were being truthful. Had they manufactured the story? Would she cover for her lover, even in a murder case?

"You made both of those calls near or at the motel?" Nicole asked.

Megan gave her a quizzical look. "Why?"

"If at some time the police do get involved, they'll subpoena your phone records. Those would reveal your location during each call."

"They can do that?"

"They can."

"But I thought us talking, me telling you what happened, would convince the police to leave me alone?"

"It might." Nicole shrugged. "It might not." She smiled to soften that. "The hope is that it will. But just in case, you don't want to lie or make any false statements. To anyone. So, were the calls made at the motel?"

"The first, I was maybe two miles away, but the second, when I was leaving, I made in the parking lot."

"Good. Hopefully it won't come to that, but if the police do check, it will support your statement."

"So that's it?" Megan asked. "We're good here?"

"I'll need to talk with the people at the motel."

"Why?"

"As you said earlier, right now it's your and Gary Wayne's word. We need harder proof if we're going to convince the police that Gary Wayne is innocent."

"He is."

"I believe you. Did he register under his own name?"

She nodded. "They require ID."

"Do they have security cameras?"

"I don't know. I wasn't looking for any."

"What kind of car does Gary Wayne drive?" Nicole asked.

"Why is that important?"

"If they have security cameras, I need to ID his car."

"It's a dark metallic gray Camaro. It has a Miami Dolphins sticker on the back window. Left side, I think." She nodded. "Yeah. Driver's side."

"That might help," Nicole said. "Thanks for speaking with me. I'm sorry to put you through this. But this is helpful."

"Enough to keep the cops away?"

"Hopefully."

She looked at Nicole. "What're you going to do now?"

"Visit the motel. Check the guest register. See if they have videos of you two coming and going at the times you said."

Megan dropped her gaze to her lap. "I want this to go away before it implodes." Her eyes glistened with tears. "And kills my marriage."

Nicole had little else to say to lessen the distraught Megan's concerns. Instead, she reached over and squeezed Megan's arm again, saying, "It'll be okay."

But would it? The potential for disaster here was real.

Nicole climbed from the car and watched as Megan drove away.

"So?" Jake asked when she settled into the driver's seat.

She related what Megan had said. When Jake asked if she believed her story, Nicole replied, "I do. I don't envy her position. Not in the least. She's walking a tightrope. With no net. If Detective Peters gets involved, there's no way that her husband won't know."

"Maybe we can prevent that."

Nicole cranked her SL to life. "Next stop the Sunset Lodge."

Her tires chirped as she accelerated toward the exit.

"Maybe we can get a room. Just for a couple of hours."

She glanced his way. "That's what it's come to? Cheap motels with threadbare carpet, age-grayed sheets, and leaky window air conditioners?"

"You're very poetic," Jake said.

"And you're a pig."

Jake feigned hurt feelings. "You don't like my idea?"

"I didn't say that. I said you were a pig." She smiled. "I meant it in the best way."

"Maybe they have a nice suite with a Jacuzzi tub."

"You're an idiot, too."

CHAPTER 20

No way the Sunset Lodge would have suites, much less Jacuzzi tubs. Not the Ritz-Carlton, but neither was it Dave's Dirty Dive. The name Pancake and I gave to the Happy Daze Inn, a place in Panama City where we had flopped. We were in high school and made a weekend run down that way to drink beer and chase girls. Didn't tell anyone. Our parents went from panicked to furious. Particularly Ray. I was grounded for a month.

Let me paint the picture. The Happy Daze had two dozen rooms that rented for twenty-two bucks a night, which should tell you something. Stained white stucco, sun-faded sickly yellow trim, much of it chipped and sagging from its moorings, and a skinny, tattooed, chain-smoking dude named Dave behind the counter. Thus, the name we gave the place. The dusty and dingy room had two single beds with mattresses as thin as a quilt. Neither of us fit, feet hanging off the end. The window AC churned with a metallic grind and the carpet smelled like mildew. We had planned two nights, but one was more than enough, thank you. The next night we slept on the beach, sharing a flattened sleeping bag and two beach towels for cover. The sand fleas had a big night. To them, we looked like a dead mackerel and a beached whale.

The Sunset Lodge sported a fresh coat of white paint and bright coral trim. Its three legs embraced a pool that looked onto the Navarre Parkway, the name for U.S. 98 as it passed through. Beyond lay Santa Rosa Sound and farther still Santa Rosa Island and the Gulf. Not an unpleasant view if you didn't mind the traffic.

Nicole pulled into a space in front of the rental office, which sat in the left elbow of the building. Two kids splashed in the pool and several adults lounged in chairs soaking up the sun, one an overweight dude already broiled to a lobster red. I suspected the array of empty beer cans on the table next to him helped reduce the pain.

A twenty-something young lady greeted us from behind the orange formica-topped counter, laying aside a frayed paperback when we entered. "Welcome," she said. "I'm Melody. What can I do for you?"

Nicole stepped up to the counter, me at her right shoulder. "I'm Nicole. This is Jake."

"Nice to meet you."

"We have a favor to ask," I said.

"Oh?"

"I saw security cameras out front." I nodded toward the ceiling behind her. "And in here."

Melody leaned back, now more cautious. "We do."

"Do they work?" Nicole asked.

"Why do you want to know?" Her hand slid toward the cell phone that lay to her left.

"Relax," Nicole said. "We're private investigators." She pulled the ID card Pancake had made for her from her purse and handed it to the now concerned Melody.

Melody examined the card and returned it. "So?"

"Someone who's a suspect in a crime said he was here with a friend. Last Monday. Late afternoon. We're trying to establish if that's true or not."

Melody didn't seem to relax much, if any. Her hand still lay near her phone and her brow remained creased.

"If you can show us your register and the surveillance video from then it would be very helpful," I said, offering her my best and most harmless smile.

Didn't seem to soften her.

"Let me explain," Nicole said. "We're investigating a murder."

"A murder?"

That got Melody's attention.

Nicole nodded. "We don't think the gentleman who stayed here was involved, but his name has come up, so we need to be sure. Your register and videos could prove his alibi, and we can go away and leave you alone."

"I'm not sure I can do that," Melody said.

"Sure you can," I said.

"It's either us or the police," Nicole said. Melody's eyebrows elevated. "We'd prefer the former. So would the gentleman and lady in question."

"You're saying someone was sneaking around?" Melody asked.

I nodded.

"And the suspect, as you call him, was here with his lover, so he couldn't be the person you're looking for?"

"Exactly."

Melody's hand moved away from the phone. "We run a family-oriented operation here. We try to avoid anything unseemly."

"And this isn't that," Nicole said. "It's two private people having an affair. Nothing more."

"We're trying to keep the police out of it," I said. "And the newspapers." I could see the questions in Melody's eyes. "We have a good working relationship with the police." Okay, a small lie but so far we had been playing well with Detective Brooke Peters. "If we can see the evidence, we can talk to the cops, and they'll not waste their and your time by coming to see for themselves."

I could sense wheels turning inside Melody's head as she assessed her options. She gazed at the countertop for a full half a minute. Nicole and I let it ride. Finally, she looked back up and nodded.

"Okay."

She slid the blue cloth–covered register book over in front of her and opened it. She thumbed back a couple of pages and turned it our way.

And right there it was: Gary Wayne Frawley, 4:30 p.m.

I glanced at Nicole. "He was here. At least he checked in."

"The security images?" Nicole asked.

"I can call them up right here on my computer." She turned the screen so that we could see it. She tapped the keyboard, opening a file folder that contained chronological video files. "You said Monday?"

"That's correct," I said.

She double-clicked and a fourplex of images appeared. "These two are out front." She pointed. "One shows the entrance, the other the parking lot and pool. This one is out back and this last one is here at the counter."

"Can you go to just before four thirty in the afternoon?"

"I think so." It took her a couple of minutes. "I've never done this before so I hope I'm doing it right." The video fast-forwarded. The time monitor whirled through the day. She stopped it at four twenty-five, then hit PLAY.

The clarity of the image suggested that the Sunset Lodge had ponied up for the enhanced package. A light-yellow Fiat and a white Camry came and went. At four thirty, a dark metallic gray Camaro pulled into a space along the left arm of the building, four slots down from the office. Gary Wayne Frawley stepped out. Then Megan's green Jeep pulled in next to him. He walked around her car to the driver's-side window and they talked briefly. He went inside, where that camera showed him signing in and paying for the room. Back outside, Megan climbed out of her vehicle and the couple entered a unit three doors from where they parked.

Again, Melody fast-forwarded through the next two hours. Quiet with only a couple of people visiting the office, people coming and going from the lot, and doing the same for the pool area, which seemed busier than it was today. At six thirty-two Megan came from the room. She stopped by her car, her phone to her ear.

"That matches the time she said she called her husband," Nicole said.

She climbed in her car and drove away. Eight minutes later, Gary Wayne came out and climbed in his car. As he backed from the slot, his Miami Dolphins rear window decal came into view.

"Looks good," I said.

"So the cops won't be coming here?" Melody asked.

"If we can convince them otherwise, no."

"Can we make a copy of this video?" Nicole asked.

Melody hesitated. "I don't know if I can do that."

"If we show this to the police, that should satisfy their curiosity," Nicole said.

Melody agreed. Nicole pulled a thumb drive from her purse. Really? She kept that in there? We made a copy and left.

"A thumb drive?" I asked as she spun onto Highway 98.

"Pancake's idea. He says you never know when you might need one." She smiled. "Looks like he was right. Again."

CHAPTER 21

THE TRAFFIC KICKED up as we rolled through Orange Beach. It was six p.m. and Nicole wasn't happy. Normal folks clogging up the road always tamped down her mood. But it was more than that. Other than muttering a few expletives at slow motorists, she had said little since we left Navarre. I knew better than to ask what was up, knowing she'd eventually get around to it.

She did.

"I feel sorry for her," Nicole said.

"Megan?"

"Yeah. She's painted herself into a corner." She braked at a red light. "I know it's her fault. She's married, and she's having an affair. But that's not earthshaking news. Or even unusual."

Was that ever true. Hell, I'd been guilty of that. Multiple times. When I was younger and stupider. Younger anyway. Regardless, that's my excuse, and I'm going to go with that. But that was my pre-Nicole era. I was different then. Did that mean I was maturing? Or worse, getting old and settling down? Not that Nicole was settling. Not in any definition of the word.

"This affair could cost her big-time," I said. "As they often do."

"Voice of experience?"

I glanced at her. "I should take the fifth, but to coin a phrase—Tammy."

"Ah, yes. Tammy, Tammy, Tammy."

"Don't do that."

Nicole passed a truck, its left turn signal activated. The car bumped over the uneven shoulder. "Don't do what?"

"I've told you this before—never say her name three times. She's like Beetlejuice."

Now she looked at me. "Did I tell you that you're an idiot?"

"You did. Many times. She's still Beetlejuice. Only worse."

We said nothing for the next mile. I waited for my phone to ring. It didn't.

"Do you think Detective Peters will accept our evidence?" Nicole asked. "Take it as a solid alibi for Gary Wayne?"

"Maybe. But the truth is I think she'll check it out herself. She seems pretty focused."

"I agree."

"Maybe she can call Megan or discretely meet her. Keep it as quiet as possible."

"It'll still be part of her records, which would then include Megan's name."

"Those are private," I said.

"Unless Gary Wayne is guilty or becomes the prime suspect. That would change things."

"It would."

"Or if the killer is found and goes to trial," Nicole said. "A good defense attorney would try to cloud the issue with as many alternative suspects as possible. Reasonable doubt and all that. That could include Gary Wayne and drag Megan into a courtroom."

"And divorce court," I said.

My phone buzzed. Caller ID read "Tammy." Which proved beyond any reasonable doubt that Tammy was Beetlejuice's long-lost sister from hell. Which wasn't fair to either Beetlejuice or hell.

I angled my phone toward Nicole. "See? I told you."

"Put it on speaker. I don't want to miss this."

Here's the thing. Tammy, my certifiably insane ex, loves to call me with her myriad of imagined troubles. Things I can't fix and have zero interest in. Our marriage, such as it was, ended years ago, cost me a bundle, and then she married her attorney, Walter Horton. Why she didn't take her troubles to Walter is an ongoing mystery, but I suspect that Walter's smart enough to avoid her delusions. Yet, he married her. I did too, so there is that.

Nicole is the opposite of helpful here. She loves to insert herself in the conversation and use whatever is said to heckle me later. Yes, heckle. As in badger, torment, needle. She excelled at that.

Avoiding Tammy, a speed-dial maven and master of wars of attrition, was impossible as she would continue to call until I gave up. So, I answered.

"Jake, where are you?"

"Orange Beach."

"Doing what?"

"Not that it's any of your concern, but I'm riding with Nicole."

"Oh. Hi, Nicole."

"Hi, Tammy," Nicole said.

"When're you going to dump this creep?"

"Maybe he'll dump me," Nicole said.

Tammy gave a soft laugh. Not a funny one. "Right. You're the best thing he's ever had. Except for me."

So very Tammy. Here, let me compliment you and then backhand you upside your head.

"What do you want, Tammy?" I asked. Not that I wanted to know, but moving this conversation along seemed the best plan. Like ripping the Band-Aid off. It might hurt, even bleed, but done is done.

"I need you to talk with Walter," Tammy said.

"Why?"

"He's being a jerk. I need you to tell him I'm sensitive and need his support."

"You think I'm the best person for that?" I asked.

"Of course. That's why I called you."

"All this time, I thought I was a heartless Neanderthal."

"You are. Which makes you the perfect person. If Walter sees that a prick like you thinks I'm sensitive and in need of support, he'll feel bad and do what I want him to do."

See? It always comes back to Tammy.

"Which is what?" I asked.

"A big fundraiser. Next weekend. For some kids charity. I forget what." Tammy, the sensitive one. "We were going and now Walter says he can't. Something about needing to go down to Panama City for some stupid meeting. Some client in trouble or something like that. Anyway, I bought this killer new dress just for this event. Where am I going to wear it now?"

"To Panama City?" I asked. "You can go to the Waffle House while Walter's in his meeting. You'd be a hit."

"You're such an ass."

"I try my best."

"Tell me about the dress," Nicole said.

I looked at her, giving her my best why-are-you-stirring-the-pot face. She suppressed a laugh. It's a conspiracy. I swear it is.

"Oh, you'd love it," Tammy said. "It's black, sleek, short, and shows off all my assets."

I wondered if it came with a matching muzzle. Okay, Tammy is hot. I'll give her that. Blonde, blue eyes, and fit from all her yoga and Pilates. But she's insane, which becomes apparent every time she opens her mouth. That tends to cool the hotness. Like dropping a hot poker into an ice bath. Thus, the need for the muzzle.

"Sounds great," Nicole said. "Where'd you get it?"

"That little shop—oh—what's the name? The one in Pensacola Beach."

"I think I know the one you're talking about. I can't think of the name either."

"So, Jake, are you going to talk with Walter?" Tammy asked, returning to her current issue.

"No."

"Why not?"

"Because I have nothing to say to him."

"What about me? I need you to do this."

"It'll work itself out. It always does."

"What does that mean?"

Where to start. Maybe that this is a nonissue. That it's the crisis of the moment and another will appear in a hot minute and this one will fade into oblivion. That it's a dress, and she has a closet full of them. That it's a fundraiser filled with people Tammy doesn't like, and she'll get wound up when she realizes they only want her there for Walter's money. I'd seen this before. Tammy liked to envision herself as part of society and charitable and all those touchy-feely things, but in reality she was so self-absorbed that no one else mattered. I came close to saying exactly that, but tugged on the reins before such thoughts escaped.

Instead, I said, "It means that Walter's a smart guy. He'll see that you're hurt and that you want to go to this event. He'll change his plans and all will go off as planned. You're new dress will be the hit of the party."

"You think so?"

I should've felt guilty throwing Walter under the bus but I didn't. He was the guy that emptied my wallet when I divorced Tammy, after all. So, deal with it, Walter, old boy.

"I do. Just wait. He'll come around."

"That's great. I can't believe I was worried for no reason." She hung up.

"You're welcome," I said to the phone.

"You're diabolical," Nicole said.

I smiled. "I work at that, too."

"You do."

"But I think I only kicked the can down the road. Walter has work to do. He doesn't let much get in the way of that." I shrugged. "We haven't heard the last of this."

CHAPTER 22

IT WAS SIX THIRTY by the time Nicole and I walked past Pancake's truck and into Captain Rocky's. His presence meant that my budget and supply chain were under siege. Around here we call that Tuesday, or Wednesday, or Friday, actually any day. Pancake ate Captain Rocky's food at least once a day. Seemed to be an addiction. Maybe I could get him into rehab. Does McDonald's Hamburger University have such a program? Probably not. Why would they? They want people addicted to their food. I had to admit that I did at times jones for a Big Mac.

On the positive side of the ledger, the place was lively and jumping. Carla had the music cranked up, and every table filled. Alcohol-boosted laughter wedged itself into the classic rock soundtrack. A large group had melded several tables together into a flotilla of nachos, wings, jalapeño poppers, beer mugs, and margarita schooners.

Maybe I could afford Pancake this week.

We found Pancake ensconced at my table with Detective Brooke Peters, who laughed at something he said, one hand on his arm. I doubted they were discussing the case.

In a Machiavellian way, this could be a good thing for our case. Listen to me. Our case? I had to admit that this situation was more engaging than Ray's usual crap. Still, it was Ray's crap, meaning it would become a hot mess with no way to bob and weave out of it.

But if Detective Peters was on our side, or at least allowed us access to information, things might go more smoothly. So far, the transfer of information had gone from Ray and Pancake to her. The two-way street had yet to materialize.

A platter of nachos and two margaritas sat before them. Pancake doing his best to pry open the gate.

"There you are," Pancake said. "We thought you'd gotten lost."

"Traffic," Nicole said.

"We know how you deal with that."

Nicole smiled. "Nothing a hood-mounted rocket launcher couldn't resolve."

"Good thing Mercedes doesn't offer that option," I said. "She would've vaporized a couple of pickups on the way here."

"Well-deserved vaporizations," she said.

We sat. Libby came our way. Nicole and I ordered margaritas.

Peters, still dabbing laughter tears from her eyes with the corner of her napkin, said, "You didn't tell me Pancake was so funny."

"He's not," I replied. "But I've heard all his stories." I snatched a nacho and shoved it in my mouth. "Hell, I lived most of them."

"So he said." Peters sipped her margarita. "He was telling me about a teenage trip to Panama City. What did he call it? Dave's Dirty Dive?"

Karma, the cosmos, the ether, whatever you wish to call it, works in curious ways. Earlier, that trip had crossed my mind. That thought had shaken the Earth's molecules, which in turn invaded Pancake's mind. He then felt the need to tell Peters the story. I mean, I know that Google and Facebook and all those techie companies have access to your entire life and can predict what you're going to do and think, and buy, often before you're aware of it. How many times have you thought of something and bingo ads for it appear on your computer? The miasma we call the cloud. Spooky. But when Mother Nature's ether projects your thoughts, that's something else again. It's disconcerting to think that my thoughts can enter the linguini of Pancake's brain, a place that needs no help finding weird. I don't know about you, but that scares the hell out of me.

"Not our best idea," I said.

Pancake drained his margarita. "But we got a good story out of it."

Libby returned with four margaritas on a tray. "Thought I'd save time and bring another round." She nodded toward Pancake. "Looks like one of those nights."

No doubt, Libby possessed a firm grasp of the ropes around here. Or was she tapped into the world's cloud storage?

Peters drained her margarita and took a sip of the fresh one. "Are you trying to get me drunk?" she asked Pancake.

"You're a big girl," Pancake said. "I think you can handle that all by your ownself."

"For the record," Peters said, "it's not my night on squeal."

"Squeal?" Nicole asked.

"That's what we call frontline duty. The one that catches the calls. The squeals."

"Detective first call is better than uniform first call," Pancake said.

Peters nodded. "No doubt. We have four detectives and we take turns. But, I well remember my days in uniform. First on the scene and all that comes with that. Drugs, fights, sometimes guns.

Family, friends, neighbors—always nosey, often angry. Not know-ing who's a victim, who's a bad guy, who's a witness, who in the crowd is armed, and willing to use a weapon. Domestics definitely being the worst. We detectives get called after the frontline guys have assessed the situation. If they can handle it, fine, but if not, if someone gets killed, or at least shot, and sometimes bigger rob-beries, we get the squeal."

"Then drink up," Nicole said. She raised her glass, tilting it toward Peters.

"Anything new?" I asked.

"This guy"—she nudged Pancake with an elbow—"is a genius."

"Don't pump up his head any more," I said. "It might explode and release enough shrapnel to doom the planet."

Pancake grunted.

Peters laughed, and again touched Pancake's arm. "We ran through the numbers that showed Mitch Littlefield raided the cookie jar for three years, and for well over three hundred thousand."

"Most likely," Pancake said. "Once you give me the files you grabbed at the realty company, I can put a bow on it." Pancake bounced an eyebrow. "Copies will do."

Peters glanced at me. "He's relentless. He's been singing that tune all afternoon."

"He's annoying," I said.

"That too." Another laugh. "But fun nonetheless."

The transformation was unambiguous. I'd seen it before. The all-business Peters had morphed into an infatuated schoolgirl. The Pancake effect.

"So he's still the prime suspect?" I asked. "Littlefield?"

"So far, top of the hit parade. We don't have a smoking gun yet, but we're looking." A sip of her margarita. "A couple of uniform guys grabbed videos from several businesses along the route Littlefield said he took home. Most proved worthless, but one service station camera gave us a glimpse of the street. A car matching Mitch's black BMW rolled by at the time he would be headed home. No license plate visible, so it might not have been him."

"So he could have backtracked to the office?" I asked.

Peters shrugged. "Possible."

And there it was. A bit of reverse information flow.

"What about Dustin?" Nicole asked.

"Again, we only found one useful video. Him going into a grocery store that's halfway between his office and home. That matches what he and Savannah said."

"So, they both might be off the hook?" Nicole said.

"Not ready to say that." Peters looked at Nicole and me. "What about you? Anything?"

"We talked to Gary Wayne Frawley's mistress," I said.

"How'd you manage that?"

"We told him that if she talked to us," Nicole said, "we might be able to convince you he wasn't a viable suspect and maybe avoid her name coming into it."

Peters shrugged. "Not likely. But go ahead. Convince me."

Nicole told her of the stories Gary Wayne and Megan, without giving her name, had told us and that they matched. That we had visited the motel where they were and had copies of the security footage that corroborated their story.

"Really?" Peters asked.

I waved to Carla. She came our way. I asked her to grab my laptop from my office.

"Your leg's broken?" she asked. "I'll call the medics." She smiled. "Back in a sec."

She returned with my computer. I fired it up and Nicole slipped in the thumb drive. I slid it toward Pancake. He could handle the videos in a fraction of the time it would take Nicole and me.

"Let's see." His fingers worked the keyboard. Nicole and I stood and moved around behind him to get a view of the screen.

"Go to four twenty-five," I said.

He did and started the video. Soon, Gary Wayne's Camaro appeared. He parked and stepped out as Megan's Jeep slid in beside him. A few words between them and Gary Wayne headed into the office.

"Go to that file," Nicole said, pointing.

Pancake opened it. The check in counter video. He raced to four thirty and Gary Wayne appeared. He signed the register, paid with cash, and walked from view. Back to the outside camera, he and Megan entered a door near their cars.

"Now go to six thirty," I said.

Pancake did. We watched Megan exit the room, climb in her car, complete her call, and drive away. A few minutes later, Gary Wayne followed the same pattern.

"See the Miami Dolphins sticker on his rear window?" Nicole asked. "It's his car."

"Clear video," Pancake said. "I should be able to enhance both license plates. "

"For a small motel, this is amazing," Peters said. "Hell, I've seen worse in multimillion-dollar homes." She nodded toward the screen. "What's the woman's name?"

"We'd rather not say," Nicole said. "We told her we'd protect her. That's the only way she agreed to talk with us."

"I can grab it from her licenses plate so save me some time."

That was true. So why aggravate her? The two-way street had eased open and closing it wouldn't be smart. Not to mention that Pancake might strangle me—literally—if I messed things up for him.

"You promise not to go see her?" Nicole asked.

"No." She smiled. "But with this, I'm inclined to push Gary Wayne off the front burner. Hell, even off the stove. I never liked him for the killer, anyway. Too big a stretch motive wise."

"Her name is Megan Varner," Nicole said. "She's scared and humiliated. If this came to light, it would crush her husband. They have a three-year-old."

Pancake copied the files to my laptop, ejected the thumb drive, and handed it to Peters.

"So, this is everything you need?" I asked.

"I'll still have to talk to her. I'll keep what you said in mind and do so quietly. Maybe only a phone chat. If she satisfies me that this is as it seems, she'll simply be a footnote in my murder book."

"Let me call her first," Nicole said. "Let her know that you'll call and to not get freaked out."

"That'll work," Peters said.

Libby appeared. "Another round?"

"Sure," Peters said. "Why not."

Yeah, why not.

CHAPTER 23

I WOKE UP at six thirty, my face buried in my pillow. A little groggy, a tad stiff, but rested. Last night, Nicole and I reached her place around nine, downed some tequila, jumped in bed, did our thing, and by eleven were in a coma. I rolled onto my back and stretched out the kinks.

I heard Nicole in the kitchen. I slipped on my jeans and followed the aroma of coffee that way.

"Did you sleep well?" Nicole asked.

"I did."

"Grab some coffee and then jump in the shower."

"You going to join me?"

She lifted a coffee mug. "For coffee, yes, but I've already showered."

How did I miss that? I must've really been out. I mean, to miss that opportunity. "Wouldn't hurt to have another one."

"Are you saying I'm dirty?"

"Yes, but in a good way."

"Go take a shower, Jake."

"What's the rush?"

"Do you ever listen to me?" she asked.

Uh-oh.

Moving on, she said, "We're meeting Savannah this morning."

Did I know that? A vague niggling rose in the back of my mind but I couldn't be sure. "Why?"

"To see how she's doing and if she has any more insights on Mitchell Littlefield." She drained her coffee cup. "But first we have to feed Pancake."

Of course we did.

So showered, shaved, and clad in jeans and a gray golf shirt, we swung by Captain Rocky's and then to Ray's, finding him and Pancake on the deck. I placed the bag of breakfast burritos on the table. Pancake snatched one, unwrapped it, and took a huge bite.

"You're a lifesaver," he said. "Ray ain't got shit to eat around here."

"We're headed over to Savannah's," Nicole said.

Now I remembered. Sometime during our drinking with Pancake and Peters last night, Pancake suggested we, really Nicole, go by and see Savannah. Not just to check on her and to keep her up to date on things, but to see if she had given Mitch Littlefield any more thought. Maybe some subtle change in his behavior. Maybe even such changes in her father, or in the dynamic between the two. Any hint of trouble between them. Mitch already occupied the top slot in the suspect list, but if he knew Carl had discovered his financial shenanigans, it would push him way out front. So far, we had no evidence of that.

Savannah had earlier told us that everything seemed normal to her, but she was in shock from her father's death. Now, a few days later, she might recall something useful. That was Pancake's thinking. Peters agreed. Nicole called and arranged to meet her at eight thirty this morning.

"Anything new we should relate to her?" Nicole asked.

"Yes," Ray said. "Pancake dissected the partnership agreement between Carl and Mitch."

"I thought you didn't have that," I said.

"Turns out it was in a mislabeled folder in the materials Carl gave us last Friday."

"And?" I asked.

Pancake shoved the last chunk of his first—not only, mind you—burrito into his mouth. He opened a folder and shuffled through the pages inside, finding the one he wanted. He slid it toward me. "I doubt you want to read it, but there it is."

Before I could say anything—like no, I didn't want to read it, I wanted him to give me the thumbnail—Nicole picked up the page and scanned it.

"Bottom line is if either partner dies," Pancake said, "his share goes to his heirs as spelled out in his individual trust and will. Standard stuff. Interestingly, though, if either partner is convicted of a felony, his ownership shares go to the other partner. Completely, totally, and without contingency." Pancake unwrapped his next burrito. "Doesn't matter what outside arrangements the felonious partner might have made—wills, contracts, whatever—this supersedes it, and any outside claims on the realty company or its assets are null and void. The convicted partner owns nothing as far as the company is concerned."

Even I understood that. If Mitch goes down for embezzlement, or murder, or both, Savannah owns the company outright. Her inherited half and Mitch's surrendered half. This was huge. She stood to gain millions of dollars and a successful company that should generate many millions more as the years rolled by.

Was Savannah involved in her father's death? Did she not know about Mitch's embezzling as she claimed? Was she aware of the details hidden in the partnership agreement? She had said she knew little about her father's business, but was that true? If she knew everything, did she spin up a plot to kill her father and grab everything?

Money, big money, makes folks do strange and immoral things. I had sensed nothing but shock and grief from Savannah, but was she the devil in disguise?

I hoped not. I liked her.

CHAPTER 24

SAVANNAH APPEARED LESS frayed than the last time I saw her. No red eyes, no bags beneath them. She wore a floral summer dress and sandals, makeup adding a rosy glow to her cheeks. Big change. No longer an emotional wreck, she appeared sweet, innocent, and undamaged.

"How're you doing?" Nicole asked as we sat down in her living room

"I'm not sure. Good days, bad days. Good hours and tough hours. I managed to sleep last night. And make Dustin breakfast this morning. Poor dear, he's had to stop for donuts the past couple of days. He hates to eat junk food, but I couldn't drag myself out of bed in the morning."

"Looks like you did okay today," I said.

"I feel better. Enough to get moving anyway. I guess the shock is fading. Not the grief. I've decided to stop dwelling on the negative and begin putting things back together." She gave a headshake. "Still not sure how, but I'm working on it."

"One day at a time," Nicole said. "One step at a time."

"That's what they say." Savannah gave us a weak smile. "But each step seems heavy. Like I'm walking in molasses."

I flashed on when my mother died. That's how it felt. My entire body numb, heavy, standing a challenge. Walking a labor. Thinking or talking sensibly impossible. The world indistinct, as if viewed through fog, or ground glass. Even breathing became difficult.

"How's the business going?" I asked.

"Frantic, according to Dustin. He and Mitch have to take over Dad's accounts, so he's been working longer hours the last two days. He feels guilty about leaving me alone, but I told him he has to take care of things and keep the business going. That I'll be all right. Not sure that's true." She sighed. "I wish I had something to do. I mean, something important, something I couldn't put off or ignore. Instead, I sit here all day and think too much."

"That's the main reason we wanted to come by," Nicole said. "To make sure you're okay."

"That's so kind." Her eyes glistened. "It means a lot."

"Have you given any more thought to Mitchell Littlefield?" I asked.

"A lot. It's hard to believe he stole from my father." She folded her hands in her lap and gazed at them. "I don't understand any of it. It makes no sense. But to answer your question, I've racked my brain trying to remember anything that seemed off. I came up with nothing. Neither Mitch nor my dad behaved differently in any way. Except maybe Dad being a little distracted. Now I know why, but I still don't understand why my father didn't tell me what was going on." She looked at me. "I feel clueless. Out of touch. Like I was busy living life, actually doing very little, and not paying attention. And now I feel . . . lost."

"Don't be hard on yourself," Nicole said. "It's a common feeling. People don't focus on details until they have to, and when something like this happens, they feel out of touch. Like they should've predicted what happened. Known it was coming."

"But that's rarely the case," I said. "These things come out of the blue. It's natural to think you should've seen it coming, and prevented it. Unfortunately, life isn't that way."

She nodded. "I know. And now I have to deal with Mitch being a bad guy. A thief."

"We don't know that for sure," I said. "It just smells that way. Once Pancake gets the materials Carl had for him, he'll know more. Right now, the police have them and are holding them close."

"When do you think they'll let you see them?" Savannah asked.

"That's up to Detective Peters."

"It can't be soon enough," Savannah said. "I need to know what's going on." She looked at Nicole, then me. "How else can I get through this?"

Wasn't that the truth? Her father dead, his lifelong friend and partner in the middle of it as a thief and possibly a killer, and a business that needed tending. I imagined to Savannah it felt like juggling butcher knives. Blindfolded.

"There's one other thing," I said. "Pancake went through the partnership agreement. You do indeed inherit your father's ownership interest in the company."

"I thought so but I didn't know. Dad's mentioned it in the past, but I didn't really pay attention." She sighed. "I guess I thought he would live forever and I didn't need to think about such things."

"There's more," I said. "A morals section, clause, whatever it's called. It says that if either partner is convicted of a felony, that partner's share is forfeited to the other partner."

"I don't understand," Savannah said.

Did she? Was that knowledge that kicked off this entire chain of events? I hated thinking that, but it was too obvious to ignore. Every murder has a motive and money is often in the mix.

"It means that if Mitch is convicted of embezzling, you'll own the entire company," Nicole said.

"No," Savannah said. "That can't be true."

"It is. According to Pancake, it looks solid."

"I didn't know that." She rubbed one temple. "Dustin did mention that might be the case. He said a lot of companies and partnerships have such provisions, but he didn't know for sure if Dad and Mitch had done so in their agreement." She took a deep breath. "To be honest, I'm not sure how I feel about it. I mean, Mitch and my dad had been friends forever. They built the company from the ground up."

"He stole from your dad," I said. "From you too."

"I don't know anything about real estate or running a company or any of that. I wouldn't know where to start."

"That's why people hire managers," Nicole said.

"I'm thankful I have Dustin. He knows real estate and has a head for business."

"He can be the manager then," I said.

"He'll be more than that. We're moving the wedding forward. Our plan was to wait a few more months and have a big deal. A beachfront venue, bridesmaids, caterers, the whole thing. But with Dad gone, that seems wasteful." She knuckled a tear from one corner of her eye. "I so much wanted him to walk me down the aisle." She let out a stuttering breath. "He did too. Now I guess it'll be before a justice of the peace or at the courthouse. Simple and quiet."

"When?" Nicole asked.

"We don't know yet. Soon. Maybe in a few weeks."

"If you need," Nicole said, "we'll show up and be witnesses."

"That would be very welcome." Another tear knuckled away. "I'm so glad my dad hired you guys. And so glad I know you. Your support means a lot."

CHAPTER 25

NICOLE AND I stood and were ready to say goodbye to Savannah when a thought came to me. Yes, I sometimes have those. What followed was an absolute miracle. A gold mine. A game changer. And that's being modest.

"Did Carl do any work from home?" I asked.

"Sure. He has an office."

"Does he keep any business-related papers in there?"

"I believe so. Dad was compulsive about keeping duplicates. Both digitally and hard copy. He'll definitely have everything in his cloud storage, and I bet he has paper copies in his office."

"Didn't the police take them?" Nicole asked.

She shook her head. "Just the stuff from the realty office. If I remember correctly, Detective Peters said that's all they needed, but if she found she needed something from here, she'd let me know. I told her she could have anything she wanted."

"So if he had copies of the files he had put together for Ray and Pancake, they might be here?" Nicole asked.

"Maybe. Want to check?"

Did we ever.

Carl's home office was a converted bedroom, since it had a closet and an attached bathroom. His desk faced a large picture

window that offered a view toward the pool and beyond the boat
dock and Belleview Bay. Savannah began opening drawers. The
upper left one was empty. Except for a handgun. I recognized it as
a .38 revolver. Nickel plated, short barrel.

"That's Dad's," Savannah said. She stared at it for several seconds. "I didn't like him having it, but I understand why he felt the
need. You just never know." She looked at me. "I wish he'd had it
at the office. Maybe he could've defended himself."

She pushed the drawer closed and slid open the upper right
one. She lifted a small blue hardback notebook and extended it
toward me.

"Would this help? It has all his passwords."

"Yes, it would."

She smiled. "He had one of those encrypted online password
programs, and he actually used it. But he was old school and liked
to write them down."

Thank you, Carl. Pancake will go crazy when he sees this.

When I asked where he might have kept any company papers,
Savannah pointed to an old and dented file cabinet in one corner.

"He keeps important stuff in there," she said. "He's had that
thing forever. Mom and I kidded him about it, but he said it
worked, so why swap for a new one?"

I walked to it and tugged on the top-drawer handle. Locked.

She rummaged toward the back of the desk's middle drawer.
Her hand came out with a key. She gave a soft laugh.

"He didn't know I knew where this was. Dad had a sweet tooth.
He'd hide candy in that cabinet to keep it away from me. One day
I found the key and the candy. I'd pilfer goodies all the time."

"He never knew?" Nicole asked.

"If he did, he never said anything."

"Maybe he put the candy there knowing you would find a way inside," I said. Ray tried that with alcohol, but Pancake and I found the key to the cabinet and helped ourselves, replacing what we took with water. Did Ray know? Probably. Ray knew everything.

Savannah laughed. "I never thought of that. But that would be so like him."

Inside the filing cabinet's top drawer, I found several gray envelopes. Those with the little metal closure clips. One labeled "Private" in handwritten black block lettering and another toward the back that was thick and unlabeled. I took both of them to the desk, sat, and began going through their contents.

The "Private" one held a stack of pages. A sticky note planted on the first page read, "Copies." The pages behind held columns of numbers. Hieroglyphics to me. I noticed the dates covered the last six months.

"This might be the information he had for Pancake," I said. "What we were going to pick up."

"Really?" Nicole asked. She moved behind me and looked over my shoulder. "That would be amazing."

No doubt.

The unlabeled envelope held important personal docs. A copy of the house deed, two automobile pink slips, a copy of his will, and a copy of the corporate papers for Orange Coast Realty.

"Can we take this stuff to Pancake?" I asked.

"If it will help, sure," Savannah said.

"If this is what I think it is, it will."

I collected the files and the password book and we walked toward the front door. We said our goodbyes to Savannah, adding that we'd call and give her an update soon.

CHAPTER 26

I FELT GUILTY. A sensation I almost never encountered. Pancake says it's because my life is boring. Vanilla was the word he used. I reminded him of our childhood, where we were always guilty, whether we felt it or not. Whether we did it or not. We got blamed for everything off kilter in the neighborhood. I guess they were playing the odds. We failed at discretion and stealth as Ray and my mom knew what we were up to long before we did the deed. At least it seemed that way. We preferred being caught by Pancake's parents. More forgiving than Ray. To him, we were heathens, barbarians, and master criminals.

My current guilty feelings had nothing to do with my childhood. Rather, my brain had concocted a cluster of nasty scenarios. Most right out of a B movie script. Like how and why Savannah might've hired someone to kill her father in a murderous plot to take over the company and the estate. That she and Dustin had hatched the scheme together. Or that Mitch and Dustin conspired to control the agency. That Savannah and Mitch were tangled in some cabal, maybe an affair—no, surely not. Was it possible that Savannah knew of the embezzling and was part of the plot?

I hated that my imagination went to those places. Each down and dirty and dark. I mentally ran through every encounter I'd had with any of the players in this tragedy, but none of these storylines fit.

Nicole would say I watched too many of those true crime shows. I believe I read too many of her screenplays. Always dark and dangerous stories.

Yeah, that's it. It's Nicole's fault.

"What do you think?" Nicole asked, breaking my reverie.

We had motored down Ono Boulevard and hopped on the bridge that led off the island. Our destination: Ray's place.

"I don't know what to think."

"You were contemplating something," she said. "Or were you having a waking dream?"

"Well, you were driving sensibly for a change, so rather than holding on for my life I might've dozed."

"Wimp."

"Not what you said last night."

"You do have your moments. But let's not relive past history. Tell me what's in your head."

She turned west onto Perdido Beach Boulevard toward Gulf Shores. I ran through each of my scenarios. After we crossed the bridge over the inlet to Bayou Saint John and approached Orange Beach, I looked at her and smiled. "Aren't you glad you asked?"

"I am. It amazes me that your pretty little brain came up with all that."

"You've never seen my brain," I said.

"It's behind your pretty face so it must be pretty too."

Good grief.

She laughed. "But with a twisted mind like that, you should write screenplays."

"I'll leave that to you."

"Each of those could be a movie."

I gave a half shrug. "Probably already are."

"That's true. But the devil, and the difference, is in the details. I mean, there are really only two types of story."

"Only two?"

"Somebody comes or somebody leaves. That's it. Someone, some thing, or some situation comes into your main character's life and knocks it off balance. The story is how they rebalance life. Or, the hero goes somewhere, gets involved in a stressful situation, and must solve the riddle. Stranger in a strange land sort of thing."

"I never realized screenplays were so easy."

"Try it sometime. See if you feel the same."

"Again, I'll leave that to you."

The pickup in front of us slowed, turned on its left turn signal, and rolled to a stop, waiting for a break in the oncoming traffic. Not deterred, Nicole strayed on to the shoulder and passed it.

"Okay, so let's plot each of these stories," Nicole said. "Let's say it's Savannah. How would she pull this off?"

"She could've hired someone."

"Who?"

"A friend, a lover, a pro."

"All good possibilities," Nicole said. "Her motive would be easy. An estate, a company, and a boatload of cash."

"Old and reliable motives," I agreed.

"Was Dustin involved?"

"Possible. Maybe he figured the money, the business, and that wonderful house would make good wedding presents."

Nicole smiled. "A dowry of sorts."

"Exactly."

"I think that's unlikely, but moving the marriage forward does add a certain element."

I glanced at her. "That's what I thought."

"Could Mitch be involved in this little conspiracy?" Nicole asked.

"That's more difficult. If Pancake's right—and isn't he always? —Mitch is headed to court, maybe jail."

"Which hands the entire company to the newlyweds."

"But, if Mitch was part of the conspiracy, wouldn't he bargain his way out of any embezzlement charges? Squeal long and loud and bring them all down?"

"He might. Let's move on. What if only Mitch and Dustin hatched the plan?"

"To me, that makes more sense," I said. "I don't see Savannah killing her own father. She seems truly damaged by his death. So if it's only those two, we again have the problem of Mitch's thefts."

By now we had left Orange Beach behind and approached Gulf Shores. The traffic light. Thanks for small favors.

"I see a way around that," Nicole said. "Dustin says he needs Mitch to run the company. That it's too big for him alone. That Mitch has all that institutional memory needed to keep things going."

I nodded. "Mitch agrees to pay restitution, which would make good financial sense from the company's point of view, the charges are dropped since Savannah, and Dustin, refuse to press charges, and life goes on."

"Not for Carl."

"No, not for Carl."

"In the end," Nicole said, "if I had to pick someone, I'd still go with Mitch. He has the most to gain. And avoid. Either he did it or had someone do it."

"He could afford it," I said. "With the money he stole."

Nicole slid to a stop among the pylons that supported Ray's house. I saw Ray's black '66 Camaro SS but not Pancake's big Chevy Dual-cab.

"Wonder where the big guy is?" I asked.

"You might not want to know."

We found Ray on his deck, as usual. Computer open in front of him, a Mountain Dew nearby.

"We're headed over to Captain Rocky's," I said.

"Why?" Ray asked.

"Carla wants to go over a few things with me."

Ray smiled. "Again, why?"

Why are people, meaning Ray, Pancake, and Nicole, always questioning my involvement in the nuts and bolts of my business? Okay, not a good question.

"We brought you a gift," I said. I handed him the two envelopes and the blue password book Savannah had given us.

"What is it?" he asked.

"Copies of the papers Carl had collected for Pancake, I think,"

"Really?"

"And his password book," Nicole said.

Ray tugged the pages from the envelope labeled "Private" and rummaged through them. "Where'd you get this?"

"Savannah," Nicole said. "Carl had a home office. He kept copies of important documents."

I explained the locked filing cabinet and how Savannah knew the combination from her childhood candy hunt.

"I hope you brought Pancake some candy," Ray said.

"Just this stuff," I said.

Ray laughed. "You better hope he doesn't find out."

CHAPTER 27

"WHAT'S ALL THIS?" Detective Brooke Peters asked.

"Thought you might be hungry," Pancake said.

She slid into the booth across from him. Between them sat two steaming cups of coffee and two plates, one with three ham and cheese croissants and the other with six blueberry muffins.

"Are you expecting someone else? Like a family of eight?"

"No. Why?"

"This is a bit much, don't you think?" Peters said.

"Looks about right to me." Pancake grinned.

"I had some Cheerios before going to the office earlier."

"That's not breakfast. That's not even a snack."

She laughed. "For you."

They sat in a window booth at Black Kat Koffee, a popular local hangout on Perdido Beach Boulevard in Orange Beach. Near Peters' office, which is why Pancake suggested it when he called earlier.

A young woman with purple hair and a lip ring appeared. "Can I grab you guys another coffee?" she asked.

"I haven't touched this one yet," Peters said.

"I'll check back later." She headed toward a nearby table, asking the same question.

"Dig in," Pancake said.

"I'll pass."

"Not even a nibble?" Pancake picked up a croissant and took a bite.

"Maybe half a muffin."

"There you go."

She broke off a piece and took a bite. "Hmmm. These are good. I've seen this place forever but never been here. It's quaint."

"Glad I made the right choice."

"Which brings up the question, why're we here? You were cryptic on the phone."

"That's me. International man of mystery."

"You're mysterious all right." Peters sipped her coffee, examined him for a few seconds, another sip. "So, again, why're we here?"

"Because I wanted to see you again." She started to speak, but he continued. "I enjoyed working with you yesterday. Particularly at Jake's place last night. You were more yourself, relaxed and funny."

"You don't know that. Maybe last night was an anomaly."

"Anomaly. I like that word." He finished one croissant and snatched up a muffin. "Doesn't work here though. I can read people and last night was the real you."

Another smile. "Maybe." She glanced around the room, out the window, back to him. "But this"—she waved a hand his way—"whatever this is, isn't really appropriate."

"In what way?"

"I'm working a murder case. You're working for the victim, or now, the victim's daughter. Don't you see the conflict?"

"Since we're both on the same mission, to find out who killed Carl Davis, I'd call it a partnership."

"My boss might not agree."

"Unless we can, together, crack this case."

"Crack the case? You sound like a 1940s cop, or P.I."

"Part of my misspent youth reading Chandler and Hammett."

"I bet you did." A sip of coffee. "For the record, so did I."

"Any conflict here is more imagined than real. Ray and I've worked with law enforcement agencies too many times to count. Comes with the territory. Some got a little wonky but most were effective collaborations with excellent results. There're things your department can do that we can't, and things we can do that you can't. Seems like a good marriage."

"And this? Coffee and small talk?"

"You have an odd definition of small talk." That drew a soft laugh from her. "Besides, I have something for you." He broke off a piece of muffin and ate it.

"Let's have it," Peters said. "Maybe I'll feel better about this."

"The partnership agreement between Mitch Littlefield and Carl Davis has a morals clause. If either partner is convicted of a felony, he forfeits his ownership to the other."

"Define ownership."

"Everything. One hundred percent. All ownership and all assets. And to answer your next question, yes, it appears airtight. Ray has an attorney looking into the details, but I've seen a few of these and this one is right down the line." Another bite of muffin. "I'm sure your guys will look into it too and come to the same conclusion."

"They're already dissecting it." She took another nibble of her muffin. "So if Mitch Littlefield goes down, Savannah gets the entire company?"

Pancake nodded.

She stared at him, the corners of her eyes crinkled as she considered that. "You're not saying that Savannah killed her own father, are you?"

"Not really. In fact, I don't see her doing that."

"And you read people well." Peters smiled.

"Touché. I could be wrong, but I don't think so. Plus, I'm not sure Savannah was aware of the agreement details. She's not involved in the company, and from what I've seen, isn't all that interested in it."

"Except she benefits from the money it generates."

"But the gravy train depends on her father's continued success."

"What about the fiancé? Dustin?"

"I'd for sure consider him. But again, that would probably involve Savannah. In the end, everything points to Mitchell Littlefield."

"Motive, means, and opportunity," Peters added.

"Definitely a motive. If Carl discovered his thefts, which he did evidenced by him hiring us, and if Mitch knew he had and knew he could lose everything if that ever entered a courtroom, he'd have to act."

"The added threat of jail time would only sweeten the motive," Peters said.

"Self-preservation is the strongest motive of all." Pancake opened his palms toward her. "See? This is a business meeting."

She gave a headshake. "You're very clever, Mr. Pancake."

"I am."

"And modest."

"That, too." He leaned forward, forearms on the table's edge. "The truth is that I could have called you with this, but I wanted to see your smiling face again."

"Yes, you could have. But I'm glad you wanted to see my face."

"Speaking of which, dinner tonight?"

"Don't push your luck."

"That's not a no."

She eyed him. "No, it's not. Let me think about it."

"I'll make a reservation."

"You're very confident," Peters said.

"Don't forget modest."

CHAPTER 28

PETERS FOLLOWED PANCAKE into the parking lot, where he stopped in front of their vehicles. He gave her a hug before climbing into his massive truck. She felt uncomfortable, even guilty, with that intimacy. She looked around, sure the entire world was watching and judging her. No one seemed to care. A woman corralled three kids into a van; a young man carried a giant to-go cup out of Black Kat Coffee, his phone to his ear, talking animatedly; a young couple sat at an outdoor table, sipping cappuccinos, chatting casually, paying her no attention.

Now she felt silly for worrying.

The warmth of Pancake's body lingered, and a slight thrill crept up her spine.

Jesus, Brooke, get a grip.

She climbed into her car, cranked the engine, then jacked up the AC, directing the vents toward her flushed face. What was wrong with her? She was acting like a high schooler, not an adult, not a police officer. She watched Pancake's truck turn out of the lot and roll out of sight. He had red hair for Christ sakes. She didn't even like guys with red hair. She wasn't sure where that came from, maybe the uncle she had that drank too much and talked too loud, and stood too close. He had red hair.

Not to mention Pancake was so big. She had never gone for the big burly football player type, preferring the tall and slim guys. Of course, each of those had turned out to be jerks. Like most guys in her experience. So why did she feel this . . . what was the word? She couldn't even define it. Gaga, giddy, girly? Damn it, she was none of those. She was tough and prided herself on that fact.

In the academy, she earned top notch marksman grades, tore up the obstacle course, and knocked more than a few of the guys on their butts during pugil sticks combat. She had wrestled meth-amped guys, one memorable dude with fifty pounds on her, to the ground and snapped cuffs on them. Once, she risked a fiery death to drag an unconscious woman from her car after it struck a power pole, flipped on its roof, and ignited the gas that spilled from the ruptured fuel tank.

Through the windshield, she focused on the couple at the table. Happy, smiling, holding hands, and then they leaned in and shared a kiss.

That wasn't helping.

She backed from the space and turned onto Perdido Beach Boulevard, her destination Savannah Davis' home. Not that she didn't feel that Pancake was right in his assessment—he probably was—but she wanted to take her own face-to-face read on Savannah. Assess her thoughts on possibly taking over the entire multimillion-dollar company. Her cop mind said that was a potent motive. Money made people do insane things, including patricide. She had seen it before. Family members, business partners, best friends turning on each other, even to the point of murder, over fortunes big and small. This one was big and came with a strong future. Well, maybe. With both Carl and Mitch out of the picture, would the company continue to prosper, or even survive? Could Savannah and Dustin keep the gravy train rolling? Would they hire a professional manager, or even sell it to someone who could keep it on track?

Or was Savannah so shocked and confused that she couldn't make such plans?

Those were the questions that drew her over the bridge to Ono Island and Savannah's front door.

Savannah answered her knock after a full minute. She looked tired and stressed, but less anguished than the last time she had seen her. Time was working its magic. Somewhat.

"Sorry to bother you," Peters said.

"No. It's okay. I was just doing . . ." Savannah glanced back toward the interior. "Actually nothing." She tugged the door wide. "Come in, please."

They settled in the living room.

"Truth is," Savannah said, "I don't know what I'm doing. I have so much to take care of and yet I can't seem to get organized. I can't even begin. I think about one thing and then something else intrudes and I seem to spin in circles." She exhaled a breath. "See? I'm rambling about nonsense."

To Peters, Savannah's welcoming smile, gracious manner, even her floral dress, seemed a facade. One that cloaked her internal turmoil. Peters feared the young woman might break down at any minute. "Under the circumstances, not unexpected. This has been traumatic, I'm sure."

Savannah sniffed. "It has. But this isn't me. I'm always so together."

"This situation you've never faced. It's personal. There's no playbook here."

Savannah gave a headshake. "Isn't that the truth." She fingered a tear from one eye. "Look at me. Not a very good hostess. Can I get you something? Coffee or a soft drink?"

"I'm good," Peters said. "Just relax. Take a few breaths and you'll be okay."

Peters' cop mind analyzed everything she saw. Facial expressions, body language, words, emotions. She had seen many truly distraught and overwhelmed people, and a few that could fake it. Which was Savannah? She favored the former. Savannah hadn't known she was coming and had no time to prepare for her visit, or contrive an act. Looking at the young woman now, Peters saw only a wounded soul. One check for Pancake's ability to read people.

"Why're you here?" Savannah asked.

"I wanted to see how you were doing."

A half laugh escaped with a rush of breath. "Not well. But I guess that's evident."

"Not really." Peters flashed her a smile. "You look fine."

"It's like I'm inside a plastic bag. Everything's blurred like a weeping watercolor painting. Like there isn't enough oxygen and I need to take deep breaths all the time." Which she then did. "It reminds me of my freshman year in college. School was suddenly harder, and I was away from home for the first time. All the usual stuff, I guess. I saw a local doc. He gave me one of those meds that smooths things out. After a few days, I felt detached from the world, as if I was inside a bag. Sort of like now. I stopped the med and things got better. Right now I don't know what to stop, or start, or anything. I don't know what to do."

"I'm sorry to intrude," Peters said. "I just wanted to check on you and I certainly don't want to make things harder for you."

"Actually, I welcome someone to talk to. It makes me feel less isolated. With Dustin working, he now has so much more to do, I'm lost in this big house."

Peters let that hang for a minute before speaking. "Can I ask a couple of questions?"

"Sure."

"Have you given Mitchell Littlefield any more thought? Remembered anything out of place in his relationship with your father?"

Savannah shook her head. "No. Jake and Nicole were here and asked the same thing. I've racked my brain, thinking I must've missed something. I see him all the time. Here or at the office when I drop by. Sometimes at dinners. I know him well. He's like family. I've come up with a big fat zero. Nothing he did or said seemed out of place. No change in his attitude, or anything. I would think that if he was stealing from my dad, he would show at least some level of guilt."

"Some people hide things well."

"I guess."

"The evidence against him is getting stronger by the day," Peters said.

"I'm having trouble believing it."

"So far everything suggests he siphoned money from the company." Peters smiled to soften her statement. "Just to be clear, neither you nor Dustin have said anything to him about this. Right?"

"Absolutely. I haven't seen him and Dustin has said nothing." She sighed. "He said it wasn't easy since he sees Mitch every day. It's a lot of stress on him."

"I imagine so."

"But don't worry. He understands the need for secrecy."

Peters studied her as she asked her next question. The one she came to ask, and to gauge Savannah's reaction. "I assume you know that, according to their partnership agreement, if Mitch is found guilty of theft, you could end up with the entire company?"

"I didn't but I do now. I just found out, what? An hour ago? When Jake and Nicole dropped by."

"How do you feel about that?"

"I don't know." She sighed. Her eyes glistened. "This, everything, is so confusing."

"I'd be surprised if it wasn't. If you do inherit the entire business, what will you do?"

"I have no idea." A sadness fell across her face. "I can't believe this is happening. I assumed Dad would always be here. I never gave any thought to what I'd do if he wasn't around. And now?" She looked out toward the pool area, her gaze unfocused. She wiped a tear from one eye. "I guess Dustin and I will keep it going. He's good at business and I suspect I'll have to learn about real estate and we'll march on."

Peters admired that attitude and told Savannah so. "I think you two will do well. Whether it's half the company or all of it."

"I wish I was that confident. One thing is that we're moving our wedding forward."

"Really?"

Savannah nodded. "We were going to wait a few more months and have a big to-do. Chapel, reception, the perfect dress. All that stuff you dream about. But now, without Dad to walk me down the aisle, that seems silly. I guess we'll head down to the courthouse and do it in a couple of weeks."

Peters found nothing clever or soothing or supportive to say so she simply said, "I'm sorry."

"Me, too. It's a day that I wanted to share with him since I was a little girl. But, as they say, life gets in the way. Anyway, Dustin and I want to get it behind us so we can move on."

*   *   *

Back in her car and headed toward the Ono Island bridge, Peters ran through the conversation she had just had with Savannah. She agreed with Pancake. Savannah wouldn't kill her own father. She seemed distraught and disoriented. Still, the cop in her said not to close that book just yet. Maybe Savannah taking over the business and getting her marriage behind her would bring things into focus. In many ways, Savannah had never grown up. Daddy pampered, college was fun, and living back home was easy street. Now she got hammered with an unimaginable loss and a need to grow up fast. Welcome to adulthood.

CHAPTER 29

PANCAKE STEPPED ONTO the deck where Ray sat. He tossed a paper bag on the table. "I brought us some blueberry muffins."

"Us?"

"You can have one if you want. I got half a dozen. There's three left."

"Maybe later."

"Suit yourself." Pancake opened the bag and lifted one out, taking a big bite. "Pretty damn good."

"You say that about everything."

"Except liver. Don't like liver. And kale. I don't get kale. I don't think even cows or pigs eat that."

"How'd your sit-down with Detective Peters go?"

"Fine. I told her about the partnership agreement."

"And?"

"She agrees with us. Sure piled more motive on Mitch's plate."

Ray took a slug of Dew and leaned back. "Murder to hide his embezzling."

"Like that case we worked a few years ago," Pancake said. "Up in Foley."

"Looks that way," Ray agreed.

Foley, Alabama. A cute little town just a stone's throw due north of Gulf Shores and the home of Alabama football legends Kenny Stabler, DJ Fluker, and Julio Jones. The case? Two dudes owned a used car dealership. The successful venture made each of them good money. Then one partner wanted more, as is often the case, and began siphoning off cash. The other found out, and that was that. It differed from the Carl Davis–Mitch Littlefield scenario—possible scenario—in that in the killer was the aggrieved partner and the victim the embezzler. Fit of anger stuff. A heated exchange, a pushing and shoving and fist flying altercation, a gun, bang, done. One partner dead, the other a lifetime resident of Holman Prison near Atmore.

"Peters have anything new for us?"

Pancake shook his head.

"You could've called her with this information."

Pancake raised an eyebrow. "I needed some fresh air."

Ray nodded toward the Gulf. "You mean like this?"

Pancake raised his hands. "Okay, you win. She's rather easy on the eye and I wanted to see her again."

"What's her take on you playing lovesick puppy?"

"Pit bull, you mean."

"Same concept."

"She's—what's the word?—hesitant."

"Smart woman," Ray said.

"But we'll probably be having dinner tonight."

"So hesitant doesn't mean no."

"So it would seem."

"Jake and Nicole brought that stuff by for you." Ray indicated the two gray envelopes and the small blue notebook on the table.

"What is it?"

"Haven't had time to give them a detailed look, but Jake said it might be what we were looking for."

"What're you busy with?" Pancake asked.

"That Biloxi case."

"Will that ever end?"

"Looks like it's winding down. At least our involvement."

Pancake sat, slid the stack of papers from each envelope, and for several minutes thumbed through them. "This is exactly what we needed. Copies of the recent financials for Orange Coast Realty." He glanced at Ray. "How'd Jake get these?"

"Savannah gave them to him. Apparently, Carl kept copies of everything at home."

"Well, God bless him. As much as it pains me to say so, Jake too."

"See anything useful?" Ray asked.

"On first glance, looks like the same story. It'll take a bit of time to run through them more thoroughly."

When Carl Davis first hired them, he had analyzed nearly three years of accounting info, working from the most remote toward the most recent. He had completed reviewing and organizing two and a half years of records when he realized what the numbers were telling him. Mitch was stealing from the company. That's when he called Ray. He sent over the information he had gathered and Pancake had done his own dissection, agreeing with Carl's conclusions. Ray and Pancake were waiting for the final six months before putting the package together and, along with Carl, going to the police. Carl had finished that task and was going to give the papers to Jake and Nicole the night he was murdered, which changed everything. The police now had the originals and the copies and were reluctant, despite Pancake's efforts and charm, to allow them access to the information.

"Does that mean dinner is off?" Ray asked with a smile.

"Not hardly."

"Didn't think so."

Now Pancake picked up the small blue booklet. He opened it. "Well, hello."

"What is it?" Ray asked.

"The Rosetta Stone. Carl's password list."

"Really?"

"Time to excavate."

Pancake lifted his MacBook Pro from his satchel and opened it. He began digging and scratching through Carl Davis' private life. Emails, texts, Facebook, everything.

An hour later, he closed his laptop. "It gets curiouser and curiouser."

Ray looked up. "In what way?"

"Carl was seeing someone."

"Who?"

"A younger woman. Twenty-seven according to her company profile. She works at that Paloma Resort on Pensacola Beach. Name's Denise Scholander."

"What does she do?"

"Marketing. Also teaches tennis, it seems. The emails and texts between the two date back six months. Lots of lovey-dovey stuff, arrangements to meet, at her place, sometimes motels, sometimes restaurants down near Pensacola. Didn't see any for local places."

"Carl kept it on the down-low."

"Looks that way. She doesn't appear on his Facebook page and likewise no sign of him on hers. Just emails and texts. Phone calls of course."

"She married?" Ray asked. "This Denise?"

Pancake shook his head. "No evidence of that."

"Why all the secrecy then?"

"Maybe Carl didn't want Savannah to know. Maybe he felt their age differences might raise some eyebrows. Maybe she had a boyfriend. Maybe he simply didn't want the world in his business. Take your pick."

"Could be any or all," Ray said. "I guess we need to chat with her. Where does she live?"

"Pensacola. She has a condo near the resort."

CHAPTER 30

"WHAT'S UP?" I asked as Nicole and I walked onto Ray's deck. Ray held a can of Dew, Pancake hunched over an array of papers, the ones we had retrieved from Savannah.

"Did you finish all your work?" Ray asked. "Is that dive of yours going to stay afloat?"

I shook my head but said nothing.

Ray hated Captain Rocky's. To him, it was a frivolous waste of time and the main obstacle for me not working for him. Truth is, the obstacles were numerous, Captain Rocky's not even making the list, which included things like Ray, actually working for a living; Ray, sticking your nose in other people's lives; Ray, gunfire; and not necessarily in that order.

"Good work getting these," Pancake said, indicating the papers.

"It was Savannah," I said. "She said Carl kept copies of everything in his office."

"Is it the stuff we were picking up the day we found Carl?" Nicole asked.

Pancake nodded. "It is." Then he asked, "Where's my candy?"

I glanced at Ray. "You had to tell him about that?"

Ray smiled but said nothing.

"Savannah ate it all," I said.

"Skinny little thing like her?" Pancake asked. "Pardon me for not buying that."

"That was when she was a kid," Nicole said. "Carl did that because he knew Savannah would find it. He no longer had a candy stash or we'd have brought you some."

"My parents never kept candy around for me," Pancake said.

"You ate all of it right out of the grocery bag," I said.

"You helped."

"Not true—Maybe a couple of pieces—"

"Want to take a road trip?" Ray asked.

"Absolutely," Nicole said. "What do you need, boss?"

Two very bothersome things. "Road trip" meant fear and car sickness and enraged citizens, while "boss" meant this was another Ray deal.

Ray nodded toward Pancake.

"Carl was seeing someone," Pancake said.

Not what I expected. "Really?"

"Based on what I've uncovered so far, a woman half his age."

I don't know why I was surprised. Carl had been good-looking man, his wife had passed two years earlier, he had money, and he probably had fits of loneliness, so why wouldn't he be seeing someone?

"Who?" Nicole asked.

"Denise Scholander," Pancake said. "She's twenty-seven and works over in Pensacola at the Paloma Resort."

"How long has this been going on?" I asked.

"About six months."

"Savannah doesn't know," Nicole said. Not a question.

"What makes you think that?" Pancake asked.

"A feeling more than anything else. If Carl was seeing someone, and if Savannah knew, she'd have said something. I'm sure of
that."

"How sure?" Ray asked.

"As sure as I can be without actually knowing. My take on
Savannah is that she's a kind and caring person. She would've
hurt for her father's lover. She would've talked about her. Probably
called her. Since she never mentioned anything, I think she wasn't
aware of it." She shrugged. "That's my take anyway."

"How do you know this?" I asked Pancake

"Email, texts, phone calls. A lot of them."

"Couldn't she be a business contact?"

Pancake grunted, meaning he didn't think so. "Let's see, dinner
arrangements, meetings at her condo, hotel hookups. Probably
not business. I'll know more when I dig a little deeper."

"Okay," Nicole said. "If Carl and this Denise woman are an
item, why would he keep that from Savannah?"

"Maybe he thought she'd feel hurt, or betrayed," I said. "Like
he was forgetting about her mother, or cheating on her in some
sense."

"Well, look at you," Nicole said. "Getting all psychoanalytical."

"That's me. Jake Freud."

Nicole laughed. "You couldn't psychoanalyze a lump of clay."

I smiled. "Neither could Freud. He just thought he could."

"I'd bet the entire psychiatric community would disagree.
But on this, I agree with you," Nicole said. "If this woman's
twenty-seven, she's Savannah's age. Maybe Carl felt it would be
awkward."

"We have to talk with Denise," Ray said. "See what she says.
That's why I'd like you two to pay her a visit."

"Why us?" I asked. I knew the answer but I couldn't simply roll over. I had to put up some resistance. Not that it would do any good since Nicole was already "on it," as she liked to say.

"Because, we'll be less threatening to her," Nicole said.

"Bingo," Pancake said. "Besides, Ray is knee deep in another case, and I still have a lot to do on these records." He waved a hand. "It would be helpful if you two had a chat with Ms. Scholander. See what she has to say about Carl and if there's anything we need to know. It's a simple errand."

"Like picking up papers from Carl Davis?" I asked.

No response.

Nicole stood. "We're on it."

See? Of course we were.

CHAPTER 31

"MORAN SAID YOU wanted to see me, LT," Brooke Peters said.

LT, short for lieutenant, what everyone called Lieutenant Buddy Scoggins, head of the Orange Beach Police Department's Investigative Division, and Peters' boss.

Peters' mental image of Buddy Scoggins, a square, crew-cut gym rat with thick shoulders and arms, was a linebacker, which he had been in high school, or a drill instructor, which he wasn't during his tour with the Marine Corps. He should've been. Large and in charge, few people challenged him.

"Come in," Scoggins said. "Grab a seat."

She sat in the uncomfortable—no doubt planned that way—wooden ladder-back chair, adjusting the holster and gun along her lower back to lessen the pressure. Most visits to Scoggins' office were simple briefings or chats, but some were harsher encounters, Scoggins barking about a case that progressed less rapidly than he wished.

"What's up?" she asked.

"My exact question. Where do we stand on the Davis murder?"

She ran through the case, most of which he already knew. But Scoggins liked summaries, complete summaries, the big picture sprinkled with crucial details. Who was who and what was what.

Kept everyone on the same page was his position. She knew he believed such repeated summaries kept his investigators organized and focused, their eyes on the prize, and not wandering too far afield. She agreed with him, even if these sessions could be tedious. More to the point, each was a test of how well she knew her own case and how she was pulling things together.

"I guess this means that Mitchell Littlefield is still your primary suspect?" Scoggins asked.

"More and more. I just talked to the computer guys downstairs and they agree with Ray Longly and Pancake that Littlefield skimmed over three hundred thousand in the past three years."

"Pancake?"

She smiled. "Ray Longly's partner. His name is Tommy Jeffers, but everyone calls him Pancake."

"Including you?"

"When in Rome."

Scoggins' face hardened, forehead creased. "What's their involvement in your investigation?"

"None. Not officially anyway."

"Unofficially?"

"They've been helpful. Their work pointed us to Mitchell Littlefield from day one. They learned of the embezzlement a few days before the murder."

"We would've gotten there," Scoggins said.

"That's true. They had a head start, so got there first. They also found that the partnership agreement has a morals clause. If Littlefield goes down, Savannah Davis owns the entire shebang."

"I didn't know that."

"I didn't either until Pancake—Tommy Jeffers—told me earlier today."

Scoggins raised an eyebrow but let the Pancake reference pass. "Do you believe Savannah Davis was involved in her father's murder?"

"Possible, but I don't think so. I've seen nothing in her, or her fiancé for that matter, that points that way."

"Still?"

"Exactly. It's only a gut feeling, so they're not free and clear by any means."

"What else?"

"Have you decided whether we can share the financial data we got from Carl's office with Ray Longly?"

He studied her, his eyes piercing. Heat rose in her face.

"Why would we?" Scoggins said.

"They've been helpful. Mr. Jeffers seems to be some sort of computer whiz and financial guru. It can't hurt."

"Except it's evidence. Evidence we don't want leaked."

"I'm sure they're aware of that."

He gave a brief nod. "Why are you so enamored with Longly Investigations?"

Enamored. The word struck home. Is that what this was? Was she enamored with Pancake and this merely a ploy to see him? No. No way. She knew they could assist, enhance her investigation. That's all it was.

"I think they can help," Peters said. "We aren't exactly over-staffed here. A little outside help might be beneficial."

"You know how I feel about private types. They don't play by the same rules."

Which might be a useful thing, she thought. Too often laws and rules and regulations, and of course bureaucratic BS, tied their hands. She suspected little, if anything, restrained Ray Longly's or Pancake's hands.

"They've been helpful in other ways," she said. "Besides the financial and the embezzlement issues."

"Such as?"

"Remember the disgruntled former employee, Gary Wayne Frawley? The guy Carl fired a year ago for problems he had created with several clients?"

"Yeah. Didn't you clear him?"

"I did. He moved on to another realty firm in Fort Walton Beach. We had a chat. He had an alibi. He was with a woman he was seeing. A married woman. He refused to give her up. Even after I told him that without her substantiating his alibi he remained in the suspect pool." She shifted in the uncomfortable chair. "But Jake Longly, Ray's son, and Nicole Jamison, his girlfriend, pried her name from Frawley. They then met with her. Megan Varner. She confirmed his alibi and told them where they had hooked up that night. The Sunset Lodge over in Navarre. They visited the motel and grabbed a copy of the security footage, which showed Frawley and Varner coming and going as they had said. Clear as day."

"Okay? So?"

"The point is, we might never have gotten her name from Frawley and might never have been able to clear him. That would only muddy things and waste resources."

He nodded, lips pursed.

"While I'm not ready to let them in the henhouse, we can use their help in certain areas."

Scoggins leaned back in his chair. It creaked under his weight. "Remember, these guys, even those with solid reputations like

Ray Longly, are in it for the money. This is a business endeavor for them." He gave her that Scoggins look. "You've made a compelling argument, but I need to think about this." His features softened. "I'll let you know."

She stood, readjusted her gun and holster. "Thanks, LT."

"This is why you need a partner. To keep you from painting outside the lines."

"Isn't that a good thing?"

"For most people. But you don't seem to know how far to push it." He smiled. Not a common occurrence. "That's why Leo was good for you."

Leo Martini. Her former partner who taught her the ropes when she left uniforms and pinned on her gold shield. A legend around the department, he had a nose for evidence, and for BS, and knew how to interrogate even the most hardened criminals into submission. She missed him, could still hear his voice in her ear, teaching, guiding. But working alone suited her.

"You got anybody in mind? Someone who doesn't want to stop at a donut shop every fifteen minutes?"

Another smile. "I'm working on it."

She walked back to her office and called Pancake. She gave him the highlights of her chat with Scoggins. "I think he's softening on the materials you need."

"No need now," Pancake said.

"What?"

"I have them."

"How? When?"

"Just now. I was planning to call you."

"Where'd you find them?" Peters asked.

"Savannah. Carl kept duplicates of everything in his home office."

An uncomfortable tickle danced up her spine. She should've considered that. Should've asked Savannah if Carl kept any important papers at home. Why hadn't she? Was it because Savannah was distraught and damaged and she felt the need to comfort her rather than do her job? Was she too soft? Too unfocused? Did she need Leo?

Stop it, Brooke. Don't do this. Don't second-guess yourself. On that day, Savannah was a heartbroken daughter whose father had just been murdered. Nothing more. Peters had no knowledge of the embezzlement or the partnership agreement that potentially made Savannah a very rich woman. She wasn't even on the radar as a suspect.

Plus, the examination of the documents taken from Carl Davis' office was far from complete. No holes in the data had been uncovered so there was no need to probe Davis' home.

Still, she should've asked. Leo would have.

Scoggins would pitch a fit if he knew this. Worse, what if the information Pancake had wasn't in the files she took from the Orange Coast Realty? What if they contained the smoking gun she needed? The proof that Mitch had planned Carl's murder? That could be a career disaster.

Her approach, approved by Scoggins, was to keep everything wrapped tight. Not let Mitch Littlefield know they were aware of his thefts. Keep it clean, a generic murder perpetrated by an unknown intruder. Make him believe he was a witness, not a suspect. Until they hammered out the money trail. Until they had enough to arrest him for murder, not just embezzling.

"I wish I'd known this ten minutes ago," Peters said. "Before I begged my boss for the data."

"I'm sorry. But I just finished going through the info, and a few other things."

"Like what?"

"Still working on it," Pancake said. "Let's say we'll have a lot to discuss at dinner tonight."

She could picture Scoggins' face when she referred to Pancake by his nickname. What if he knew she'd met him and his partners in a bar to discuss an active investigation? Or that she had met with Pancake for breakfast earlier in the day? That she had exchanged information with him? He would be apoplectic, and she just might be unemployed.

Suddenly, she felt uncomfortable with where this was headed.

"I'm not sure about that," she said. "I still think it's a potential conflict."

"You got to eat."

She laughed. "It's not the eating that's the issue. It's the person across the table."

"It's a business dinner," Pancake said. "We'll have a nice dinner, a few laughs, and I'll enlighten you on everything I've uncovered."

"*Enlighten?* That's a big word."

"I'm a big guy."

CHAPTER 32

THOSE WORDS AGAIN—"WE'RE on it." Engaged, focused, and ready for duty, "sir, yes, sir" being the implication. But when Nicole uttered them, they led to another of Ray's rabbit holes. To be fair, I didn't expect any confrontations or brawls or gunfire at the Paloma Resort, but with Ray driving the train, you never knew what might come down the tracks. The old cliché about the light at the end of the tunnel being a locomotive crossed my mind. I mean, just a few days ago we went on a Ray mission and stumbled on Carl Davis' body.

See what I mean?

Nicole harbored no such concerns, so despite my unease, we blasted off in Nicole's rocket ship. She attacked the more sane and polite motorists who had the audacity to be on "her" highway, this one Highway 98, eastbound. With the SL's top lowered, the bright sun and clear blue sky felt warm, but not hot. The humidity a notch lower than usual for this time of year.

Doing a good twenty miles an hour over the speed limit, we passed a patrol car going the other way. I expected him to brake, pull a U-turn, and run us down. Instead, Nicole waved at him. He waved back and kept going. Amazing.

We rolled along in silence for a few miles, and then Nicole said, "This whole thing is becoming a soap opera."

"At least," I replied.

"Everyone is screwing someone besides their spouse."

"Got to love America," I said.

"It's universal. Hell, the French've been doing it for centuries. Hollywood for decades."

"Let them eat cake," I said.

"That and champagne are what starts all that rolling around in the hay."

"Around here, it's beer and nachos."

"Same principle." She glanced at me. "Tequila works on you."

"You work on me."

She flashed a smile. "You're so charming."

"I am."

"When we get there, keep your irresistible charm in your pocket."

"Why? My natural-born charisma might be useful. After all, I am the chief schmoozer at Captain Rocky's."

"The Paloma isn't Captain Rocky's."

"Same principle though."

"All your earthshaking elan might be a distraction and we need to get information from her."

"*Elan?* Speaking of the French."

"Just let me handle the talking and you sit and look pretty."

"With *elan.*"

"I knew I'd regret that word choice as soon as it came out."

"But you said it with such *elan.*"

"See what I mean?"

The Paloma Resort and Spa occupied a prime chunk of beachfront real estate on Pensacola Beach. Mediterranean style, coral walls, white trim, and a massive porte cochere. Clusters of specimen palm trees enhanced the vibe. Cool, exclusive, expensive. Welcome to your personal oasis. Relax, have a cocktail, chill out in the sun, while we excavate your wallet.

A young man in black pants and a crisp white shirt tugged open Nicole's door. "Welcome to Paloma," he said. "Checking in?"

"No. We're here for a meeting."

"Very good. I'll have your car right up front when you're ready to leave." He nodded toward a row of vehicles along one side of the entry drive. I saw two Bentleys, a Ferrari, and a dozen more pedestrian Mercedes, BMWs, and Porsches. Good advertising for a resort that cultivated its high-end image. The average Joe pulling up in his Camry or Prius would feel they had granted him access to an exclusive club. If it cost a week's salary, so be it.

We entered an open lobby, a marble reception counter to the left, a matching concierge desk to the right. We continued straight ahead to where an intricate wrought iron rail separated the upper and lower lobbies. We looked over a massive and buzzing bar with sofas and clustered chairs for eating, drinking, and chatting. When on vacation, or simply hanging out at a resort, happy hour could be any hour. Beyond, twenty-foot windows opened onto the pool complex and the Gulf, framed by more palm trees.

We descended the steps and veered left down a hallway.

Earlier, Nicole had called Denise Scholander, telling her we needed to ask her a few questions. About what? When Nicole mentioned Carl Davis, Denise audibly inhaled. Nicole told her to relax, that we only needed a few minutes and everything we said would be confidential. Denise attempted to act confused, as if Carl Davis had nothing to do with her, but Nicole explained that we knew of their relationship.

"How could you?" Denise had asked.

"Emails, texts, datebooks."

Denise said nothing for a full half a minute. "I can't believe any of this."

"It won't take long and it could clear up a few things," Nicole said.

Denise hesitated. Nicole continued, saying there were questions that had to be answered, either to us, or the police, and that we might be able to keep the police out of her life if Denise would simply chat with us. Denise relented.

Once again, the threat of police involvement proved to be the key that opened the door. No doubt we were tricking Denise. No doubt we'd have to tell Brooke Peters about this chat. And more likely than not, she'd also visit the lovely Paloma Resort, and Denise's office.

At the end of the hallway, double-frosted glass doors served as the entrance to the spa. Before reaching them, we turned left and passed through another double doorway—the home of the marketing and customer relations department. The young, attractive, efficient, and helpful receptionist directed us to Denise's office.

Small, neat, classy, its large window looked onto a garden with azaleas and more palm trees. Denise sat behind her desk. Blonde hair, blue eyes, very tan, trim, and fit. She didn't smile but was pleasant as we introduced ourselves and took the two chairs that faced her desk.

"Thanks for seeing us," Nicole said.

"I didn't seem to have much choice," Denise said.

"I'm sorry," Nicole said. "I didn't intend to make you uncomfortable."

"I need to ask up front—do the police know about Carl and me?"

"Not yet," I said.

"But they will?" Denise asked.

"Sooner or later they'll have to," Nicole said.

"Why? I mean, we were just . . . friends." Denise sighed, deflated. "That's not true. We were more than that."

"Which is why we're here," Nicole said.

"The harsh truth," I said, "is that someone murdered Carl, the police have no real suspects, and since you and Carl had a relationship, they'll have to look at you, and the other people in your world."

Denise released a long sigh. "I suppose that's true." Then to Nicole she said, "What's this to you? You said something about being private investigators. Isn't this a police matter?"

"We're helping the police with their investigation," Nicole said.

I added, "Carl's daughter hired us to find out who might've done this."

"Savannah?" Denise said.

"Do you know her?"

She shook her head. "No. We've never met, and I don't think she even knows about me and Carl. But Carl talked of her so often that I feel like I do."

"Tell us about you and Carl," Nicole said.

She glanced toward the window and the garden, gathering her thoughts. "After you called, I mulled over how best to tell the tale." She looked at Nicole. "I guess I should begin at the beginning." She slid a stack of papers aside and squared her shoulders.

"We met six months ago. At a Chamber of Commerce mixer in Orange Beach. He was handsome and funny and charming, and I liked him immediately. We ended up having wine in a bar that night." She smiled. "We talked until after midnight. I guess you could say I was smitten. I knew he was twenty years older than me, but that wasn't a problem." She shrugged. "Maybe that was part of the attraction. My recent experiences with guys my age haven't been the best."

"Like fine wine," Nicole said, "it takes guys time to mature." She flashed me a smile. "Jake here is still a work in progress."

Denise smiled. "Must be a universal problem."

Outnumbered, I knew enough to simply return her smile and keep my mouth shut. A mature move, I think. Besides, Nicole didn't want my charm and charisma and elan oozing into the conversation.

Denise continued. "After that night, we started seeing each other. Soon it became a romantic situation."

"A serious one?" I asked.

"We were on that path, for sure. We talked about the future." She closed her eyes and dropped her head for a beat. "We would've been good together." She looked up. "That's why this is such a shock." Tears welled in her eyes. "I still can't believe it. I keep seeing his face, hearing his voice. I keep thinking about what could've been." She pulled open the drawer to her left and tugged out a tissue. She dabbed both eyes. "We could've had a good life together."

"You never met Savannah," Nicole said. "Why?"

"Carl's reluctance. He feared she wouldn't take it well. Losing her mother was a blow to her. According to Carl, even now, two years later, she wasn't dealing with it very well."

"If your relationship continued and became more serious, wouldn't she have to be told?" I asked.

"We'd decided to do exactly that." She sniffed. "Next week. I was going to drop by and we were going to tell her everything and that we were serious about each other." She dabbed her eyes again.

"If it helps any," Nicole said, "from what I've seen of Savannah, she would've handled it well."

She sniffed. "That's good to hear. It would've meant a lot to Carl. Me too."

"Did you get together at your place?" I asked.

"No. Various hotels and motels. Carl's home was obviously off limits and my condo wouldn't have been smart."

"Why?"

"My ex. Boyfriend, not husband."

"Oh?" I asked.

"Tucker Moss. You might've heard of him."

I hadn't and told her so.

"He drives race cars. Sort of a local celebrity in that circuit. Hooking up with him wasn't one of my best decisions. We met at a race a few years ago. He has a body shop and drives sprint cars. And he's an asshole."

"In what way?" Nicole asked.

"The same old story. At first, he was nice and charming, his racing world exciting. He actually suggested we move in together. My place, of course. Thank god I declined. He quickly showed his true colors. He became controlling and demanding. Demeaning would be a better word. Aggressive and abusive."

"Physically?"

"Not really. He grabbed me a couple of times, left bruises on my arms, pushed me down once. But he never hit me." She shook her head. "Yet I felt he might. He definitely had the temperament. So I bailed. He wasn't happy."

"Do you still hear from him?" I asked.

"Occasionally. Mostly texts and calls, which I don't answer. He did bang on my door one night while Carl and I were there. We didn't answer and he finally gave up." She wadded the tissue in one hand. "That was the last time we met at my place."

"Was he angry about Carl?" Nicole said.

"Oh yeah. But he didn't know Carl. Or anything about him. Just that he was older and I was seeing him. Called him an old worn-out dude and a loser. Carl was neither."

"Did he blame Carl for your breakup with him?"

Denise shook her head. "No. We broke up months before I met Carl. Tucker simply didn't want me seeing anyone. He wanted me to himself even though I made it crystal clear that would never happen. That we were done." She gave a weak smile. "I try not to repeat my mistakes."

"Is he dangerous?" I asked. "A threat to you?"

"I want to think not, but the truth is, he could be. The last few weeks Tucker and I were together, I felt like I was sitting on a time bomb. The tiniest thing could set him off on a rant. Oh, he threw a lamp at me once." She looked at me. "You don't think he had anything to do with Carl's death, do you?"

"Do you?"

"No. Surely not."

"But possible?" Nicole said.

She nodded. "He has a short fuse. But he doesn't know Carl. At least I don't think he does. I've never told him his name or anything about him. I don't see how his anger could've been directed at Carl. He'd be just as angry with any man I brought into my life."

"Unless he made it his business," I said. "To find out who you were seeing."

"We were very careful," Denise said.

"Stalkers, and that's what we're taking about here, can be clever and relentless," Nicole said. "They stay in the shadows and gather information, and become adept at following their victims. They might use rental cars and employ friends to help follow and keep tabs. They track licenses plates and even put GPS devices on cars." Nicole shrugged. "Anything and everything is in play."

"Sounds like you've had some experience in this."

"I have. And I know it's scary. I wouldn't underestimate this Tucker character."

A soft moan escaped Denise's throat. "God. It would kill me if I was the cause of what happened to Carl. He was such a sweet and thoughtful man."

"It's not your fault regardless," Nicole said. "You were living your life, following your heart."

She exhaled loudly. "No doubt."

"You loved Carl, didn't you?"

"I did. And he loved me. I'm sure of that. That's why we planned to go to Savannah and let her know we were serious."

"So this Tucker Moss races cars," I said. "Is that what he does for a living?"

"Yeah, plus he owns Moss Sports Cars here in Pensacola. They work on exotics and race cars."

"We'll have a chat with him," I said.

"Be careful," Denise said. "He's a rattlesnake, and his crew is just as bad. I only went there twice. I felt too uncomfortable around them to stay very long." She brushed her hair from her forehead. "It was like Tucker had told them about me. Intimate things. Things we did together. In bed. Their attitude, their smirks and glances, their mentally undressing me, their complete lack of respect made me feel like a whore." She let out a shuddering breath. "Which is how I believe Tucker thought of me. Someone to own. To use and abuse."

"I'm sorry," Nicole said. "That you went through that."

Denise tilted her head to the left for a beat. "Yeah, well, like I said, not my best decision."

"We'll be careful," I said.

"One more thing," Denise said. "He uses meth. He'll deny it but he does."

"You sure?"

She nodded. "I found a packet in his pants pocket once. I was looking for his car keys to get something I had left in the trunk. I confronted him. He denied it. Said he was delivering it to someone else. I didn't believe him. When I thought back on some of his behavior, it made sense. That was three weeks before I broke things off."

"Sounds like a smart move," Nicole said.

"My worst move was hooking up with him in the first place. Walking away was my best."

CHAPTER 33

PANCAKE AND RAY sat at the teak table on Ray's deck, each shuffling through papers and working laptop keyboards, speaking little. How they worked. Pancake munched on the remnants of an apple fritter. Ray worked on a fresh can of Mountain Dew. Pancake closed his laptop and gazed toward the Gulf. Calm water, a sailboat interrupting the horizon.

He had sifted through Carl Davis' emails, texts, and his Facebook account, looking for clues, connections, something that pointed to anyone other than Mitchell Littlefield. To avoid tunnel vision, you had to explore other possibilities and not lock onto a convenient target. Yet after two hours of digging, nothing appeared out of line. No enemies, or threats, or conflicts. The only thing remotely off kilter was his clandestine affair with Denise Scholander. Even that held no sinister overtones. A widower and a younger woman sneak off for quality alone time. Happens all day, every day.

Denise's name decorated his emails and texts. Each friendly and loving. His deeper dive into Carl's social life confirmed what he had found earlier. Denise didn't appear in any of his Facebook posts, not even "friends" on any of the social platforms. Likewise,

Carl didn't surface on any of her social media. Such posts were public, so if they desired to keep their relationship on the down-low, blasting it into that uncontrolled chaotic world wasn't the best idea. Not that texts and emails were secure, but Facebook was a megaphone screaming, "Hey, look at me."

Reviewing the six months of their communications revealed that what started out friendly, tentative, each exploring the other's likes, dislikes, and values, drifted into more intimate territory. Not in a sexting way, but rather two people falling in love. Each message more personal and caring than the last.

Pancake's cell phone buzzed. Nicole. He answered, placing it on speaker. "What's up?"

"Nicole and I are leaving the Paloma Resort." Jake. The phone obviously connected to the Bluetooth of Nicole's Mercedes. The modest wind hiss suggested Nicole was holding her speed below ninety.

"Did you see Denise Scholander?" Ray asked

"Sure did. Pancake was right. She confirmed that she and Carl were an item. For the past six months or thereabouts."

"She said their relationship became serious," Nicole said. "Making future plans and all that. She also confirmed that Savannah wasn't aware."

Nicole then explained Carl's reluctance and Denise's understanding of his hesitation. Though Denise wanted to meet Savannah, she didn't pressure Carl on that front. They had decided to go public, so to speak, next week and reveal their affair to Savannah.

"Did you sense any trouble in paradise between them?" Ray asked.

"None."

"Same with all their communications," Pancake added.

"But there's an ex-boyfriend involved that could be trouble," Jake said.

"Tell me," Pancake said.

Jake did. Tucker Moss ran a sports car repair shop and raced sprint cars. Angry, arrogant, and possessive. Meth user. Had a crew that Denise felt was cut from the same mold. Yes, Tucker was aggressive and abusive. Yes, he knew Denise was seeing someone else, and no, he didn't like it. Yes, he had made threats but there was no evidence he knew Carl's ID. At least that was Denise's take.

"So this guy, this Tucker Moss, is a bad guy with boundary issues," Pancake said. A statement, not a question. "Did she feel he was aggressive enough to have harmed Carl?"

"She wasn't sure," Nicole said. "But reading between the lines, she's afraid of him, so I think the answer is yes. She fears he could've stepped over that threshold."

"We're going to stop by his shop and chat with him," Jake said.

"No," Ray said. "I get a bad vibe about him. We'll take care of it."

"It'll be fine," Nicole said. "Jake has a couple of baseballs in the glove box. He can throw them if the need arises."

"I agree with Ray," Pancake said. "Let us handle this. I don't want you two rolling into a body shop filled with meth heads and getting into a situation. Jake's balls not withstanding. Besides, I have another job for you."

"Cool," Nicole asked.

No, not cool.

"Stop by and see Savannah," Pancake said. "She needs to know her father was seeing Denise."

"Why?" Nicole asked.

"Because she hired us to find out who killed her father. Part of that's keeping her informed. If we're going to investigate Denise's ex, and he's some miscreant who could stir things up, she needs to know."

"I guess so."

"It would look bad if she found out later that we knew about her father's affair and didn't tell her," Pancake said. "She'd feel betrayed and wouldn't trust us."

"Who knows," Ray said. "Maybe she saw something in Carl's behavior. Being away from the office and home for time periods that couldn't be explained or were a departure from his usual habits. Maybe he said something that now knowing he was seeing someone possessed a different spin. Even the smallest thing might lead us down a path other than Mitch Littlefield."

"Okay," Jake said. "We're leaving Pensacola and will swing by her place."

Pancake ended the call. "Ready for a run to Pensacola?" he asked Ray.

"Give me another hour. This Biloxi case is a can of worms, and I need to get this out today."

"What about this?" Pancake said. "You stick with that. I'll call Brooke Peters and see if she wants to tag team this guy."

"Is it her or him you want to see?"

Pancake grinned. "Both. But having the law with me might tamp down his anger a bit."

"And rev up your hormones," Ray said.

"My hormones rev just fine."

"So it seems."

"Besides, informing her about Carl's love life and including her in this little chat with the aggrieved ex-boyfriend will garner us more favor." Pancake gave a one-shoulder shrug. "Her take on this dude might be useful. Besides, she has a badge and a gun, and that never hurts."

"Okay. You head off on your playdate and I'll keep at this."

Pancake grunted, stood, and walked into the kitchen. He called Peters.

She answered after the first ring. "Peters." Muffled voices in the background.

"How's my favorite detective?" Pancake asked.

"Just a sec." Scratchy sounds as if she had pressed her phone against her chest to mute the microphone, the unmistakable sound of a door closing, and then she was back. "Sorry. I was in the squad room listening to a bunch of testosterone-infused stupid-ass jokes. What's up?"

"I have a few of those jokes in my repertoire."

"Don't advertise it. It'll cut your chances."

"Always seemed to work in the past," Pancake said.

"You need to meet a better class of women."

"Which bring us to you."

"Did you practice that?" Pancake sensed the smile in her voice.

"Daily. But to the point of my call. Make that points. First, I have us a reservation for dinner at six thirty. Does that work?"

"Is this a good idea?" Peters asked.

"You need dinner. Might as well be with me."

"I'll have to think about it."

"Don't think, just do."

She hesitated for a full half a minute. Pancake almost asked if she was still there. Then she said, "I must be crazy but okay. Where?"

"It's a surprise."

She sighed. "I hate surprises."

"Humor me."

"Not one of my best skills, but I'll give it shot. What else you got?"

"Carl Davis had a girlfriend."

"Really? How do you know that?"

"Let's say the couple left an email and text trail that wasn't hard to follow."

"You got into Carl Davis' accounts?"

"I did. Wasn't hard since I had his passwords." He told her of the password book Savannah had given him.

"When were you going to tell me about this?"

"Now. Like I am. I'll pass along the book to you so your guys can sniff around in his electronic communications too."

"Who's the woman?"

"Denise Scholander. Works at the Paloma Resort over in Pensacola."

"I know that place. A little rich for my wallet, but I hear it's nice."

"Jake and Nicole stopped by and talked with her. She and Carl were seeing each other for six months and it became serious."

"What did Savannah think about that?"

"She didn't know. Carl wasn't ready to tell her yet, but they were planning to next week. Jake and Nicole are going to sit with Savannah and bring her up to date."

"Does she really need to know?" Peters asked.

"She does. First because we always keep our clients informed, and second because of the Denise woman's ex-boyfriend."

"Now you've got my interest."

Pancake told her Tucker Moss' story. His harassment of Denise and anger with Carl, whose name he might or might not know. He concluded with, "Not sure if there's any there there, but I figured dropping by for a chat with him and his crew was in order. I said to myself, who would enjoy that? And shock of all shocks, your name came to mind."

"You already know me too well."

"I'll pick you up. Say twenty minutes?"

"That'll work. I need to chat with my boss for a minute. I'll let him know about this new lead. He might actually smile."

"Our first stop will be the Paloma so you can assess Denise Scholander for yourself. Then, we'll head over to Tucker Moss' place."

"Sounds good."

"Then we're free to have dinner."

"This whole interrogation thing is simply a ploy to trap me into dinner, isn't it?"

"You know me too well, too."

CHAPTER 34

"HEY, LT," PETERS said. She stood in the doorway to Lieutenant Buddy Scoggins' office. He sat behind his desk, a folder open before him, his biceps threatening to rip open the short sleeves of his white shirt. "Got a sec?"

He waved a hand, inviting her to sit. She did.

"Carl Davis had a girlfriend," Peters said. His chin elevated. "A woman named Denise Scholander. Works at the Paloma, that fancy resort over on Pensacola Beach."

"She a suspect?"

Peters shook her head. "Not likely. I'll know more later."

"You going to chat with her?"

"Pan . . . the Longly crew found out about her."

"Them again?"

"Yep. Tommy Jeffers discovered that she and Carl were an item. For the past six months."

"How'd he do that?"

"Savannah found her father's password book. He was old school and kept all his log-in information in a notebook. She gave it to Pancake . . . Jeffers . . . and he got into his accounts and found a series of communications. Jake Longly and his girlfriend, Nicole met with the woman. She confirmed that she and Carl had indeed been lovers for the past six months."

"Is Longly Investigations running your case for you? Is that what I'm hearing?"

"No. But they've been helpful. Like this. Finding that Carl had been seeing someone."

"Someone who isn't a suspect. Right?"

"No, but her ex could be."

Scoggins leaned forward, but said nothing, choosing to wait for her to continue.

"Race car driver and meth user named Tucker Moss."

Scoggins' brow furrowed. "Where do I know that name?"

"He's some big deal sprint car driver. Has a sports car shop in Pensacola."

Scoggins gave a slow nod. "I remember."

"Besides being a tweaker and an asshole, he's an angry young man and possessive of Denise."

"Interesting. Let's slide him onto the suspect list. Not at the top. That slot still belongs to Mitchell Littlefield."

"I agree. But scorned lovers do stupid shit."

Scoggins leaned back in his chair. "So it seems. What's your plan?"

"You aren't going to like it."

His fingers gave her a gimme waggle. "Let's have it."

"Tommy Jeffers and I are going over to talk with Denise Scholander and then pay a visit to Moss. See what they have to say."

"You're right, I don't like it."

"Look, he, they, the Longly crew, are already in this investigation. We couldn't stop that even if we wanted to. Savannah

Davis hired them to do exactly what we're trying to do. Find out who killed her father. So, rather than getting all wound up or engage in some pissing contest, I think we should work with them. We're shorthanded and they're good at what they do. If they can open the door to another line of investigation, we should walk through it."

Socggins tapped a finger on his desk. His arms and shoulders flexed, his jaw tightened. Unease climbed her spine, a feeling magnified by Scoggins' scowl. Here she was trying to shoehorn outsiders into a murder investigation, which broke a dozen rules and might blow up in her face. Too late to back away now, so she continued. "So, we're going to see Denise and then Tucker Moss. Jeffers will definitely help there."

"How so?"

"You haven't met him. He's massive and, from what I can tell, doesn't intimidate easily. Since over in Pensacola I'll be out of my jurisdiction, his presence might make Tucker more forthcoming."

"I can call the chief over there, get some of his guys involved." She cocked her head to one side. "You really want that?"

He exhaled heavily. "No."

"Then let me do this my way."

He considered that. "Okay. With one condition."

"What's that?"

"I want to meet this Pancake dude."

"I'll arrange it for tomorrow morning."

CHAPTER 35

I USED NICOLE's phone to call Savannah so it would go through the Mercedes' hands-free system while Nicole navigated traffic. Navigating being a euphemism for terrorizing. I waited through half a dozen rings before Savannah answered. She sounded winded.

"You okay?" Nicole asked.

"Yeah. Sorry. I was out watering the plants on the patio and left my phone in the kitchen. I barely heard it ringing. What's up? Anything new?"

"Yes."

"What?" I sensed apprehension in her voice.

"Don't panic," Nicole said, "but it would be better if we sat down and talked. Can we stop by for a minute?"

"Oh, I, uh, have a doctor's appointment in about thirty minutes."

"Nothing serious, I hope," I said.

"Routine girl stuff," Savannah said.

"Never fun," Nicole said. "What about later?"

"That'll work. Say around five?"

"We'll be there."

I disconnected the call. "We have a couple of hours to kill. What do you want to do?" I looked at her and smiled. "My place isn't far."

"Neither is Captain Rocky's, and I need a margarita."

"You're no fun," I said.

"I am. And I will be later. Right now I need alcohol, and maybe a couple of tacos."

Since she was driving, I had no viable argument so we headed toward Captain Rocky's. At least the day was pleasant, the sky blue, and the breeze warm. A good day to be out and about. Not as good as the four walls and firm bed of my bedroom, but still nice.

My cell buzzed.

Tammy.

The day just spiraled down the crapper.

I angled my phone toward Nicole. "See? I told you we weren't done with this."

"Try to play nice for a change," Nicole said.

"Me? She's the evil one."

"Are you in the third grade?"

"It sometimes feels that way."

"Obviously."

The phone's buzzing continued so I answered, placing it on speaker so Nicole could have her fun.

"What is it?" I asked.

"Well, there's a greeting," Tammy said. "No hello, how are you, anything like that?"

"Hello, how are you, and what do you want?" I said.

"Why do I call you?" Tammy asked.

"Bingo. That's always the question."

"Nicole? Are you there?"

"I am."

"Will you fix him? Train him? Or whatever?"

"I'm trying. It's no small task."

"Do like I did and give up while you're still sane."

Sane? The distance between Tammy the Insane and sanity was measured in angstrom units.

The bigger question? Why did I always end up the topic of conversation? I was minding my own business, enjoying the flawless day, and then boom, Tammy calls and all those good feelings crash and burn and I become the red circle in the middle of the dartboard.

Wanting to push this along, I again asked, "What do you want, Tammy?"

"You don't have to be rude."

"I can hang up."

She laughed. "You want to play the I-call-you-a-hundred-times-until-you-give-up-and-answer game? I love that one. I could play it all day. Don't you just love speed dial?"

No, I didn't. In Tammy's hands, speed dial became the electronic equivalent of a sniper rifle with a laser sight, and yes, she could launch a war of attrition that I would lose. Back to the original question: "What can I do for you?"

"That's better," Tammy said. "You didn't talk to Walter."

"Was I supposed to?"

"Jake, you promised you'd talk to him."

"I did? When? I don't remember saying that." I flashed Nicole a grin, she shook her head.

"You need a brain scan. Maybe one of those MRI things. I had one of those once. It was awful. Claustrophobic and all that banging that'll rattle your fillings out. Perfect for you."

"I don't think my fillings need rearranging."

"Your brain does."

Nicole laughed.

See why I have trouble being polite to Tammy?

Without taking a breath, Tammy continued. "It was just yesterday that I asked you to call him."

"I remember that, I just don't remember agreeing to make the call."

"You promised."

I certainly didn't agree to that. My first reaction was to say so, but instead I said, "We've been busy."

"There's nothing in your life more important than helping me convince Walter that he's wrong. That going to this fundraiser would be a smart business move for him. That people seeing us would show we care and give back to the community."

"What's the name of this charity?" I asked.

"I don't know, but it has to do with kids. I think."

So Tammy.

I flashed a triumphant smile at Nicole. Got another headshake in return.

Tammy marched on. "They're having this extraordinary auction. Trips to Europe, cruises, even one to Antarctica."

"I'm not sure your new dress would be appropriate for Antarctica."

Nicole suppressed a laugh. She loves this stuff. I was getting a headache.

"Sure it would," Tammy said. "We'd certainly have dinner with the captain one night."

Maybe on an iceberg. One that drifted away. Surely, a guy smart enough to navigate a ship through floating ice mountains would figure out that Tammy was an environmental toxin.

Tammy had more to say. Didn't she always? "Besides, all the money goes to helping kids."

Probably not. Most so-called charities lined their own pockets and maybe ten percent actually reached the intended—or advertised might be a better word—recipients. The rest consumed in "administrative" BS. Or was I too cynical?

"Plus, it's a tax write-off," Tammy added.

"Sounds like a win-win," I said.

"See, you understand. Plus, I'd get to show off my new dress."

"A trifecta," I said.

"What's that?"

A win-win-win," I said.

"Oh. That's really good."

"The bottom line is I don't think me talking to Walter would help. He's a smart guy, so give him some credit. He'll see the benefit of going. For the kids, for his taxes, for his sense of community, and to make you happy."

Tammy fell silent for a minute. A rare occurrence. I thought, hoped, the call had dropped, but then she spoke.

"You know, you're right. Walter will understand. He's reasonable and kind and all that stuff. So don't screw it up, Jake."

"How could I do that?"

"By calling Walter and confusing him."

She disconnected the call.

I looked at Nicole. "Was there even a hint of logic in any of that?"

She laughed. "No. But it was fun."

"Now I need a margarita. Drive faster."

She did.

CHAPTER 36

PANCAKE PARKED HIS big Chevy pickup near the entrance to the Orange Beach Police Department next to a black SUV, its doors white with slanted red and blue stripes and blue lettering that said POLICE. Nice design. Its twin sat several spaces away, as did a pair of unmarked black sedans and a white patrol car with a roof-mounted light bar. A woman paced back and forth near the glass entry door, smoking a cigarette, a cell phone to her ear. She gave Pancake a quick glance as she continued her conversation. Too far away for him to make out her words, her anger and agitation evident. She spoke rapidly, the cigarette bobbing between her lips, her free arm conducting an invisible orchestra. Probably talking to a lawyer, or a bail bondsman, or someone attempting to sell her a better cell service plan.

Pancake had called Peters when he was a mile away. She said he should wait in his truck and she'd meet him out front to avoid the raised eyebrows, questions, and teasing that would follow. Being one of the few female officers, Peters' social life was fair game for discussion, speculation, and good-natured needling. Better to dodge it if possible.

Peters pushed through the exit door, sidestepped the pacing woman, and came his way. She wore tan slacks, a white shirt, and an open black jacket, her gold shield attached to her belt. She climbed in.

"Nice rig," she said.

"It gets me here and there and back again."

She clicked her seatbelt. Pancake cranked the engine. He left the parking lot and turned south toward Perdido Beach Boulevard.

"You know where this place is?" she asked.

"Got it plugged in the GPS. Not that far."

"Depends on traffic."

"Doesn't everything?"

"I looked into this guy, Tucker Moss," she said.

"I did too."

"What'd you find?"

Pancake flashed her a smile. "Ladies first."

"I'm no lady." She returned his smile. "He's thirty-three, owns Moss Sports Cars, which seems to be very successful. A good reputation as a driver on the sprint car circuit. Won a bunch of races. How am I doing?"

"So far, so good," Pancake said.

"He has a record. Two arrests for assault. One the real deal, the other a minor bar fight. The real one involved him jumping a guy he had issues with and beating him in a convenience store lot. He never fessed up to what the beef was and the victim clammed up. Probably intimidated by Moss and his guys. Regardless, the altercation got Moss a few days in jail and year of probation. Plus a series of anger management visits."

"Which he didn't complete," Pancake said.

"No, he didn't."

"Could be a probation violation, which would give us leverage."

"Except, in Pensacola, I'm out of my jurisdiction."

"Moss is too ignorant to know that. All he'll see is cop."

"How do you want to handle this?" Peters asked.

The eastbound traffic was light, so they were making good time toward Pensacola.

"You're the pro," Pancake said.

"This isn't your first rodeo."

He smiled. "Then let's go with cool and calm. See what the boy has to say. If he gets horsey, we can come down a little harder."

"What about his crew?" she asked.

"If he's a tweaker, I'd bet they are too. Could make them a bit more confrontational."

"Is that why you called me?" Peters asked, a smile on her face. "To protect you from the bad guys?"

"You have a badge and gun."

She laughed.

"It's about four," Pancake said. "They close at five. Gives us time to talk with Denise and get to Tucker's place at closing time."

"Sounds good."

"If we're lucky, most of his crew will head out about then. If not, we can always hang back for a few and wait for the tribe to dwindle to a manageable level."

"What's a manageable number?"

"Four or thereabouts."

They rode in silence for a few miles, then Peters asked, "Any thoughts on whether this guy is a viable suspect?"

"On paper he fits the profile. Anger issues and no virgin to violence. According to Jake and Nicole, he harassed and stalked Denise to the point that she became afraid of him. Didn't like his meth use. Said he was a mean drunk, and druggy."

"Meth will do that." She shifted in her seat, twisting to better face him. "Did he know Carl Davis?"

"Denise said no. He knew she was seeing someone and that it was becoming serious. That ramped him up. As long as she was unattached or uninvolved, he believed he had control. Still had a claim on her. He probably believed that if he ever wanted to reignite things, he could turn on the charm, dial up the pressure, and she would wilt and crawl back. His ego told him that her current rejection was a temporary and weak reluctance. Eventually she would fold. But if she entered a committed relationship, he would fear his grip slipping. That makes sociopathic control freaks crazy."

"Very insightful."

"That's me. Mr. Insight."

She laughed again. He liked it. Soft and musical, despite her tough cop image.

"If his anger boiled up, he'd see two options," Peters said. "Go after Denise or the guy she's seeing."

Pancake pulled into Paloma Resort's expansive circular entrance. A valet appeared.

"We'll only be a few minutes," Pancake said, handing the guy the keys.

"I'll keep it right over here, sir."

"Is she expecting us?" Peters asked as they entered the lobby.

"Yeah. I didn't want to show up unannounced. Might alienate her. I didn't tell her you were coming, though."

"So I'm crashing the party?"

"You're my plus one." He bounced an eyebrow.

"I feel so special."

"I want to get your take on her, and indirectly, Tucker Moss."

The meeting with Denise Scholander was brief. Even though she hadn't expected Peters, she handled it in stride. As if she figured police involvement was a given. Her only concern was that if Tucker found out she was talking to the police about him, he might react unpleasantly. Her word. Peters assured her that no one knew about this meeting.

Denise told them of how aggressive Tucker was with his stalking and threats. How he followed her, called and texted, annoying at best, dangerous at worst. How he banged on her door one night while Carl was there. How that moved their meetings away from her condo and to various motels.

Yes, she was afraid of Tucker. Yes, he was angry and a tweaker. Yes, now that she had given it some thought, she believed he could've killed Carl. She reiterated what she had told Jake and Nicole that she didn't think Tucker knew who Carl Davis was. Not even his name. Only that she was seeing someone seriously.

"You're sure about that?" Peters asked.

Denise hesitated a beat. "Jake and Nicole said that stalkers like Tucker had ways of finding out about their perceived rivals. Following their target, GPS tracking, stakeouts, that sort of thing. I guess it's possible he could've done that, but I believe that if he had known who Carl was, he would've thrown his name in my face every chance he got. It's in his nature. He would've harassed Carl, too."

"Maybe he did," Pancake said. "With a gun."

CHAPTER 37

SAVANNAH PICKED UP the two magazines that lay on the sofa, *Southern Living* and *Coastal Lifestyle,* and placed them on the side table. "Sorry. This place is a mess. I haven't had enough energy to clean."

The living room looked fine to me. Much neater than mine. Not that mine was messy, but a couple of magazines on my sofa wouldn't cause concern.

"Don't apologize," Nicole said. "You have a lot going on right now."

We sat on the sofa, Savannah in the chair at the end of the coffee table.

"Too much. Funeral arrangements, trying to figure out what's going to happen with the business. The whole Mitch thing." She sighed. "Which I'm still having trouble with."

"Understandable," I said.

"Dustin's working long hours. Like today. That's why he's not home yet. So much to do to keep things up and running at the office."

"My impression is that Dustin will do fine," I said.

"He's very organized and a hard worker. But right now he has so many balls in the air. Managing all the showings and closings, keeping the sales force intact, reassuring them that things will go on as usual."

"Are you losing agents?" I asked.

"Not yet. Dustin said a couple of them were nervous and asked about how my father's death would change things. Dustin spoke with each of them and he thinks everyone will stay."

"One less worry," I said.

"So, what's this news you have?" Savannah asked.

I glanced at Nicole. We had earlier discussed how best to handle telling Savannah of Carl's affair. We saw no way to predict her reaction. Anger and denial? Shock and dismay? Sadness and depression? Would she turn on the messengers? Or did she already know, or at least suspect? The decision was for Nicole to tell her and to do so straight up.

"Was your father seeing anyone?" Nicole asked.

"Not really. He had a couple of dates. Months ago. Maybe even a year. I can't remember it's been so long. Lately he's been working too hard. Why?"

"What if he had been? Would you be okay with that?"

She looked from Nicole to me and back to Nicole again. "What are you saying?"

"Carl had been seeing a woman for the past six months."

"What?" Her hand went to her throat.

"A woman named Denise Scholander," Nicole said. "She lives in Pensacola."

"I had no idea." Savannah's initial shock faded, replaced by . . . what? An understanding? A resignation? A sadness? "Why didn't he tell me?"

"He wasn't sure you'd be thrilled."

A slight recoil, an intake of breath. The hand near her throat descended to her chest. "I knew about the few dates he had had. Many months ago. But they were one or two and done. So why not this one?" Her eyes widened. "Because this woman wasn't like the others, right? This one was more serious."

"Yes," Nicole said. "This was much more serious. Carl feared you might not take it well. That you might see it as a betrayal of your mother."

Tears welled in her eyes. "I still miss her. I still see her, hear her, feel her presence."

"Carl knew that. That's why he hesitated telling you."

Savannah bent forward, forked her fingers into her hair, and stared at the floor. She gave a slight headshake, then looked up. "I feel so selfish."

"Don't," I said.

"My father found someone and he couldn't tell me because I wasn't adult enough to deal with real life." She swiped a tear from one eye. "The truth is I've been that way my whole life. The only child. Spoiled. Ungrateful."

"You're being too hard on yourself," Nicole said. "You have every right to mourn your mother for as long as you need."

"Not if it interfered with my father's happiness."

"This might help," I said. "They had decided that it was time to tell you the truth about them. They planned to do it next week."

"Really?"

"Really," Nicole said.

Savannah sniffed. "I take it you got this from her? From Denise?"

"That's right," I said.

Savannah nodded. "Who is she?"

"She's pretty and bright," I said. "Very together. You'd like her. She works in marketing at the Paloma Resort in Pensacola. She also teaches tennis."

"They met at a Chamber of Commerce event six months ago and hit it off," Nicole added. "Their relationship grew and became a big deal for both of them."

"And my father didn't tell me because he feared my reaction." She wiped one eye with the back of her hand. "Now he'll never be able to share his joy with me."

"He wanted to," Nicole said. "He planned to."

"There's one more thing," I said. Savannah looked at me. "The woman, Denise, had an ex-boyfriend. A bad guy. Abusive, drug user. He didn't take her affair with Carl well. He harassed her, stalked her, threatened her."

Savannah paled, held her breath for a beat. "Are you saying he killed my father?"

"We have no evidence of that," Nicole said. "Ray and Pancake are on it. They're going to talk with him. He's a car racer and owns an exotic car repair shop in Pensacola."

"But he could be the guy?"

I nodded. "It's possible. Let's see what Ray and Pancake find out before jumping to any conclusions."

"How did my father get involved with someone like that?"

"He didn't. He didn't even know this guy. Denise doesn't think that Tucker, that's his name, knew Carl. He knew she was seeing someone and that it was serious but he never met Carl and Denise never told him Carl's name."

"But if he was harassing her and spying on her, he could have followed her," Savannah said. "And discovered who my father was."

"It's possible," Nicole said.

"Look," I said. "We don't want to sugarcoat this. Tucker's an angry and controlling ass. People like that are capable of anything. If he was involved, the truth will come out. But Denise? She's a sweet and kind lady. She loved your father. They were planning a future together."

"That's why they were going to sit down with you and Dustin next week," Nicole said. "They wanted you to know and wanted to share their happiness with you."

Savannah broke. Sobs racked her, her shoulders lurching. She buried her face in her hands. We sat and let her expel her grief. After two deep stuttering breaths, she said, "Sorry."

Nicole slid to the end of the sofa, bent forward, and clasped Savannah's hands in hers. "It's okay. This is a lot to a absorb."

Savannah nodded. "I want to meet her."

Nicole smiled. "I hoped you'd want to. I believe Denise would welcome it."

"We'll arrange it," I said.

CHAPTER 38

UNTIL TUCKER MOSS popped up, Pancake had never heard of Moss Sports Cars. He cared little for car racing and sports cars. As a teenager he had had a brief fascination with Corvettes, but even then he couldn't fit into the driver's seat. His massive pickup suited him just fine.

Larger than Pancake expected, Tucker's operation occupied half the block, with seven work bays, a cinderblock office building, and a side lot that held half a dozen cars. Two Vettes, a Porsche, a Mercedes SL and SLC, a BMW 650, and an older Ferrari. Four of the bays housed cars undergoing repair. A Porsche Turbo, an old Ferrari 308, a twenty-five-year-old BMW 850, and a bright blue sprint racer, complete with the elevated rear wing spoiler. Black lettering on the side indicated its sponsor was none other than Moss Sports Cars. Tucker's racing ride, no doubt.

Pancake rolled past the shop to check it out before he pulled a U-turn and swung into the lot of the strip center across the street. A pharmacy, a nail salon, a bagel shop, a clothing store, and a donut shop caught his eye. Especially the donut shop. His stomach growled. He parked, the nose of his truck aimed at Tucker Moss' domain.

"There he is," Pancake said.

"Which one?" Peters asked.

"The lanky dude in the red tee-shirt."

Tucker wore dirty jeans, the aforementioned tee shirt, and a black cap with a red Ferrari logo on the front. A cigarette hung from one corner of his mouth. He stood before the racing car, chatting with the five remaining employees.

"You sure?" Peters asked.

Pancake lifted his cell from the center console, tapped the screen a few times, pulling up the photo he wanted. He turned it toward Peters. "This is his booking photo from a couple of years ago. After his bar fight arrest."

"Where'd you get that?"

"From his Facebook page."

"No, you didn't," Peters said.

"I'm a private investigator. I have my ways."

She raised a palm toward him. "Don't tell me. I might have to arrest you."

"Would that include cuffs?"

She laughed. "It might."

"Then I'm in."

"You're incorrigible."

"It's been said."

"So, what's the plan?" Peters asked.

"Based on his history and what Denise told us about old Tucker, we can expect a hostile witness. Maybe a boot on his throat will alter his attitude."

"I guess being polite is out the window?" She had a slight smile on her face.

"After everything he's done to Denise, and maybe Carl Davis? Not sure he warrants the consideration. So, his window for civility is narrow."

"Just don't break anything."

Pancake raised an eyebrow. "You're no fun." He nodded toward the shop. "Looks like they're closing up for the day. Let some of the troops scatter, then we'll have a chat."

Two of the guys split from the group. One climbed in a pickup. The other swung a leg over a Harley, settled his shiny black helmet into place, and fired up the machine. He followed the pickup from the lot and both disappeared up the street.

"Small enough for you now?" Peters asked.

Pancake glanced at her. "You looking for a fight?"

She laughed. "Always."

"My kind of girl. Let's go."

They crossed the street. The three men looked up as they approached.

"We're looking for Tucker Moss," Pancake said, as if they didn't already know which of the men was him.

"That's me." Relaxed, laid back. He dropped his cigarette to the asphalt and crushed it with his scuffed brown work boot. "What can I do for you?"

"A couple of questions."

Less friendly. Shoulders elevated, eyes narrowed, face arranged into a smirk. "About what?"

"It's private," Peters said, nodding toward the other two men.

Tucker looked at her, all of her, and then to Pancake. "If you got something to say, say it. Otherwise, we're closed, so you can be on your way." Much less friendly.

"Denise Scholander," Pancake said.

Tucker flinched but retained his aggressive poster and scowl. "Who are you?"

"I'm Pancake. A private investigator." He tilted his head toward Peters. "This is Detective Brooke Peters."

Concern settled over Tucker's face, but he recovered, his smirk returning. "I don't have to talk to you about her or anything else."

"No, you don't," Peters said. "But it'd be best if you gave us a few minutes of your time."

"Best for you? Or best for me?"

"Both."

"Fuck you. You can't come in here and threaten me."

"No one's threatening you," Pancake said. "Yet. But if that's how you want to play this, have at it." Before Tucker could respond, Pancake said to the men standing to his left, "Why don't you two run along? This doesn't concern you."

They shuffled their feet, glanced at Tucker for direction.

"They don't have to go anywhere," Tucker said. "But you do. Get off my property."

Pancake ignored him and stepped toward the guy closest to Tucker. He towered over him, looked down, into his eyes. "Either leave or I'll toss you in the street." He smiled. "Maybe down the block."

"Hey," Tucker said. "You can't do that."

Pancake remained focused on the man in front of him. "I can. I will. And I'd love to oblige." He glanced at Tucker. "Your call."

Tucker looked toward Peters. "If you're a cop you can't let this happen."

"I am." She lifted the lower edge of her jacket, revealing her gold shield. "All I see is a friendly chat."

"He's threatening us."

"Looks more like a teaching moment to me."

Pancake suppressed a smile and remained focused on the man before him. He grabbed the guy's throat, squeezing just enough to abort any resistance. He held his grip, walked him back several steps, then said in a low voice, "Get the fuck out of here before I get angry. You've wasted enough of my time."

"Let them go," Tucker said. "This is an assault."

"Not yet," Pancake said. "But we're getting there." He smiled and released his grip. "Now, are you boys going to do the smart thing, or do we have to ramp things up?"

The pair glanced at Tucker but got nothing but a blank stare in return.

"Hit the road," Pancake said.

No hesitation now, no getting cues from Tucker. The two men scurried to their vehicles, a white Camaro and a black Vette, and climbed in. Engines cranked to life. Pancake watched as they swung out of the lot and, like a pair of scalded cats, accelerated up the street.

Pancake turned toward Tucker. "Now, back to the reason for our visit."

"I don't have to talk to you." Tucker raised his chin, defiant. "This is harassment."

"File a complaint," Pancake said.

"You can bet on that." He looked at Peters. "You're a witness to this."

Peters hooked a thumb in her belt. "You see, my momma dropped me on my head as a child. My memory's not so good."

Pancake stifled another smile, not wanting to give Tucker even a sliver of hope.

"What about those anger management classes?" Pancake asked. "You ever finish them?"

"How do you—"

"Like I said before, I'm a P.I. My job is to find out things."

"Which means you've violated the terms of your parole," Peters said. "With a simple call, I can have you behind bars in less than an hour."

"Come on. That was a long time ago."

"Not in the eyes of the law."

"Those classes were a waste of time."

"Apparently," Pancake said. "Doesn't look to me like they took. Maybe you need a refresher course."

"You can't push me around with this bogus crap," Tucker said. "I know my rights."

Pancake closed the space between them. He jabbed a finger into Tucker's chest. "You do not have the right to remain silent. You do not have the right to an attorney. You do not have the right to avoid getting things broken." Pancake moved even closer, his chest almost against Tucker. "Where do you want me to start? What's your least favorite bone?"

That did it. Tucker's defiance drained away and his shoulders sagged. "Look, man, I don't want any trouble. I just don't like people coming to my business and threatening me."

Pancake smiled. "Just a couple of questions."

Tucker nodded. "About what?"

"Like we said earlier, Denise Scholander," Peters said.

"What about her?"

"You dated her," Pancake said. "She dumped you. Now you're harassing her." Tucker started to interrupt but Pancake silenced him with another finger to his chest, this one firmer. "She's scared of you. She's told you it's over but you won't accept that."

"Did she put you up to this? Is that what's going on? She's a lying bitch."

Why were people so hardheaded? Why did they keep poking the hornet's nest to see what might happen?

What did happen was that Pancake gripped Tucker's throat and lifted him from the ground. He let him dangle until his face purpled, then lowered him to his feet. He relaxed, but didn't release his grip. "I don't like you. I think you're a sociopathic punk who stalks and abuses women. I also think you just might be a killer."

"What?"

Pancake released his throat. Tucker rubbed it.

"Carl Davis," Peters said, moving up beside Pancake.

"Who's that?"

"The guy Denise was seeing. The guy that got murdered a few days ago."

"Whoa." Tucker raised his hands, took a step back. "I don't know anything about that."

"Sure you do," Pancake said. "You've stalked Denise for months and threatened her over her relationship with Carl Davis."

"I don't know him. Never heard of him." Tucker was now in full panic mode, grasping the seriousness of the proceedings. "Look, I knew she was seeing someone, but I had no idea who. She kept it a secret."

"Maybe she was afraid something might happen to him?" Peters said.

"She knows I wouldn't do anything like that."

"You sure about that?" Pancake asked.

Tucker had no answer.

Pancake studied him. Fear dripped from Tucker, but was he lying? Did he really not know who Carl Davis was? Denise had said he didn't, but she might not have known. Pancake favored him lying over being clueless. Sociopaths like Tucker could lie with a straight face. He had seen it more than a few times.

"Here's the problem I have," Pancake said. "It wouldn't be difficult for you to find out who she was seeing and where he lived and worked."

"I wouldn't even know where to start doing something like that."

Pancake gave his best smirk. "It doesn't take a heap of brain power. Even you could figure it out. You follow them, see his car, get the plate number, run it through the DMV. Or you follow him home, check the mailbox, grab his name. Or maybe one morning after he and Denise parted ways, you tailed him to his office. The scene of the crime. See, not all that difficult."

"But I didn't. I swear." He took a deep breath and let it out slowly. "Yes, I was upset that she was seeing someone. Yes, I gave her some grief about it."

"Not sure I agree with your definition of grief," Pancake said. "More like stalking and threatening."

Tucker's shoulders drooped. "Maybe I did go too far." He looked at Peters. "I still love her. I didn't want to lose her forever. That's what I thought was happening."

"Which is a common motive for murder," Peters said. "One of the most common. Abused women are in the most danger when they try to leave or extricate themselves from the situation. It's an old and common story. Sometimes the dumped ex thinks eliminating the rival is the right answer."

"But I don't know this Davis guy. I never heard his name until you told me. I know nothing about him. I know nothing about whatever happened to him."

Pancake's read skewed. Before, he felt Tucker was lying and was a viable suspect. Now, he wasn't so sure. He leaned toward believing him. Still, what he thought and what happened were two different things.

"Where were you Monday evening?" Pancake asked.

"What time?"

"Let's say late afternoon or early evening."

"Here at work."

"You never left here?" Peters asked.

Tucker hesitated. "We had a race down in Lake City on Sunday. We didn't come back up here until Monday."

"Lake City isn't that far," Pancake said. "What took so long?"

"We won, so we got drunk. Stayed up too late. Closed the bar. Slept in. Then we had to go by the track garage where we kept the car overnight. We cleaned and trailered it. We didn't get on the road until near noon. It was around two in the afternoon when we got here."

"And later in the day?" Pancake asked.

"I had to go over to my buddy's parts store to get some stuff."

"Which is where?" Peters asked.

"In Gulf Shores."

Pancake cast a glance at Peters. "Gulf Shores, huh? You got to go right through Orange Beach to get there."

"Yeah. So?"

"That's where Carl Davis was murdered."

"Wait a minute." Tucker was on the verge of unraveling. His breathing erratic, his eyes wide. "I didn't do nothing."

"What time did you go over to Gulf Shores?"

"I left here before four. Got there around four thirty."

"And back?"

"I only stayed long enough to pick up what we needed. I left around four forty-five. Before five for sure. We got back here around six."

"What took so long?" Peters asked.

"You live in the area, I assume. Traffic. It was fine going over but it gets ugly around quitting time. Took over an hour to get back to the shop."

That was true. Traffic was never light along the Gulf, but rush hour could be brutal. Even though only thirty miles separated Pensacola from Gulf Shores, it could take an hour, sometimes much longer, to motor from one to the other. Try doing it during spring break. Better pack lunch.

"So you had motive and opportunity," Pancake said.

Tucker took another half step back. "What the hell are you talking about?"

"The Davis murder took place about the time you'd be sliding through Orange Beach."

"I don't like what you're insinuating. Don't like it at all. I didn't do nothing to this guy. I didn't even know him. Nothing about him."

"Except that he was stepping in on what you considered your turf," Pancake said.

Tucker again had no response.

"You said *we*," Peters said. "Did someone go with you to Gulf Shores?"

"I was with one of my guys."

"Who?"

"I don't want to jack anybody up."

"Too late for that," Pancake said.

Tucker knew he had lost the argument. "Patrick was with me. He'll tell you."

"Does Patrick have a last name?"

"McCall. Patrick McCall."

"When you two got back here," Peters asked, "who was here?"

"No one. The boys had locked up. We dropped off the parts and went home."

"Can anyone corroborate that?"

"I live alone, if that's what you're asking. But I don't need no corroboration. I didn't do anything."

"What about the store in Gulf Shores?" Pancake asked.

"Which one?"

"Custom Auto Parts," Tucker said.

"Hank Duggans' place," Pancake said.

The look on Tucker's face was priceless. The last thing he expected was Pancake knowing his parts buddy. Truth was that Jake had gotten replacement parts for his '65 Mustang there and Pancake had met Duggans when they stopped by to pick them up. Nice guy. Nothing like Tucker.

Tucker found his voice again. "Yeah."

"We'll have a chat with him," Peters said.

That elevated Tucker's mood. "You do that. He'll tell you I was there."

"Which would mean that, according to your timeline, you had the perfect opportunity to kill Carl Davis after you left there," Pancake said.

Tucker deflated as he realized that his so-called alibi actually made things worse for him.

"We'll have a chat with Duggans and Patrick," Peters said. "We'll reach out again if we have more questions."

"I'm sure you will." Tucker's smirk returned.

"Bet on it."

Pancake glanced at Peters, gave a slight jerk of his head. She got the message, turned, and walked toward Pancake's truck. Pancake remained, stepped into Tucker's space. "Listen up, Tucker. You might or might not have killed Carl Davis. We'll sort all that out. But there's another issue we need to cover. Denise. From this moment forward, she doesn't exist for you. You don't go near her home or work. Consider it a restraining order. If you see her walking down the street, you cross to the other side. If you contact her, or harass her in any way, I'll be back. If she gets hit by a truck, or falls down the stairs, or god forbid suffers a lightning strike, I'll be back." He smiled. "Next time I might be in a bad mood."

Pancake left Tucker to ponder his threats and walked to his truck, where Peters stood.

"What was that about?" she asked.

"Needed to deliver a message to old Tucker."

"Which was?"

"That he lived on a different planet than Denise and that if he liked things like walking, talking, and breathing, he'd keep it that way."

She laughed. "Love it." She cocked her head. "You're kind of fun."

"One of my many excellent qualities." He cranked the truck's engine.

"Along with that modesty thing."

"That too."

"All that worked up an appetite," she said. "Where's dinner?"

"So you decided it's a date, after all?"

"We'll decide over some wine what kind of dinner it is."

CHAPTER 39

"THIS PLACE IS NICE," Peters said.

"You've been here before?" Pancake asked.

"Right. I'm a lowly cop. The Waffle House is more my budget. But I've heard good things about it. Kudos on your choice. I'm impressed, and flattered."

"Nothing but the best for a pretty lady like you."

She smiled. "You trying to turn this into a date already?"

"Why wouldn't I?"

Amici's, an Italian seafood restaurant in Orange Beach, had indoor and outdoor seating and overlooked the Gulf. It catered to an upscale crowd with linen tablecloths, actual silver flatware, and deep and delicate wine goblets. Prices to match. A corner table on the deck, a warm night, a cloudless sky, and calm waters made for a near perfect evening.

Their server appeared. A young woman, probably a college kid, this her part-time job. She wore tan slacks and a black open-collared shirt, a script *Amici's* embroidered in white on the left front pocket. She smiled. "How are you doing?"

"Great," Peters said.

"I'm Katie. Can I get you something to drink?"

Pancake glanced at Peters. "Wine?"

"That would be nice."

"How about a bottle of your Safreddi Super Tuscan," Pancake said to Katie.

"Excellent choice. Back in a sec."

"What's a super Tuscan?" Peters asked.

"I'm not sure." He smiled. "I know it's from Tuscany, which I guess is apparent. My wine knowledge isn't very broad. I'm more of a beer and a bourbon guy."

"I'm sure it'll be wonderful." She looked toward the Gulf. "As is this evening."

Katie reappeared, two glasses and a bottle of wine in hand. She showed the label to them and then went through the whole opening, tasting, and pouring ritual.

"Very good," Peters said, after taking a sip.

"It's one of our best," Katie said. "I'll grab some menus." She walked away.

Peters took another sip of wine. "This really is amazing."

"As are you," Pancake said.

She eyed him over her glass. "Are you trying to woo me?"

"Woo? Haven't heard that in a long time."

"You know what I mean."

"I do, and yes I am."

"I assumed this was a business dinner." She gave him a mischievous smile.

Pancake shook his head. "No, you didn't. A business meeting would be at your Waffle House. Amici's is for special occasions." He smiled. "Like wooing a pretty lady."

Katie approached with a pair of menus, opening one for each of them. "We also have two specials. A swordfish with a lemon, butter, and caper sauce. That comes with black Asian rice and sautéed veggies. Also, an excellent veal chop with a red wine and balsamic reduction. That comes with fingerling potatoes and asparagus. They're both great. I'll give you a few minutes to look over the menu and then I'll check back."

They chatted, sipped wine, examined the menu, discussed a few of the options, and made their selections. Katie returned.

"We'll both have a Caesar salad, a shrimp cocktail, and the veal chop, medium rare." Pancake glanced at Peters. She nodded her agreement.

"Excellent. I'll get the salads out in a minute."

Peters took another sip of wine. "This might be the best wine I've ever had."

"I agree." Pancake tipped his glass toward her.

"Before we down too much of it, let's talk about this case."

"This is play time, not work time," Pancake said.

"Humor me."

"Okay. You start."

"Number one on my suspect list, no doubt, is Mitch Littlefield. He had motive, means, and opportunity. If he knew Carl was wise to his skimming cash and, of course, the details of the contract, he also knew he stood to lose everything. Unless there was no Carl and no proof. Other than you guys, I found no one who even suspected he was embezzling. Not Savannah, not Dustin, no one."

"But we did know," Pancake said. "So did Carl, of course."

"Are you sure Mitch didn't know Carl hired you?"

Pancake gave a headshake. "As sure as I can be. We met with Carl only three days before his death. On Friday. Not at his office. Carl demanded that. He came to Ray's and brought what he had with him. Part of the deal was that we remained off the radar, in the shadows, until we had something. We did data analysis. No interrogations or chats with the employees. So I doubt Mitch would've known about us. Or that Carl knew of his activities."

"Unless he discovered that Carl had copied records and put two and two together."

"Possible. That's why we sent Jake and Nicole to pick up the papers well after hours. When only Carl would be in the office."

"If Mitch knew Carl had hired you guys and knew that he was planning to pass along damning information on Monday evening, he might've panicked. Killed Carl before the handoff could occur."

Pancake shrugged. "If so, why would he leave the papers there? Why not take them with him?"

"Yeah, that's a problem. And why I agree with you. I believe Mitch had no idea what was headed his way."

"Which begs the questions, why would he kill Carl? And why did he choose Monday night?"

Peters parked a stray strand of hair behind her ear. "Maybe he felt he'd played the game long enough and that, if he continued, sooner or later someone would discover his thefts. That killing Carl and destroying or altering the ledger, the unbalanced ledger, would cover his crimes."

"And give him de facto control of the company," Pancake said. "Savannah isn't up to running it, and my read is that she doesn't want to. He could've bought her half at a discount, a distress sale, so to speak. He would then own a multimillion-dollar outfit."

"A powerful motive."

"You bet."

Katie arrived with their salads. "I'll have the shrimp out in a minute."

"This salad is huge," Peters said. "You over-ordered."

"Not possible."

She laughed. "In your case, I imagine that's true."

They ate in silence for a minute.

"I agree with your take on everything," Pancake said. "But with a couple of lingering questions. Mitch and Dustin left together. If Mitch shot Carl on the way out the door, wouldn't Dustin have heard it? The office isn't that big."

"That troubles me too. Dustin said he talked with Carl about ten minutes before he left. A client issue and what Savannah had planned for dinner. Mundane stuff. He then made a couple of calls in his office and walked out with Mitch."

"Makes for a narrow window of opportunity with complicated logistics."

Peters nodded. "Ten minutes would be enough. But risky with Dustin in the office. Dustin could've finished his calls and gone back to Carl's office before he left, and that would've blown the whole thing up." She shrugged. "Plus the gunshot noise."

"The other thing is, where did he dump the weapon?"

"Maybe he didn't," Peters said.

"Which would be stupid."

"You know the old adage that a cop's best friend is a stupid criminal. And most are." She took a sip of wine. "There're plenty of places between point A and point B where he could've dumped it. A ton of water, marshland, sand dunes, and forested areas."

"Assuming he traveled a straight line between point A and point B," Pancake said.

"We did catch a car matching his on that bank video. If that's him, the timeline matches his story."

"Whether it was or not, I still favor Mitch backtracking to that semi-desolate area we saw, entering through the back door, which he had unlocked before he left, doing the deed, and walking away."

"That makes the most sense."

"Okay, next on your list?" Pancake asked.

"Dustin, with or without Savannah. They had the motive, her for sure. Dustin too, once they get married. Which, incidentally, they moved forward." She shrugged. "But again, the same problems. If Dustin was the shooter, Mitch would've heard a gunshot. Where is the weapon? We have Dustin documented on the grocery store's security cameras. His tracks fit his story of stopping at the store on the way home."

A busboy appeared and whisked away their salad plates. Katie waited until he moved aside, then placed a shrimp cocktail before each of them. "I love these. My favorite thing on the menu. But be warned, the sauce has a bite."

"Perfect," Pancake said.

And they were. The shrimp plump, the sauce spicy.

"What if Dustin and Mitch were in on this together?" Pancake asked. "That would solve the non-shooter hearing the gunshot problem. One of them shoots Carl and they both drive away."

Peters nibbled a shrimp. "Possible. If so, Mitch and Savannah, and after the marriage, Dustin, would own the company. But that would be a lateral move for Savannah. She would gain little."

"The truth is, it would be worse for her."

"How so?" Peters asked.

"Her father, the guy who ran the business, paid the bills, and took care of her, would be dead. Would she have wanted that? I don't see it. My take is that she and Carl were very close. That only child thing. She was devoted to him, and him to her." He dabbed some cocktail sauce from the corner of his mouth. "She knows little about the business. With her father running things, she enjoyed the benefits and had no responsibilities. A cushy situation. And eventually she'd inherit her father's ownership anyway."

"Good points," Peters said.

Pancake shoved an entire shrimp in his mouth. "Who else you got on your list?"

"Gary Wayne Frawley has a motive. Being shown the door by Carl and he for sure wasn't happy about it. But that was a year ago, and he has a solid alibi. Supported by Megan Varner and the video evidence. Same with Everett Lowe. He had motive, his anger at Carl, but that anger dissipated once he looked at the situation. He likewise had a solid alibi." She shrugged. "For me, those two possibilities are remote."

"What about Tucker Moss?" Pancake asked.

"He's a different story. He's an aggressive ass and a tweaker. A combination that can lead down a dark road. Tomorrow I'll visit Hank Duggan at his parts shop in Gulf Shores and see what he has to say."

"I'll go with you," Pancake said.

"I can handle him."

Pancake feigned being hurt. He gave a pout. "You don't like my company?"

"I love your company."

"Then it'll be our second date."

She rolled her eyes. "I have a better idea. You visit Duggan since he's in your neighborhood, and I'll see this Patrick dude since he's closer to mine."

"You trying to avoid a second date?" Pancake asked.

"Not at all. We'll have to meet to compare notes, won't we?"

"I like it." He ate his last shrimp. "The funny part here is that Tucker put himself near the crime scene. If what he told us is true, he would've been in or near Orange Beach around the time of Davis' murder."

"But he has this Patrick character as an alibi," Peters said.

"An employee. Someone he likely controls and dominates. Someone who could be an accomplice."

"That's true," Peters said. "Alibi, accomplice, or whatever, Tucker's still high on the suspect list and now so is Patrick. Not above Mitch Littlefield but up there anyway."

"Tucker's a nasty SOB. A stalker and a tweaker and I don't like him." He smiled. "If he's smart he'll take everything I said to heart and leave Denise alone. Otherwise, I'll pay him a visit, and enjoy doing so."

"Don't tell me if you do. I'd hate to have to arrest you." She smiled.

"Are you threatening me with handcuffs again?" He bounced an eyebrow.

She laughed. "I could be. But before we go down that road, back to the case. Our major suspects are Tucker Moss, who has motive, means, and opportunity; some random dude, which I don't buy since this doesn't look like a robbery, but still possible; and Mitch Littlefield, the guy with everything to gain."

"I agree," Pancake said.

"It might be time to bring Mitch in for an official chat."

"Will you let him know that you're aware of his embezzling?" Pancake asked.

"Not at first. Better to tap-dance around that and focus on the murder. See what he might know and who he might suspect, that sort of thing. Not like he's suspect one. See if he stumbles. We can then use his thefts as leverage to rattle him."

"I like that."

"The truth on the embezzling front is that, right now, there hasn't been a complaint filed. Unless Savannah does so, we can't move forward on the missing funds."

"Let us handle Savannah," Pancake said. "We can get a better feel for where her head is at if we don't go in with badges and guns."

"Now, my feelings are hurt."

"No they're not."

Their meals arrived. They ate. Everything was perfect. They ordered a second bottle of wine. Once the meal was complete, Pancake ordered desserts—a crème brûlée and a Linzer torte. They shared them, then sat back to finish the wine.

"That was beyond wonderful," Peters said. "Thank you."

"Did you get enough?"

"Lord yes. Enough for the next three days."

"Is the business meeting concluded? Can we have fun now?"

"We can." She touched her wineglass to his. "To first dates."

CHAPTER 40

STANDING PROVED DIFFICULT, walking even more so. Me, the ex-pro athlete. The hot swirling water, the bottle of Petron tequila we had damaged, and Nicole's acrobatics made climbing out of the hot tub and staggering inside a labor. The term *swoon* came to mind. I'm not sure why since I'd never heard that word used in conversation. I must've read it in a book. What did it mean anyway? I felt light-headed, off balance, and feeble. Sort of swoony. Was that a word?

Nicole was not sympathetic. She laughed at me. She did that a lot. It would've hurt my feelings, but I was too numb to feel much.

"What?" I asked.

"You remind of one of those old dudes on the beach looking for coins with a metal detector."

My tight back resisted straightening. "You're picking on an incapacitated man."

"Ha. That wasn't the case a few minutes ago."

"I faked it."

"No, you didn't." She slapped my bare ass. "Now get in bed. I'm not through with you."

True to her word, she wasn't finished. Not even close. An hour later, we lay there, glistening with sweat, pleasantly exhausted.

"That was fun," Nicole, said. "I might keep you around."

"Lucky me."

"Yes, lucky you." She nuzzled against me. "Lucky me too."

We lay there for several minutes, melted against each other, our breathing in sync.

"What's on the agenda tomorrow?" I asked.

She tilted her head and looked me in the eye. "You don't remember?"

Uh-oh. I had missed, or forgotten, something. Again. This was becoming a habit. Maybe I needed a brain scan. Or one of those MRI things. I tried to fake it. "Sure I remember."

"Okay, I'll play. Tell me what you remember."

I hated it when she called my bluff. But, I wasn't ready to concede. "I forget the details."

"The broad strokes will do." She raised an accusatory eyebrow.

I said I needed to go pee, she said I didn't, I asked how she could know that, to which she responded that I was avoiding the question. She rolled on top of me.

"It's not that your teeth are floating, it's that your mind is empty," she said.

She had a point. The only thing floating was the one thing I needed to remember. It rattled around in my head somewhere, but I couldn't pin it down. My brain needed a better filing system. I wondered if the Dewey decimal system would work here. I made a mental note to work on that but wasn't sure where to file the memo.

Thinking there still might be a way out of this trap, old stubborn me still had hope. I needed to come up with the right words that were noncommittal and general enough to create the illusion that I knew more than I did. A Houdini act I occasionally attempted that, more often than not, made things worse. But then, doesn't hope spring eternal? Poetic me.

Okay, here goes.

"We have to go see someone," I said, with false confidence, hoping I had guessed right.

"Who?"

Damn. I racked my brain. Who had we talked about earlier? I remembered tequila, jacuzzi bubbles, tangled bedsheets, and Nicole, but no names. I made another mental note to pay more attention. Unfortunately, it fell on a stack of identical memos, also doomed for oblivion. Okay, back to the question. Ray? Pancake? Carl, Savannah, Dustin? Denise? I went with the most common choice.

"Pancake," I said.

She rolled off of me. "Go pee."

"See, I told you I knew."

"You aren't even close. Now go take care of your business."

"I don't need to."

"We're going to pick up Savannah and take her to lunch with Denise."

Now I remembered. Savannah said she wanted to meet Denise and Nicole planned it. During the fog of last night, she must've mentioned it to me. Another pay attention note added to the pile.

"What time?" I asked.

"I told Denise I'd call her to check her schedule and then we can make it happen."

"Getting them together is one of your better moves," I said.

"I hope they like each other," Nicole said.

"They have Carl in common so I suspect they have a lot to share."

"Yesterday when we told her about Denise, I sensed Savannah was relieved that her father had found someone."

"Seemed that way to me."

"It could've gone the other way," Nicole said. "She could've resented the intrusion on her father's affection. Or felt betrayed by his secrecy. But I didn't sense any of that."

"Me, either."

Another few minutes of silence followed. Nicole's fanned-out hair and breath warmed my chest. Contentment didn't cover it. My mind wandered. I thought about Savannah's loss. How hard it must be. About Carl. From what I had learned of him, a hard-working decent guy with no real enemies. Until his partner screwed him. And when Carl discovered the deception, Mitch Littlefield killed him. That had to be what happened.

Nicole came to the same conclusion. "Mitch did it," she said.

"Looks that way."

"No one else makes sense. No way Savannah was involved. Neither were Gary Wayne Frawley and Everett Lowe. Tucker Moss is, of course, still in play."

Pancake had called last night after he and Peters confronted Tucker. He had told us about Tucker's Sunday race and his trip up to Gulf Shores on Monday afternoon, which put him at least near the crime scene. He added that Tucker was a snake and it wouldn't take much to topple him over the edge. That nasty was his basic personality trait, and when meth entered the picture, all manner of bad behavior could follow. He ended by saying, "A quick trip out to the woodshed might do the boy wonders."

"Would Denise seeing someone else be motive enough for him to shoot Carl?" I asked Nicole. "In the head? In cold blood?"

"Sure it would."

"Seems flimsy to me."

"That's because you aren't the jealous or possessive type."

"I'm possessive of you."

"No, you're not. It's not in your nature." She smiled. "One of your best qualities."

"More than my sparkling personality?"

"And your modesty." She poked my ribs. "Tucker belongs on the suspect list, but my number one is still Mitch."

"Both had motive, means, and opportunity," I said. "What about Dustin? He was there. In fact, he might be the last person to have seen Carl alive."

"Unless that was Mitch." She looked up at me. "But why would Dustin do that? He knows Savannah was devoted to her father. Would he harm the person he supposedly loves that way?"

"Jealousy? Like Tucker, only different? Maybe he resented Carl's importance to Savannah. Maybe he wanted her all to himself."

"I guess that's possible."

"But you don't think so," I said.

"The old adage that following the money is the best advice is in play here. There are millions involved if you take the stolen money and the value of the company together. Mitch would've covered his crime and gained more control of the business with one pull of the trigger. Not in ownership with Savannah inheriting her father's half, but in operational control. If he convinced her to sell out, he'd have the entire empire. Savannah knows little about the company, and might feel out of her league. Such an offer could look attractive. Dustin has no stake in the company so it would be her decision."

"Not yet," I said. "But once he and Savannah get hitched, he will."

"Hitched? Are we in a western?"

"You were a cowgirl earlier."

"You complaining?"

"Not in the least."

"But Dustin is an interesting thought," she said.

"I'm full of them."

"You're full of something." She poked my ribs again. "But if Dustin was involved, so was Savannah. I don't see her planning and carrying out the murder of her father. He meant too much to her."

"Sure seems so," I said.

"Mitch has to be the guy. Do you think Detective Peters will arrest him soon?"

"I don't know. I mean, what does she have? Dustin saw him leave, literally followed him from the parking lot. There's at least one security camera that saw him heading home. The time between when they left the office and when we showed up is a narrow window."

"But a doable one," Nicole said.

"True. It would only take a couple of minutes for him to loop back and kill Carl before heading home."

"He knew about that sandy area," Nicole said. "He knew Carl was alone and that no one else was in the office, or likely to return. He knew the rhythm of the place. Who comes and goes and when. He could've unlocked the rear door before leaving."

"Then he had plenty of places to dump a gun between there and home," I said. "Hell, he could've dumped an arsenal. Lots of water, lots of swampy areas, lots of sand dunes."

"You're making a good case for her arresting him. A pile of circumstantial evidence there."

"Arresting is one thing, mounting a successful prosecution is another. She needs the smoking gun, literally."

CHAPTER 41

BROOKE PETERS WOKE, lying on her side, hugging a pillow. Dawn lightened the blue curtains she faced. Not her curtains, not her pillow. Not her bed or her bedroom. She sat up. To her left, empty rumpled sheets.

Last night came rolling back. Dinner, drinks, back here, more drinks, kissing, touching, clothes disappearing. Sex on the sofa. Him carrying her to bed.

She collapsed back on the pillow and stared at the ceiling, where a slow-moving fan stirred the air. Her temples throbbed.

Good lord, Brooke, what have you done?

Too much alcohol, too much laughter, and she ended up here in Pancake's bed.

More memories. Pleasant ones. In fact, outstanding ones. Still, not her best decision. This had conflict and calamity written all over it. No other way to see it. If Scoggins found out, she'd be looking for another job. Or at least be back on the streets in uniform.

The aroma of coffee reached her. Bacon too. What the hell?

She rolled out of bed, back and legs stiff, dizzy, her balance precarious. She grasped the nightstand for support. Didn't help. She sat. After a few breaths, she rose again. Better. At least she didn't fear she might fall on her face.

She searched for her clothes. Not on the floor or the nearby chair. Images formed. Slacks, shirt, bra, panties piled on the floor next to the sofa, mingled with Pancake's pants and shirt.

She shuffled to the foot of the bed where she found an oversized navy blue tee-shirt tangled in the covers. Pancake's shirt. He had given it to her. When? Why? Oh yeah. After some quality time in bed, they had returned to the kitchen for more wine, her clad in the shirt. The wine led them back to the sofa for another round of play. How she eventually got back to bed, a mystery.

She slipped on the shirt. It engulfed her, reaching her knees, sleeves beyond her elbows. She staggered to the bathroom, and then to the kitchen. The aromas of bacon and coffee intensified and were now laced with that of toasting bread.

"What're you doing?" she asked.

Pancake stood at the stove, spatula in hand, bacon sizzling in the skillet. He turned toward her. "I was getting ready to come shake you awake. Coffee?"

"Please."

He nodded toward the counter to his left, where a pot of coffee and a cup sat. She poured some and took a sip. "Good, and very needed."

"Cream or sugar?"

She raised her cup. "Perfect as it is."

"Bacon's almost done, then I'll scramble some eggs."

Hunger gnawed at her. After last night's meal she didn't see how, but her grumbling stomach didn't lie. "Anything I can do?"

"Have a seat." He nodded toward the array of stools beyond the center island, the far side raised to serve as a counter. "Enjoy your coffee, and I'll have everything ready in a sec."

"It smells great and I'm starving."

"Me, too," Pancake said.

She smiled over her coffee cup. "Aren't you always?"

He laughed. "Pretty much. Especially after an evening like last night." He bobbed an eyebrow.

"Which we need to talk about."

"We do?"

"We do."

"Okay," Pancake said. "I'll go first. You were magnificent. I think I did okay. We can try again right after breakfast. How's that?"

"As tempting as that sounds, I was referring to what my boss would say if he found out."

Pancake lifted the last of the bacon onto a plate where paper towels soaked up some of the grease. "You planning on telling him?"

"Good lord, no."

"Then how will he find out?" He poured a bowl of eggs into the skillet and began stirring.

"He's a detective. He's suspicious by nature. He can read people." She took a sip of coffee. "I'm not very good at poker."

"I am. Let me handle it."

"A P.I., a cook, a poker player, and still modest. Amazing." She grinned.

He loaded two plates with a mound of eggs, a pile of crisp bacon, and triangles of toast. He slid one plate toward her.

"Did you make enough?" she asked.

"We'll see." He sat next to her. "If not, I have more in the fridge."

"This would feed a family of four. You might have to help me."

He shoved eggs into his mouth. "Gladly."

She broke off a piece of bacon, ate it, and then dug into the eggs. "This is so good."

"Simple eggs and bacon," Pancake said.

They said nothing for a few minutes, only the tapping of forks against plates breaking the silence.

"Are we meeting with your boss today?" Pancake asked.

"He said to call this morning, and he'd see what his schedule allowed."

"He'll be available."

"Oh, you sure of that?" she asked.

"He wants to know what we know. He'll find the time."

"He also wants the papers you got from Carl's office. And that password book."

Pancake poured more coffee for each of them. "No problem. Maybe that'll endear him to us."

"He's not the endearing type."

Pancake smiled. "He hasn't met me." She gave him a head-shake. "We can swing by Ray's on the way and I'll grab them." He sipped his coffee. "Rather than letting him decide the when and where, let's just show up. Bearing gifts."

"You know, that might work."

Peters continued working on her food. Pancake carried his empty plate to the sink and began washing it.

"Is he planning to bring Mitch Littlefield in for an official interview?" he asked.

"He's considering it."

"I would. At first, all casual like. See if Mitch has come up with any possible suspects. Like he's helping solve the case. Then, I'd drop the money deal in his lap. Shift his focus. Shake him up.

Make him think it's all about the money and give no hint that he's the prime suspect in Carl's murder."

"I think that's his plan."

"I'd like to be there," Pancake said.

"Not sure that'll happen. He's a stickler for the rules."

"I'll turn on my charm."

"Don't forget your modesty."

"That too."

Peters leaned back, patted her stomach. "I'm stuffed. If I hang around you I'll weigh three hundred pounds."

"We can work it off." He smiled.

She carried her plate to the sink and placed it inside. Pancake moved behind her and massaged her shoulders. She leaned back against him. He felt strong, solid.

"What'd you have in mind?" she said.

"More of the same."

"What time is it?"

"Six thirty. We have time."

"Yes, we do."

CHAPTER 42

NICOLE AND I performed our usual morning duty of stopping by Captain Rocky's for a bag of breakfast burritos before heading to Ray's. It was just past eight, and the day promised to be perfect. Blue sky, comfortable temperature, and a gentle breeze off the Gulf. When Nicole turned into Ray's parking area, the spaces among the stilts that held the house, I didn't see Pancake's truck.

"Wonder where he is," Nicole said.

"Maybe he couldn't wait for our delivery and went out to grab something to eat."

She smiled. "Hope it doesn't spoil his appetite."

"Yeah, right."

Upstairs, we found Ray at his deck table. His laptop open, a sweating can of Mountain Dew nearby.

"Where's Pancake?" I asked. I placed the bag of burritos on the table.

"On the way. He just called."

"A little late for him," Nicole said.

"He said something came up that delayed him."

"He say what?" I asked.

"No."

I heard the rumble of Pancake's truck engine. Ray grabbed a burrito, as did Nicole and I. I placed the bag with the other three at Pancake's usual spot.

Pancake walked out, Brooke Peters behind him.

Well, well.

"Detective Peters," Ray said, standing. "I didn't expect to see you this morning."

"We're having a chat with her boss in a bit," Pancake said.

"Compare notes?" I asked.

"Hope so." Pancake glanced at Peters. "I guess that depends on her boss. But I'll bring gifts. Those papers we got from Savannah, and the password book."

"You have copies, I assume," Ray said.

"I do."

"A breakfast burrito?" Nicole asked Peters. "I'm sure Pancake will share with you."

"No thanks. We just ate."

And the plot thickens.

Peters appeared uncomfortable. Guilty even. Pancake the dog.

I should've let that sleeping dog lie, take the gallant road, but I couldn't resist. "Where'd you eat?"

Nicole elbowed my ribs.

"At Pancake's place. He cooked a great breakfast." She scanned the three of us. "Yes, we had dinner last night. Yes, I stayed over."

"That's none of our business," Nicole said, unable to suppress a smile.

Peters gave a one-shoulder shrug. "I figured I needed to kill the elephant in the room. Now he's dead and we can move on."

Good for her. I liked her moxie. I wasn't sure what that word meant, but I think it fit.

Pancake opened the bag and extracted a burrito. He held it toward Peters. "Want one?"

"Are you kidding?"

"I never joke about food." Pancake unwrapped it and took a massive bite. "Always room for a burrito or two."

Or in Pancake's case, three or four.

Pancake and Peters sat.

"Is this your office?" Peters asked Ray.

"It is. Nice, huh?"

"Very. Mine has a single window the size of a postage stamp. It's a gulag."

"Only warmer than the Russian variety," Pancake said. "Plus the beach and palm trees."

"Neither of which I can see through my little window," Peters said.

"What are you guys up to today?" Pancake asked me.

"Taking Savannah to meet Denise for lunch."

"That might be good for both of them," Peters said.

"I hope so," Nicole said. "They both loved Carl, so maybe it'll help heal their collective wound."

Pancake finished his burrito and tugged out another. Again he extended it toward Peters. She waved it away, gave him an eye roll.

"Before you do that," Pancake said, "why don't you, all three of you, go with us to the department. We can show Lieutenant Scoggins who we are and assure him we're on the same team here."

"P.I.s aren't his favorite life-form," Peters said.

"Nicole will soften him up." Pancake smiled.

Or have the exact opposite effect. Either way might be helpful.

"You're so kind," Nicole said.

"Always," Pancake said. "I want him to know we aren't a threat to the investigation and can be of help."

"Which is what I told him," Peters said. "He wasn't convinced, but meeting the entire crew might help." She glanced at Pancake. "Handing over the materials you have will definitely make him more amenable."

Pancake finished his second burrito and stood. "We better get moving." He grabbed the bag that held the last burrito. "For the road."

"Where do you put it?" Peters asked.

"That's been an indecipherable question since we were kids," I said.

Pancake gave a grunt. "You guys can poke me all you want, but I got two breakfasts today. Always a good start." He waved Peters toward the door to the interior. "We need to swing by Brooke's place so she can change clothes. Meet us at the Orange Beach PD in an hour."

And just like that, Detective Peters became Brooke.

CHAPTER 43

NICOLE AND I had an hour to kill before drifting over to the Orange Beach Police Department. We watched Pancake and Peters drive away and then climbed into Nicole's car.

"Didn't see that coming," Nicole said.

"Nor did I. But the big guy has his charming side."

Nicole suggested we stop by Captain Rocky's, or somewhere, for coffee. I countered, suggesting we stop by my place for some quality time. She countered my counter, saying an hour wasn't long enough for what she had in mind.

Oh yeah, put me in, coach.

"We can be a little late," I said.

"No, we can't."

Sometimes she's no fun.

She swung east onto Beach Boulevard and accelerated. Until we smacked into the Gulf Shores traffic that crept and crawled. Nicole tapped the steering wheel.

"Since we aren't going to my place, we have plenty of time."

"That's not the point." She now patted the dashboard. "This baby needs to run, not jerk along with these folks."

"They'd drive faster if they could."

"Not fast enough." She glanced at me. "Let's go to that place Pancake mentioned."

"The coffee shop?"

"Yeah. It's called Black Cat or something like that. It's near Peters' office."

I tapped alive my iPhone and began searching.

"Black Kat Koffee," I said. "It's not far."

"If these people will get a move on we might get there before our clothes go out of style."

Nicole wasn't what you'd call a clothes-horse, but she was never out of style. Whatever she wore looked cool and trendy. Hell, she could don a flour-sack dress and look hip. Today she wore light gray jeans and a black silk shirt, untucked. Hot and fashionable. Guys have it easier since men's fashion changed about every fifty years. I wore ten-year-old jeans and a five-year-old dark green pullover.

Beach Boulevard became Perdido Beach Boulevard as we rolled past Shelby Lakes and entered Orange Beach. To my right stretched one of the few segments of the beach that had yet to see development. I hoped it never would but such prayers aren't realistic. Land is money and developed land is big money.

Nicole, fed up with the stream of humanity in front of her, made three right shoulder passes, and we reached Black Kat Koffee with time to spare. Small, busy, and yes, trendy, we waited in the counter line to order a pair of Americanos. We grabbed the last remaining booth. The coffee strong and rich, and better than I expected. How did Pancake find this place? Not his usual as there was no barbecue, or burgers, or nachos in sight. Either he stumbled on it or someone told him about it. I mentioned that to Nicole.

"He found it online when he looked for somewhere to meet Peters away from, but near, her office."

"I'm still not sure what to think about that," I said.

"I'd say the good detective has fallen into Pancake's web. He's such a clever boy."

"That he is. But it's good to see that twinkle in his eye."

"It is. But you know it'll cost you."

"Me?"

"Pancake's appetite is hardier, if that's possible, when he's happy. He's already had two meals, and the day hasn't even started."

"I better call Carla and warn her."

"Good idea."

"A risky move on her part, don't you think?" I asked. "Brooke hooking up with Pancake?"

Nicole nodded. "Could be. If her boss finds out, I imagine she'll have some tap dancing to do."

"So we better be charming and non-threatening today. Soften him up."

"We can be charming. The threatening or not is up to Ray."

We finished our coffee, I hit the head, and then we walked out to her car.

"Do you know anything about her boss?" I asked, sliding into the passenger's seat.

"Only that his name's Buddy Scoggins and, according to Peters, a straightforward dude." She pulled her phone from her pocket. "I have a picture of him I grabbed from their website."

"When did you do that?"

"While you were primping in the men's room."

"I wasn't primping. I was washing my hands."

She smiled. "And fluffing your hair."

Okay, okay, I did. But I wasn't about to admit it. She had enough ammo to use on me, and I saw no reason to refill her quiver. And hair fluffing is not primping. It's not.

She turned her phone toward me. The image showed Scoggins in his uniform. Square jaw, crew cut, deep-set eyes, thick neck. Not someone who tolerated bullshit or deception.

"He looks like a Marine drill instructor," I said.

"According to his bio he was a Marine. Not a drill instructor but an MP."

"That's even scarier."

"Don't worry," Nicole said. "I know Krav Maga. I'll protect you."

CHAPTER 44

In person, Lieutenant Buddy Scoggins appeared more intimidating than his photo. 3D versus 2D with an added air of authority. He entered the conference room where Peters, aka Brooke, had gathered us around the long table. Scoggins greeted each of us with a firm handshake and an expressionless face. He sat at the head of the table, eyed Ray.

"It's good to meet you." He waved a hand. "And your crew. I've heard only good things."

"Always nice to hear," Ray said.

Scoggins looked at Pancake. "And you're the famous Tommy Jeffers, or Pancake."

"I am."

"Brooke here has high praise for you." His gaze lingered.

Uh-oh. Did he know about them? Was this where he took Brooke's badge and gun and showed her the door?

Scoggins continued. "Let me begin by saying I'm uncomfortable about you, or anyone, being involved in an active investigation."

"We understand," Ray said. "We've worked with law enforcement countless times and know the rules and where most of the boundaries are. Our hope is to help, not muddy the waters."

"That, of course, is the concern."

"We'll do our best to stay low profile," Ray said. He rested his forearms on the table's edge. "Savannah Davis hired us to look into her father's murder, so we're investigating the same thing as you. Hopefully, in lockstep. Free of any conflict."

"Carl Davis originally hired us," Pancake said. "To look into possible embezzling by his partner. We found that that's indeed the case."

"It looks that way," Scoggins said.

"It looks that way because it is." Pancake removed a folder from his briefcase. "These are copies of the latest information. We just got them from Savannah. They're what you already have from Davis' office."

Scoggins tugged the folder toward him, flipped it open, and thumbed through a few of the pages. "What does this tell you?"

"The same thing I'm sure your guys are seeing. Mitch stole close to four hundred K from Carl over the past three years. In small amounts covered by monkeying with the books. After matching up inflows, outflows, invoices, and bank documents, the evidence is compelling."

Scoggins closed the folder. "My guys told me just an hour ago that they found the same thing."

"Then there you go," Pancake said. "What they don't yet know is that Littlefield has three accounts in the Caymans."

"Really?" Scoggins glanced at Brooke and then back to Pancake.

"New info," Pancake said. "I'm not dead solid sure yet. I have a few more connections to follow. It appears one is legit, where he keeps some of his retirement and savings money, while the others are for the stolen funds."

"But you're not sure?"

"Not yet. But I'm getting there."

Scoggins leaned back in his chair. It looked like his chest and shoulders might rip through his white shirt. "Getting caught with your hand in a three-hundred-thousand-dollar cookie jar is a powerful motive for murder."

"It is," Ray said. "Not proof, of course, but it smells like Littlefield is the bad guy in this drama."

Scoggins nodded. "What else have you uncovered?"

Ray shrugged. "Not much. What about you?"

Scoggins hesitated.

"This needs to be a two-way street," Ray said.

Scoggins shifted in his chair. "The truth? We don't know much else. Mitch Littlefield remains our top suspect."

"Mitch was always the strongest possibility," Pancake said. "But Davis' conflicts with past employee Gary Wayne Frawley and previous client Everett Lowe made them of concern. Both, as you know, were dead ends. Then we found that Carl had been seeing someone."

"Brooke told me," Scoggins said.

Pancake continued. "A woman named Denise Scholander. Savannah didn't know since Carl didn't want to tell her until he was sure. Somewhere along the line he crossed that threshold and he and Denise were going to talk with Savannah next week." He shrugged. "Savannah had no idea Denise even existed."

"We're going to get them together," I said.

"Oh?" Scoggins asked.

"Savannah's idea," Nicole said. "She wants to meet Denise. She seemed genuinely sad that her dad hadn't told her about them. She felt as if she had clung so tightly to her mother's memory that she had interfered with her father's happiness."

"Thus the meeting," Scoggins said.

"Exactly." Nicole nodded. "They both loved Carl so they have a lot in common."

"When will this happen?"

"Lunch today."

Scoggins gave that some thought. "Does anyone see a potential conflict here?"

After a brief silence, I said, "I do." Everyone looked at me. Why do I open my mouth? What I believed to be intelligent and well-thought out suddenly seemed stupid and irrelevant. "I mean, Denise is a potential witness and Savannah a possible suspect."

Scoggins nodded.

"Except," I continued, "there's no legitimate conflict here. Savannah wasn't involved in her father's murder. No way I can see that. Denise had no role either. Except for her jerk ex-boyfriend."

"The guy I told you about earlier," Brooke said. "Tucker Moss. We—Pancake, Mr. Jeffers—and I are looking a little deeper into him."

"I agree," Scoggins said. "That Savannah, and from what you've said, this Denise woman aren't involved. But is it in fact that way?"

Well, there was that. If I was being honest, neither Savannah nor Denise was in the clear. Yet my gut said they were.

"I agree with Jake," Nicole said. "I see no way either of them could be involved."

Scoggins appeared unconvinced.

Brooke jumped in. "We're not writing either of them off. Even though the evidence is circling Mitch Littlefield."

Pancake tugged Carl's password book from his briefcase and slid it toward Scoggins. "Carl's passwords. Something else

Savannah gave us. He was old school that way. This'll give your guys access to all his accounts, his social media, and his emails and texts."

Scoggins opened the book and thumbed through the pages. "This will help. Thanks."

"That's why we're here," Ray said. "To help."

Scoggins laid the book on the folder Pancake had given him earlier. "It might be time to bring Littlefield in for a more formal interview."

"I agree," Ray said. "We'd like to watch."

"I don't know about that," Scoggins said.

"Look," Pancake said. "We know this case inside and out. We know all the players. Maybe we'll pick up on something Mitch says that could be useful. Or lead to another line of questioning." He shrugged. "It can't hurt to have extra eyes and ears on this."

Scoggins gave a slow nod. "I'll give it some thought."

"When do you think this might go down?" Ray asked.

"Sooner rather than later. Probably this afternoon."

CHAPTER 45

NICOLE AND I arrived at Captain Rocky's a half hour early for the lunch that would bring Savannah and Denise together. I'm an important cog in the machine and my presence assured all would go smoothly. Nicole disagreed, saying I was merely set decoration and that if I didn't get in the way, Carla would have everything under control. As always.

I had no comeback since that was true.

I proved my importance by stopping and chatting with a few of the regulars while Nicole and I made our way to my private table. Exhausting, but that's the price for being the owner.

A vase filled with multicolored flowers centered the tablecloth, peach, with matching napkins. Our best china and flatware completed the picture. Things I hadn't seen in years. I wasn't sure where we stored this fancy stuff. Apparently, Carla did.

Pancake, Nicole, and I didn't need such frills. The plastic baskets we served burgers and fries in were just fine. Plus, it was easier and cheaper to clean the teak tabletop than change tablecloths after one of Pancake's feeding frenzies. The boy left little in his wake. His scraps resembled a crime scene. Stains and bones and debris.

Denise quashed the original plan, to meet at the Paloma Resort, saying that Savannah had too much on her plate right now and somewhere closer for her made more sense. Captain Rocky's seemed the best choice.

I hoped this little powwow would go well, and not become awkward if the two women didn't warm to one another. Or, worse, devolved into a jealousy-driven hissing and spitting contest. Not likely, but with deep emotions in play, anything was possible.

Obviously this wasn't the same as two women, each seeing the same man, coming face-to-face for the first time. I'd seen that. Hell, I'd caused that. Never pretty. Speaking of hissing and spitting and scratching and screaming. One memorable clash resulted in the two women rolling around on the floor of an upscale restaurant, cursing, pulling hair, and even throwing punches. I ended it with both of them. Too much drama for me.

No way this meeting would resemble that. Yet, there were similarities. I had no doubt that each of them had loved Carl. Savannah the devotion a daughter, an only child, while for Denise, Carl might have been the love of her life.

Would Savannah resent Denise's and Carl's deception? That her father hadn't trusted her to accept his life choices and had conspired with Denise to hide their affair? She had now had a full day and night to mull over the situation. Hopefully, her emotions hadn't boiled into a toxic brew.

And Denise? Would guilt, like a child caught stealing or lying or doing something forbidden, rear its ugly head? Make her defensive or combative?

I had experience with the latter. Always Pancake's fault. Really, it was. He hatched most of our schemes. Each blew up because we hadn't thought them through. The look on Ray's face alone was punishment.

Would Denise's guilt construct an impenetrable wall? If so, would Savannah offer one of those Ray looks? The one that conveyed disappointment as much as anger.

I didn't think any of these scenarios would materialize. From what I had seen, Carl's murder shook and saddened each of them with no hint of anger or resentfulness.

"You're worried, aren't you?" Nicole asked.

"About what?"

"This meeting."

We sat at the table next to each other. "It could go sideways."

"It won't."

"You're very sure of yourself."

"You're just now figuring that out?" She smiled. "They need each other. They both loved Carl, and right now, clinging to someone who shares their grief is needed."

"Says Doctor Jamison."

"You're the one I'm worried about."

"Me? Why?"

"You have a knack for putting your foot in your mouth."

My girlfriend. "I'll keep my feet on the floor."

"Good idea."

I saw Savannah enter and make her way toward us. We stood and each of us gave her a hug. We sat.

Savannah appeared nervous, strained.

"You okay?" I asked.

"Just apprehensive about this meeting." She gave a strained smile. "But excited. I'm looking forward to meeting Denise."

"She feels the same way," Nicole said. "So, take a deep breath and relax."

Carla appeared with four glasses and a pitcher of margaritas. She placed them on the table. "I have some calamari working. It'll be up in a minute."

I filled three of the glasses, sliding one toward Savannah.

"Thanks." She took a sip. "This will help."

I saw Denise at the entrance. She hesitated and scanned the room. I stood and headed her way. She saw me and weaved through the tables toward me.

"Welcome," I said.

"Nice place," she said.

I smiled. "I know the owner."

She gave a nervous laugh.

"You ready?" I asked.

"Yes. A little anxious, but in a good way."

I introduced Savannah and Denise. Savannah stood and they embraced. Warm and friendly, each reluctant to let the other go. Ultimately they did and sat.

"I can't tell you how much I've been looking forward to meeting you," Savannah said.

"Me too. For months."

I filled Denise's margarita glass from the pitcher. She took a sip and looked at Savannah. "I've been more than a little apprehensive about meeting you."

Savannah laughed. "I thought it was just me."

"You're even prettier than your pictures," Denise said.

"That's so kind." Savannah sighed. "I wish we had met before. Before Dad passed."

"He wanted that. I did too. We planned to open up to you next week."

Savannah nodded. "I know."

"Carl felt guilty keeping it from you. He said you two didn't have secrets."

Savannah's eyes glistened. "We didn't." She dabbed an eye with her napkin. "I miss him so much.

This was going well. And fast. The bond between them was palpable, as if drawn together by an invisible force. That glue being Carl Davis.

Tears welled in Denise's eyes. "Me too." She turned her chair, leaned forward, clasped both of Savannah's hands with hers. "I loved your father very much. He was so special. I truly believe we were meant to be and it would've been forever."

Savannah nodded, sniffed.

"Please don't feel betrayed by us," Denise said. "Carl wanted you to know for a while now. It's just that he wanted to make sure what we had was real. Once he, both of us, realized it was, he decided to let you know."

"I understand. Mom's passing pulled the rug from beneath my feet. I was depressed and lost. Couldn't let it go and move forward. Now, I feel guilty for making him believe he couldn't tell me."

"Don't," Denise said. "If I knew anything about Carl, it was that he loved you more than anything. His work, his friends . . . me . . . anything."

The two leaned into each other and hugged. Tears followed. Their embrace broke, each dabbing eyes with napkins.

"We're going to be good," Savannah said.

"Yes, we are," Denise agreed.

Libby Sagstrom approached with a platter of fried calamari. She placed it on the table. "Here you go. Anything else right now?"

I looked around the table, got only headshakes in return. "We're good."

The conversation then turned to the murder of Carl Davis. It began when Denise asked, "Is there anything new on the investigation?"

"Not really," I said. "Detective Peters has a few folks she's looking into."

"Including my ex-boyfriend?" Denise asked.

"Tucker is on the list."

"Jake and Nicole told me a little about him," Savannah said. "Do you think he could've done this?"

"Tucker's a total asshole," Denise said. "An abusive one. It took me a few months to figure that out, though it's a mystery why it took so long." She shrugged. "I knew early on, but for some reason let it ride, hoping he would change."

"Guys never change," Nicole said. "Jake's still fourteen."

Savannah and Denise laughed.

"You're funny," I said.

Nicole raised her margarita glass. "Just stating facts."

"Do the police have any other suspects?" Denise asked.

"Only Tucker and Mitch as far as I know," I said.

"Is the primary suspect still Mitch?" Savannah asked.

"I believe so."

Savannah looked at Denise. "He was my father's business partner from the beginning. They went way back."

"Do you think he killed Carl?" Denise asked.

Savannah glanced at me. I could read her eyes. We—Brooke, Ray, Pancake, everyone—had warned her to keep Mitch's thefts under cover. Now, she wasn't sure what she could say. I rescued her.

"This doesn't leave this table," I said. I had Denise's full attention now. "Mitch was embezzling from the company."

"No." Denise's eyes widened. "I mean, I never met him. Maybe I never even heard his name. If I did, I don't remember. But who would steal from Carl? He was so open and honest."

"And trusting," Nicole said. "Which Mitchell Littlefield exploited."

I could see Denise's mental wheels turning as she mulled over this new information. "Did Carl know about the thefts?"

I nodded. "He did. He hired my father to sniff around Orange Coast Realty's finances."

"My god. He never told me anything about that."

"Me, either," Savannah said. "I only found out later. After . . ."

"Did this Mitch guy know that Carl knew?" Denise asked. "Is that why he might've killed him?"

"We don't know if Mitch knew or not," I said. "Or if he killed Carl. It sure gives him a motive. Also, he was one of the last people to see Carl alive. Since he knew the lay of the land and when Carl might be alone at work, he had the opportunity. That's why he's at the top of the list."

"I knew none of that," Denise said.

"I've known Mitch my entire life," Savannah said. "I have a hard time believing he would kill my dad. But I also would never have expected him to steal either. I guess anything is possible."

Isn't that so? Just when you think you have the world figured out and only calm waters lay ahead, someone drops a boulder in the pond. Or steals from and then shoots a longtime friend in the face.

Libby appeared to take our order.

CHAPTER 46

NICOLE AND I walked Savannah and Denise to their cars. The lunch had gone well. Each of them shared Carl stories. His kind and giving demeanor, his quirky sense of humor, and his inability to tell a joke, butchering it every time. How he loved dry martinis and barbecued ribs, and worked too much, yet never seemed overtaxed or stressed. How he gave no hint of Mitch's thefts or that trouble in paradise existed. Savannah added he had always been that way. Whatever problems he faced, he remained steady and on course.

Savannah invited Denise to her home to continue their chat, and so Denise could see "where Carl had lived." Denise made a quick call to her office, saying she was taking the rest of the day off. They said their goodbyes and drove away, Denise following Savannah from the lot.

"We did a good thing here," Nicole said.

I wrapped an arm around her and pulled her against my side. "Thanks to you. You made it happen."

My cell buzzed. I tugged it from my pocket. Pancake. "What's up?"

"Brooke's boss gave us the green light to sit in on the interrogations."

The transformation of Detective Peters into Brooke was complete. "When and where?" I asked.

"One hour. At the Orange Beach PD. Ray wants you guys there."

"Why?"

"To get your read on things. Nicole more than you."

"I appreciate the vote of confidence."

Pancake grunted.

"We'll be there." I disconnected the call.

"We'll be where?" Nicole asked.

I told her.

"Cool."

This was cool. I loved those TV crime shows, particularly the police interrogations. Watching the bad guy wiggle and squirm and try to lie his way out of whatever predicament he faced. The police giving them plenty of rope, letting their story tangle and then untangle right before their eyes. Fun stuff. Unless you were the guy sitting in the corner chair, facing a camera and two pugnacious cops.

I learned from these shows that if you're going to do some stupid ass crime, meticulously plan it and look at all the contingencies. The coming and going, the execution, and the all important alibi. If you wait until after the fact, covering your tracks is like slapping frayed and flimsy plywood over a massive sinkhole.

Nicole and I rolled over to Black Kat Koffee, again, this was becoming a habit, for a shot of caffeine, and to kill time, before the afternoon's events. While the barista cranked out a pair of Americanos, Nicole suggested we grab an assortment of pastries for Pancake. Good idea.

We didn't bleed off enough time as we arrived at the police department before Pancake and Ray. Brooke led us to Lieutenant Buddy Scoggins' office. He sat behind his desk in his buzz cut, square body, square head, square jaw, linebacker-esque posture. He didn't smile but nodded a greeting our way.

He stood. "Let's go down to the conference room. When the others get here, we can go over the ground rules."

Sir, yes, sir. It crossed my mind that breaking one of his "ground rules" might be painful. Even put you in that uncomfortable interrogation chair.

As we settled around the long table, Ray and Pancake arrived.

"What's the plan?" Ray asked.

"We're going to chat with Dustin Hobson first," Scoggins said. "Then Mitchell Littlefield. Separately, of course."

"Oh," Ray said. "I thought it was just Mitch."

"That was the original plan, but the more I thought about it, a sit-down with Dustin might prove useful. I want his take on Mitch. Did his demeanor or activities change before or since the murder of Carl Davis? Now that he's had time to think things over, he might have some insight there. I want to make sure that Littlefield has no clue he's our number one suspect. If he felt any heat, he might've altered his behavior, or attitude, and Dustin might've picked up on something."

"Aren't they both suspects?" I asked. "They were together that night and were the last two people to see him alive."

Scoggins looked at me, Nicole, and back at me. Uh-oh. I had stuck my head out of the foxhole and was about to draw fire. Keep your mouth shut, Jake. Nicole's glance said she felt the same way.

"You're right," Scoggins said. "Both make the list. But Mitch was the one stealing. Carl learned of his activities and he was about to be exposed. Which would mean loss of everything, and possibly jail time. Strong motives for senseless acts."

"We found no evidence that Mitch knew Carl was aware of his thefts," Ray said.

"Neither have we. But it's something I'll cover with Dustin."

"Are you going to confront Mitch about the embezzling?" Pancake asked.

"Not at first," Brooke said. "We want him comfortable. Like this is a friendly chat and we're seeking his help with Carl's murder. See if he remembers anything new. That sort of thing. Then we'll get to the embezzling. Ramp up the pressure. See if he cracks."

"I have something that'll help you there," Pancake said. He lifted his shoulder bag from the floor, placed it on the table, opened the flap, and tugged out an envelope. "I told you about Littlefield's three Cayman accounts. These are the details. One's simple and legit. He has a couple of hundred thousand in there. Looks like savings and investment funds. The other two are where he stashed the skimmed cash." He handed the envelope to Scoggins.

Scoggins slid out the pages and studied them for a full minute. "Where did you get this stuff?"

Pancake smiled. "It's what we do. Find out stuff."

Scoggins nodded. "I'm reluctant to say so, but if I'm being honest, you guys have helped us, helped Detective Peters. It's appreciated. That's why I'm letting you observe these interviews."

"We appreciate the opportunity to help," Ray said.

Scoggins laid the pages on the desktop and nodded toward them. "This is good. It'll ramp up the pressure on him for sure."

CHAPTER 47

A WALL-MOUNTED MONITOR looked down on the conference table and gave us a high-angle view of the interrogation room. Brooke and Scoggins left to prep for Dustin's interview. Pancake had been eyeing the pastry bag for the past twenty minutes, knowing it contained something of interest. I handed it to him.

"From Black Kat Koffee," I said.

He looked inside, snatched a chocolate muffin, and took a bite. "You're a good man, Jake Longly."

"It was Nicole's idea."

"And you're a peach, darling," Pancake said. The rest of the muffin disappeared. "I need some coffee with this."

"I saw a staff kitchen down the hall," I said. "Come on. I'll show you."

Typical office break room. Two small round tables in the center and along the back wall a counter with a deep sink, two pots of brewed coffee, one decaf, a basket of sugar packets, a stack of filters, two canisters of powdered creamer and two others of ground coffee. A large fridge sat in one corner.

As Pancake filled a cup with coffee, I heard voices behind me. I turned. Brooke and Dustin entered. Dustin did a double take.

"What're you guys doing here?" he asked.

Before we could respond, Brooke said, "They're here to go over some case details."

"Oh." Dustin looked at Brooke. "Is there something new?"

"We'll go over that when we sit," she said.

"Want some coffee?" Pancake asked Dustin.

"That would be great."

"Here." Pancake handed him the cup he had just poured and began filling a second cup. "What about you?" Pancake asked. "What brings you here?"

Pancake could play the innocent role very well, acting as if our being here was complete serendipity. It worked. Dustin's initial surprise faded.

"Same thing," Dustin said. "Detective Peters wanted to chat, so here I am."

Pancake smiled. "She don't bite much, so enjoy."

Brooke gave a headshake, Dustin a soft laugh.

"Nicole and I had lunch with Savannah and Denise Scholander today," I said.

"She told me. I called her on the way here." He took a sip of coffee. "She said it went very well. The anxiety she felt beforehand vanished after meeting Denise. They're at the house now, still sharing stories about Carl." Another sip. "Thanks for arranging the meeting. Savannah needed that."

"We hope it helps them both cope with the situation."

"We better get started," Brooke said. "So you can get back to your office."

They left. Pancake and I waited a minute and then rejoined Nicole and Ray in the conference room. Pancake dug into the bag again, this time grabbing a cinnamon roll.

On the monitor screen, Scoggins, Brooke, and Dustin entered and sat, Dustin facing the camera. Scoggins sat back a couple of feet from the small table between them, one leg crossed over the other, relaxed, unthreatening. As unthreatening as he could be with his buzz cut and all those muscles. Brooke scooted her chair up to the table and flipped open a notepad, pen in hand.

"Thanks for coming in," Scoggins said. "We wanted to get your statement on record and ask a few questions."

"No problem," Dustin said. "Whatever I can do to help."

Dustin seemed relaxed, a bit curious, but not defensive.

"First off," Brooke said, "let's go back over the day of Carl's murder. Right before you left, you talked with Carl and everything seemed okay?"

"Yes. We talked over a pending sale. That only took a couple of minutes, then I headed home."

"You and Mitch left together, right?" Scoggins asked.

"Yeah. About five fifteen. Something like that."

"The last time we talked, you said the only other car in the lot was Carl's Escalade," Brooke said. "You saw no one hanging around and nothing suspicious."

"That's right. It was like any other day." He sighed. "Now, I feel guilty leaving Carl alone."

"Was it unusual for Carl to stay late?" Scoggins asked.

"No." Dustin smiled. "Not at all. He worked harder and longer than any of us. It seemed like he was always the last one to leave the office."

Now I felt guilty. It was an old story. A business owner, the guy who was on the hook for the whole shebang, working longer hours than any of the employees. Rocky Mason, the guy I purchased Captain Rocky's from, had been that guy. On-site day and night. Me, not so much. If I worked two hours in any week, it would be a record. I was smart enough to keep Rocky's manager, Carla Martinez, on board, and then later make her a partner by giving her a stake in the company. That move left me plenty of time to do nothing. My favorite thing.

"Then what did you do?" Brooke said.

"I called Savannah to ask if she needed anything from the store for dinner. She did, so I stopped by, picked up those things, and then went home."

"Did you ever see Mitch again after you left the lot?"

Dustin shook his head. "He was in front of me and I followed him for a couple of blocks until he turned off toward his home. I went on to the grocery store."

"So, nothing unusual?"

Dustin shook his head. "No."

"After you've had time to think about things," Scoggins asked, "do you know of anyone we should look at?"

Dustin shook his head. "I can't think of anyone who'd want to harm Carl. It makes no sense."

"Except Mitchell Littlefield."

Dustin hesitated, then gave a nod. "I guess it's possible. But I still don't believe it." He leaned back in his chair. "Even if Mitch was embezzling, I don't see him as a killer."

"If he thought he might lose everything, even get jail time, he might do something drastic," Brooke said. "We've seen it before."

"I suspect you have. But when would Mitch have had time to do that? We left together. Nothing happened before that for sure. The office isn't that large and a gunshot would've rattled the windows." He looked down at his hands, now folded in his lap. "I guess he could've come back." He looked up. "But I still don't see Mitch doing this."

"Regarding the thefts," Scoggins began, "do you think Mitch knew Carl was on to him?"

"I never saw or heard anything that suggested that."

"But you might not have," Brooke said. "Being engaged to Carl's daughter, I suspect Mitch would've been careful around you."

Dustin sighed. "I suppose. But I didn't sense any standoffishness from him or anything out of the ordinary. I mean, he's saddened by Carl's death, and I believe that's genuine, but otherwise he seems normal."

"To be clear," Scoggins said, "he doesn't know you're here today and you haven't said a word to him about any of this?"

A quick headshake. "You told me not to and I haven't." He looked toward Brooke. "That goes for Savannah too. She hasn't told anyone."

"Good."

"Do you really believe Mitch did this?" Dustin asked.

"He's a person of interest," Brooke said. She laid her pen on the pad before her. "He doesn't need to know that either."

CHAPTER 48

FORTY MINUTES LATER, we returned to the conference room. The time gap between the two interviews afforded Dustin ample time to leave before Mitch arrived. Scoggins and Brooke didn't want Mitch to know they had talked with Dustin. Not today, right before his own interview.

Best if Mitch had no clue he was the main suspect in Carl Davis' murder. Brooke wanted him relaxed and helpful. Of course, today's conversation would alter that. Confronting him with his thefts would add pressure, and maybe Mitch would fumble the ball and say something incriminating. She hoped for Mitch's confession to his embezzling. Having that in her pocket gave her leverage to push him on Carl's murder. It required careful handling because the one thing she didn't want was Mitch lawyering up. That would alter the dynamic.

I'd seen this head-fake tactic employed many times on true crime shows. People confessed to a lesser crime, hoping it would protect them from more serious charges. Made no sense to me. Why confess to anything? The problem? During such confessions, the culprit often let slip facts that put them square in the center of the more substantial charge. In this case, murder.

Keeping Dustin low profile was a smart move. It allowed him to become an inside source for information. He saw Mitch every day, and could observe, listen, and maybe detect any change in Mitch's demeanor. But only if Mitch trusted him. If he feared Dustin had conspired with the police, he might become close-mouthed. And, again, invoke his right to a lawyer.

Of course, this would be a moot point if Mitch confessed to everything today. The thefts, the murder, everything. If not, going forward, Dustin could prove a valuable asset.

Now, with the table set, it was time for the main event. The official interview of Mitchell Littlefield.

Mitch sat in the same seat Dustin had earlier occupied. He seemed more nervous than Dustin had been. Which made sense. He was guilty of theft, and maybe murder.

I understood. I had sat in a similar chair a few times, fielding questions from an unfriendly cop or two. In high school, Pancake in another room getting peppered with identical questions. Why'd you do this or that? What the hell were you thinking? What do you think we should do with you? We, of course, had no answers for any of it.

Would Mitch have answers? Or would he hang himself right here, right now?

Brooke went through the same questions she had asked Dustin. Mitch, too, had chatted with Carl before leaving. He also felt guilt for leaving Carl by himself, but he underscored what Dustin had said. Carl, a workaholic, was on most days the last to leave. He said Carl had always been that way. Even back in school. Yes, he and Dustin left together, Dustin following him from the lot. Only Carl's car remained, and he saw no one in the area. He went straight home and the first he heard of Carl's murder was when Brooke came to his door.

His story matched Dustin's perfectly. Too perfectly? The idea that they engineered this whole thing together remained out there. I didn't like it. I didn't believe it. Maybe I didn't want it to be true because Dustin's involvement dragged Savannah into this mess. Yet there it was. Like a fog bank obscuring a clearly defined horizon over the Gulf. Was a conspiracy secreted in the haze?

If there was, I prayed it didn't include Savannah. Of all the players in this drama, I liked her best. I didn't want her to be one of the villains.

Brooke tapped her pen on her pad and asked, "What's your relationship with Dustin?"

Mitch looked perplexed. "What do you mean?"

"He's the new kid. The future son-in-law. How do you two get along?"

"Very well. He's a bright kid and possesses all the skills to be an excellent broker. No doubt an asset."

"No issues?" Scoggins asked.

"No. Why would there be?"

"There shouldn't be," Brooke said. "But he's a young buck, becoming part of the family, maybe even taking over for Carl before too long." She shrugged. "I'm just curious if that caused any issues between you and him."

Mitch considered that. "I can see where you're coming from, but the fact is, I enjoy working with him. I wish he would've taken over more of Carl's duties months ago. Carl worked too hard. Harder than he needed to. Who knows? Maybe had he done that,

Carl wouldn't have been in the office last Monday night and none of this would've happened."

"Do you see that as the future? You and Dustin running the company?"

"After what happened? Sure. Savannah owns half the company and if they do indeed get married, I expect Dustin will slide into Carl's role."

"You're okay with that?"

"If you're asking would I rather Carl still be here and doing all he does, then yes, I wish he was. If you're asking if I believe Dustin can carry that load, the answer is also yes. He'll do just fine."

"So you guys are buddy-buddy?" Scoggins asked.

Mitch released a soft laugh. More relaxed now. "I wouldn't go that far, but we have a strong working relationship." Mitch watched Brooke scribble something on her notepad. "Dustin and I don't socialize, if that's what you mean. We're a few too many years apart for that. On a business level, we each have our work, though we help each other out."

"How involved is he in the business end of things?"

"Not a lot. Carl and I handled that." He sighed. "I guess he will be now."

"Speaking of the business," Brooke said. "How're things going?"

Clever. Her transition into the real purpose of today's sit-down couldn't have been smoother. I exchanged a glance with Pancake. He thought so too.

"Excellent. Steady growth." He sighed. "But now, I do have concerns. I'm more the numbers guy. Carl, the face man, so to speak. His loss could impact our business. I think Dustin, though he's no Carl, is personable and likable, so hopefully he can dampen the blow of Carl's loss."

So far, everything Mitch had said made sense. Straightforward and free of deception. But then, the questions up to now had been softer than soft.

"Let's talk about the numbers," Brooke said.

Here we go.

Mitch shifted in his chair. "What about them?"

"Any issues with them?"

More shifting, as if his seat had become uncomfortable. Which I suspected it had.

"I'm not sure I understand."

"What if I told you we had evidence that the numbers are unbalanced. They don't fit cleanly into any profit and loss accounting."

"Sure they do." Mitch glanced toward the door as if he wanted to run through it.

Brooke slid a folder from beneath her notepad. She flipped it open, shuffled through the papers inside. Mitch's brow creased. Brooke selected a few pages and slid them toward Mitch.

"What are these?" Mitch asked.

What those were was the product of Pancake's genius. A three-year timeline of missing money. Pancake had mined the data and put it into a clean summary.

"Why don't you tell me?" Brooke said.

Mitch thumbed through the pages. He appeared to be reading them, but to me, he was buying time. Trying to come up with something to say.

"I've never seen these. I'm not sure what they represent."

"Let's cut to the chase," Brooke said. "An analysis of the invoices, the incomes, and the outflows at the realty company shows that during the past three years, over three hundred thousand dollars have gone missing. Unaccounted for."

Now he slid to the front of his chair. "Where'd you get these? Who made all this up?"

"It's not made up. It's all too real. So, where did the money go?"

"How would I know?"

"You're the numbers guy. I thought maybe you had some quirky accounting system that would account for the discrepancies."

That was a clever move. Brooke offered him an out. In reality, a shovel that might dig an even deeper hole. If Mitch created some convoluted explanation for the missing funds, he'd literally tie himself in knots. He didn't bite. Not that it mattered.

"This information isn't correct."

"It is. Our guys, as well as an outside firm, dissected it. Both agree with these numbers. So, where are the missing funds?"

"I have no idea." Another glance at the door. He even leaned that way.

Brooke lifted several other pages from the folder and slid them across the table. "Perhaps these will refresh your memory."

Mitch scanned the documents, then read them more carefully. His body deflated. I thought he might melt to the floor.

"Yeah," Brooke said. "Your accounts in the Caymans. Want to tell us about them?"

Mitch shuffled through the pages, again buying time, searching for an alternative explanation in a situation where there was only one. He drooped forward, his forehead resting on the tabletop. No one said a word, giving him time to sort it out and realize the trap was airtight. Mitch lifted his head and looked from Scoggins to Brooke. "How'd you find out?"

"We're not at liberty to discuss that right now," Scoggins said. "But all in good time. Right now, tell us about it."

Mitch did. How he skimmed a few dollars, then a few more, and saw how easy it was and simply continued. More and more. How he moved it offshore in small amounts, low enough to avoid raised eyebrows by the feds or the banks. A few thousand here, a few thousand there. He laid out the entire scheme. He ended with, "I'm so ashamed. I can't believe it got so out of control."

"Why'd you do it?" Brooke asked. "You were making good money. Had fat bank accounts from what we've seen."

He cupped one hand over his forehead and massaged his temples. "I don't know. I guess it started as a game. Something like that. I'm not really sure. Then it took on a life of its own."

"Did it ever," Scoggins said.

Mitch sighed. "Am I going to jail?"

Brooke shook her head. "No. What happens now is up to Savannah."

"Oh god. Does she know?"

Brooke nodded. "She does."

"Did Carl know?"

"He did. He hired someone to look into it."

"Ray Longly?"

"Yes."

"I can't believe this." His gaze sagged to the floor. "What have I done?"

"Which is my next question," Brooke said. "What have you done?"

"Isn't this enough?"

"It is. But it's also a motive for murder."

It was as if Brooke had slapped her words on the table. Whap. Mitch recoiled as if punched in the chest. His eyes popped open. "What? No. No way."

"You stole money. Carl discovered it. He confronted you. You reacted." She opened her palms toward him.

"I swear. I had nothing to do with that. If Carl knew what I had done, I didn't know he did. I loved the man. I respected him. He was my best friend. I would never do anything to him."

"Except steal from him," Scoggins said.

Mitch deflated further, as if the weight of his crimes might crush him completely. He took a deep breath, then another, but said nothing. What could he say? He was the definition of getting your hand caught in the cookie jar.

"Can we clone your phone?" Brooke asked.

Mitch raised his head. "What?"

"Make a copy of your cell phone. That'll let us see who you might have called and where you were at all times last Monday."

"I told you. I went straight home. I didn't call anyone."

"Then your phone will reveal that," Brooke said.

Mitch sighed. He lifted his phone from his pocket and slid it toward her.

CHAPTER 49

WHILE THE TECH guys downloaded the contents of Mitch's cell phone, we gathered in the parking lot. Brooke laid out her plan. Nicole and I would visit Hank Duggans at his auto parts store to get his take on Tucker Moss. Was Tucker there on that Monday afternoon? What was his attitude? Did he say anything odd? Was Patrick McCall with him? That sort of thing. Pancake and Brooke would drop Ray at the office and then visit Patrick McCall. See if he corroborated Tucker's tale. Who knows? He might say that he helped Tucker kill Carl Davis. Wouldn't that be cool? Like firing a bottom-of-the-ninth fastball past your opponent's cleanup hitter for the third strike, third out. A pitcher's equivalent to a walk-off home run.

Whether Tucker was guilty or not, I didn't think that was likely. If this Patrick guy was with him, and if Tucker did the deed, Patrick would be in it up to his Adam's apple. Why would he break ranks if he was going down with the ship? Two answers to that. Plea bargain, and Pancake. The big guy could be persuasive.

After agreeing to meet later and compare notes, we each headed off on our errands. It was good to see Duggans again. It had been a while.

It was six o'clock by the time Nicole and I reached Captain Rocky's. Pancake had called ten minutes earlier saying he and Brooke were on the way. A little late due to traffic on the highway from Pensacola.

Nicole ordered a glass of Pinot, me Blanton's bourbon on the rocks. Carla said she had nachos working and had warned the kitchen staff Pancake was on the way. He and Brooke arrived just as the nachos appeared. An extra large platter.

"Perfect timing," Pancake said. "Carla, you're the best."

"Yes, I am." Carla waited until Pancake and Brooke sat. "What can I get you guys to drink?"

"A margarita for me," Brooke said.

"Beer," Pancake said. "Whatever you have the most of." He attacked the nachos.

"How do you afford to feed this guy?" Brooke asked.

"Afford is a relative term," I said.

Pancake looked at me. "You're funny. You really are."

"I remember reading once that, back in the day, CBS had an entire division devoted to Elvis. We do the same thing here. We have the restaurant inventory and we have the Pancake inventory. Bet you can guess which is the bigger number."

Brooke laughed.

Another look from Pancake. "You should have your own TV series."

Carla returned with the drinks and took food orders.

"How'd your visit go?" Brooke asked.

"Fine," I said. "I know Hank Duggans. Good guy. He's tracked down parts for my Mustang for me before. He confirmed Tucker was there that afternoon, along with Patrick McCall. Around four forty-five."

"That matches what Tucker told us," Brooke said. "Did he say how Tucker seemed? Anything stand out?"

"Not really." I glanced at Nicole. She nodded. "He said Tucker was his usual self. Paid his invoice, loaded up the parts, and they left. He said Tucker placed another order. One he'd pick up next week." I shrugged. "To him, it was business as usual."

A platter of fish tacos appeared. We ordered another round of drinks. Pancake devoured a taco in two bites.

"What about that Patrick dude?" Nicole asked.

Pancake's mouth was full, so Brooke picked it up. "He confirmed he was with Tucker last Monday. After they left Custom Auto, they went straight back to the shop. They didn't stop anywhere, specifically Carl's place of work. Their timeline, according to him, matched what Tucker had said."

"Did you believe him?"

Brooke smiled. "Normally, the answer would be no, but in this case, I do. Patrick remembered Pancake from our last visit."

"Boy needed motivation," Pancake said.

"He got a little more motivation today. We waited until he left work, followed him to a nearby bar, and intercepted him in the parking lot." Another smile. "Pancake offered him a little more incentive to tell the truth."

Pancake grunted. "He's a weak dude. A scared little rabbit."

Neither needed to elaborate. I could picture the scene. Pancake backing him against his car, or a wall, or some immovable object. Probably fisted his shirt, or arm, or throat. Might even have dangled him. Pancake liked doing that. A disgruntled Pancake towering over you will definitely motivate you to do as he says. In this case, tell the truth.

"So Tucker's no longer a suspect?" Nicole asked.

Brooke gave a headshake. "He's still on the list. I don't understand how, but Patrick might be more afraid of Tucker than Pancake. So, regardless of what I believe, he could've lied."

Another taco, another grunt from Pancake. Meant he disagreed. "I should've leaned on him more."

"You leaned on him plenty," Brooke said. "Any more, and he would've needed orthopedic care."

Pancake shrugged. "Bones heal."

"Of more importance," Brooke continued. "Mitch Littlefield's cell phone shows he left the office and went straight home. He remained there until I went by to make the death notification."

"So, the embezzler is in the clear?" Nicole asked.

"No one's in the clear here. It's still possible Carl's murder happened before Mitch and Dustin left the office. If so, it wouldn't require any backtracking."

"But would require them being in it together," Nicole said.

Brooke nodded.

We had discussed this before. Such a cabal would profit each of them. Mitch would have more control of the company, and Dustin, after marrying Savannah, would own the other half.

"That brings up a couple of questions," I said. "First, such a conspiracy would suggest that Mitch and Dustin planned to own the company. After the wedding, of course, and with no Carl. But Dustin knows that Mitch embezzled a pile of cash. How could they work together after that?"

"Forgive and forget," Pancake said. "Or pay it back. Or split it. It'd be tax-free income for each of them. Maybe they came to some money and power sharing agreement that would kick in once Carl Davis was out of the picture. A few hundred thousand is a lot of money; a few million is a lot more."

That made sense. If Mitch pulled a *mea culpa* and shared his Cayman cash with Dustin, millions awaited each of them. Or maybe dividing up the stolen funds was part of the original plan all along. Diabolical didn't cover it.

"What was your other question?" Brooke asked me.

"Is Savannah safe?" No one responded for a half minute, so I continued. "If Savannah isn't involved, if Dustin is in this with Mitch, and if they did kill Carl, is the ultimate plan to also eliminate Savannah?"

CHAPTER 50

"I LIKE HER more and more," Nicole said, meaning Brooke Peters.

"Me, too. So does Pancake."

"No doubt."

We stood in Captain Rocky's parking lot next to Nicole's SL and watched as Pancake held open his truck passenger door for Brooke to climb inside. Always the gentleman.

"Want to make a bet?" I asked.

"About what?"

"Right or left?"

Right led toward Pensacola and Peters' car at the PD. Left toward Pancake's place.

"You're on. I'll take left."

I laughed. "Then no bet. I take left too."

Pancake's truck rumbled across the lot, turned left, and disappeared up the road.

Nicole slapped my butt. "I think they have the right idea. My place or yours?"

"Orange Beach."

"What?"

"I want to see the scene of the crime again," I said.

"Well, look at you. The big-time investigator."

"Humor me."

"As long as you humor me later," she said.

"All the humor you can handle."

Twenty minutes later, we reached Orange Coast Realty. I directed Nicole behind the closed building to the sandy area we had visited before. Once out of the car, I scaled the dune that blocked our view of the realty office. Nicole followed. The empty building displayed only a couple of interior security lights. No cars, no activity. Beyond, traffic crept by on Perdido Beach Boulevard. I did a three-sixty, examining everything from this elevated vantage point.

We descended the slope and crossed the uneven terrain, weaving among the scrub brush that dotted the area, until we reached the water. The tail end of Bayou Saint John. Across the water sat several large homes, each with a dock and boathouse. One had a party in progress, and I could see a couple of dozen people on the rear deck, music sliding across the water toward us. I picked up a small rock and skimmed it across the water.

"What is it?" Nicole asked.

"We're assuming that this wasn't random. Not some dude coming in off the street, popping Carl, and fading into the sunset. Rather that either Mitch, or Dustin, or both, or Tucker did this."

"Okay."

"Each of them knows this area. Knows it's isolated. At least Mitch and Dustin do. Tucker maybe not. Unless he did some recon beforehand." I pointed to the east. "There are a few houses down that way. And that little marina." I swiveled to the west. "A few businesses and more houses down that way. But here, there's nothing. Just this vacant area and the empty lot next door."

"It is dark here."

"Less so at six o'clock, but still isolated. Hard to see anyone here." I pointed across the bayou. "Maybe those people over there, but it's unlikely they'd notice anyone."

"Where are you going with this?"

"If I killed someone, the first thing I'd want to do is get the hell out of there. And dump the weapon. Somewhere where it wouldn't be found."

"The water?"

"Exactly."

She stepped closer to the water's edge. "If the killer tossed it a hundred feet out there, it would never be found."

"That's what I'd do."

Nicole gazed over the water. "Both Mitch and Dustin said they spoke with Carl within minutes of leaving. Separately, but each at least said goodbye."

"So, either they're in this together, or one of them circled back and did the deed, tossed the weapon, and went on with life."

"We know that, according to Mitch's cell data, he didn't come back," Nicole said.

I walked to her side, draped one arm around her shoulders, pulled her against me. "I don't like where my head is going."

"Dustin?"

"He's as big a winner as Savannah here. Or will be."

"So is Mitch. So you're thinking it's both or it's Dustin, with or without Savannah?"

I nodded. "I hope Savannah isn't involved."

"Me, too."

"I need to call Pancake."

I did. It went to voice mail. I left a message.

"He's busy," I said.

"Why don't we go get busy?"

"Why don't we."

CHAPTER 51

Last night, Pancake returned my call an hour after I left a voice mail. Spoke well for his blossoming relationship with Brooke. My cell buzzed just as Nicole and I had poured tequila, shed our clothes, and hopped in her hot tub. I told him of our visit to the crime scene and my thought that the weapon could be nearby. He listened, saying nothing, but then voiced his agreement. He added that my engagement with the case was impressive. Almost as much an my coming up with a useful thought. My friend.

He said he'd loop in Ray and they'd take care of it. Whatever that meant.

We found out this morning when Pancake called and said we should meet him at the vacant lot adjacent to Orange Coast Realty. That way, if any of the realty company employees saw us, they'd think we were working on that property and they'd be less inclined to question our presence. So here we were once again on the banks of Bayou Saint John, this time with Pancake and Brooke. She wore the same clothes she'd had on last night. Guess they hadn't yet found the time to go by her place for a change.

The morning sun slanted across the water. It was quiet and still. I saw a sailboat in the distance but that was about it.

An unmarked black van sat near the water, its side door open. Inside, I saw half a dozen scuba tanks on the floor. Regulators, hoses, and swim fins hung on the far wall. Out in the water, bubbles agitated the surface above the two divers who endeavored to find the proverbial needle in a haystack. They had been at it for an hour and had just changed to fresh tanks, before descending into the murky water once again. Not before saying it was slow going, but they were making progress.

They continued their grid search, moving back and forth parallel to the shoreline, expanding their probe outward with each lap. So far, nothing.

My brilliant idea spiraled toward stupid. What was I thinking? There were dozens, no hundreds, of places the killer could've tossed the gun. Swamps, forests, the ocean. Plus the killer might still have it squirreled away in a secret hidey-hole. Why toss it near the crime scene and not far away? Maybe to reduce the chance of getting caught with it. Best-laid plans often jump the rails when least expected and in the oddest ways. A car accident, or a routine traffic stop, or something as mundane as a mechanical failure or flat tire might expose the weapon to law enforcement or an observant citizen. I mean, if the car had to be towed, the killer would need to retrieve the weapon from wherever he had stowed it before the car was hooked onto the tow truck. That could prove a risky move. So would tossing the weapon in the water well before sunset. With the houses across the water, someone might have seen it. Not in any great detail as the distance was too great, but enough to sense it was odd behavior. They might not think much of it at the time, but later, when the news of Carl Davis' murder came out, they might remember it. As well as the vehicle and a general description of the person.

A million things could go wrong.

The divers, friends of Ray's and former Navy SEALs, had formed a successful group for search, rescue, and recovery. I felt guilty for dragging them out here, for wasting their time, when they could be tracking a lost child, or a missing swimmer or diver, or searching for some lost object. Even a gun. One that actually existed. My faith in my hunch faded with each lap they made.

"Maybe there's nothing to find," I said.

"Give it time," Brooke said. "These things are always tedious."

"Might be a complete waste."

"We won't know until we know." Pancake smiled. "Like Schrödinger's cat."

I knew that one. Sort of. Something about not knowing whether a cat in a box was dead or alive until you looked inside.

"Hopefully, the cat's alive," Nicole said.

My cell rang.

Tammy.

Great. Just great. She had elevated calling at the worst time to an art form.

I showed my cell screen to Nicole. She laughed. I walked away from the group before answering. Nicole followed. No way she'd miss this.

As was her nature, Tammy jumped right into it. "Jake, you were wrong again. Not that that's news."

"Nice chatting with you too."

"You didn't call Walter."

Didn't we decide that I shouldn't do that? Not that I would anyway, but I distinctly remember Tammy warning me not to call Walter. Not to screw things up.

"No, I didn't," I said.

"Why?"

"Maybe because I didn't want to. Maybe because you told me not to. Maybe because none of this is all that important. Maybe because I'm busy. Take your pick."

"You said he'd come to his senses, and see it my way."

If Walter ever came to his senses he'd kick Tammy to the curb and walk away. Hard to understand why a smart guy like Walter hadn't already reached that conclusion.

"I'm shocked he didn't."

"Are you being sarcastic?" Tammy asked.

Yes. Yes, I was. "No. I'm just amazed an intelligent guy like him wouldn't see the wisdom and benefits of attending the fundraiser."

"Exactly. So call him."

"You know I have no influence with Walter. Right?"

"Maybe this time he'll listen to you," she said.

"I have a better idea. Prepare a nice dinner, put on something sexy, convince him."

"You know I don't cook."

How could I forget? "Takeout would work if your outfit has enough pop."

"Really? You think so?"

No, I don't. "Sure. You know Walter can't resist you."

"That's true."

"Got something." The voice came from the water.

"I've got to go," I said.

"What about me?" Tammy asked.

"Go seduce Walter. It'll work out." I disconnected the call.

The something turned out to be a gun. The diver extended it above the water, the handle grasped between his thumb and index finger. He churned toward shore and climbed up the shallow bank. Not bothering to remove his fins, he flapped toward where Brooke stood. He dropped the weapon into the plastic evidence bag she held.

Peters sealed the bag. "It's a nine-millimeter Glock. Right caliber." She glanced at me. "Good call."

"Sometimes he's a clever boy," Nicole said.

Pancake grunted.

Here we go. I'm back in the crosshairs.

Pancake and Brooke thanked the two divers, Pancake saying he'd let Ray know it was a successful hunt. They nodded, said to tell Ray hello, and began packing up their gear.

We walked toward our cars.

"I need to get this over to the firearms guys so they can do their thing," Brooke said. "And update Scoggins."

"Sound like a plan," Pancake said. "I'll be your chauffeur."

"I'm sure Scoggins will love that."

"He loves me," Pancake said. "More so after you show him the Glock."

"You overestimate your charm and underestimate my LT's ill temper."

Pancake smiled. "Good thing you'll be there to protect me."

"What about us?" Nicole asked.

"It's Saturday. Take the day off. Tomorrow too. It'll be Monday before we have anything back on the Glock. I still need to pry more deeply into the worlds of Mitch and Dustin."

"So I have to entertain Jake for two days?" Nicole said.

"Buy him some ice cream," Pancake said. "Or milk and cookies. He'll be fine."

I like ice cream. And milk and cookies. But I like tequila and
Nicole better so a couple of days away from Ray's world could
be fun.

"Or use your imagination," Pancake said. "I'm sure you'll come
up with something."

Nicole smacked me on the butt. "I've got a thing or two in
mind."

CHAPTER 52

PANCAKE AND BROOKE, bagged gun in hand, headed to the police department, after a stop at Brooke's condo. She didn't want to face Scoggins, or anyone else in the department, in yesterday's clothes. With Pancake standing beside her. Why arouse curiosity and instigate the tongue wagging that would follow?

"I'm the target of enough BS," she said. "No need to pour gasoline on that fire."

Pancake eyed her as he wheeled his truck into a space in front of her condo. "I thought you enjoyed stirring the pot."

"I do. But not in my personal life. They make up enough crap about me without me supplying the ammo."

"They all want to sleep with you."

She eyed him. "As tempting as that sounds, I'll pass."

Her condo project contained eighteen units in three south-facing buildings. Her third-floor, two-bedroom layout was neat and orderly. While she changed, he drew open the living room slider and stepped onto the deck. A peaceful swath of marsh-land greeted him. A pair of snowy egrets stalked the shallow water, one poised on a single leg, head angled downward as if stalking a delicacy. In the distance lay Perdido Beach Boulevard, the constantly expanding row of beachfront hotels and condos, and the Gulf. Going to be a good day. A warm breeze, not a cloud visible.

"All set," Brooke said as she stepped outside.

She wore fitted jeans, a dark blue blouse, and a black jacket. Her badge and gun too. "You look hot."

"Not what I was going for," she said. "I think Scoggins would prefer I look like a cop."

"You do. A hot cop."

"Is this a ploy to get me into the sack again?"

"It is."

She playfully punched his arm. "Keep at it. It just might work."

"Love your place," Pancake said. "The view is cool."

"I like it. Maybe we'll stay here some time."

"I'm free tonight."

"I bet you are. Let's roll."

At the Orange Beach Police Department, Brooke signed over the gun to the firearms lab. They then met with Scoggins. Brooke brought him up to date.

"Do you think it's the murder weapon?" he asked.

"Could be," Brooke said. "It was behind Carl Davis' office and near that open area where we thought the killer might've parked. Right caliber. It had the usual bottom silt clinging to it but no rust or corrosion. It hadn't been in the water long."

"The implications here are striking," Scoggins said. "But, even if it is the murder weapon, unless it has some specific evidence clinging to it, it doesn't help us ID who tossed it."

Pancake nodded. "True that. Mitch and Dustin know the lay of the land and either one or both might've pre-planned tossing the weapon in the water to get rid of it as soon as possible. A place where it would never be discovered. I mean, what would be the odds of anyone finding it in Bayou Saint John?"

"Apparently not as generous as they had hoped," Scoggins said.

"It could still be some random dude who simply saw an opportunity to dump the weapon," Brooke said. "Or the gun could be some random gun and have nothing to do with Carl Davis' murder."

"What about Tucker Moss?" Scoggins asked.

"Still on the radar," Brooke said. "He could've cased the place and saw the river as a good dumping ground. Or figured that out on the fly. His guy vouched for him but I don't think it's much of a stretch to assume he'd cover for him regardless. His job depends on it. Tucker's definitely the alpha in the group so intimidation also enters the picture."

"I don't see Tucker being smart enough to toss the gun into the water," Pancake said. "Or dump it at all. He seems to be the kind that wouldn't give up a weapon, or anything else. He'd think he's too smart and that his shop has too many hiding spots for anyone to find it even if they looked."

"I can't argue with that," Brooke said. "He's one of those guys that thinks the world revolves around him. Too clever to be trapped by anything."

"Yet he and his dumb-ass alibi were moronic enough to put themselves near the scene around the time of the murder."

Scoggins seemed to like that. "Anything from Mitch Littlefield's cell phone?"

"The GPS data matched his story," Brooke said. "He left the office, went straight home, and never left. He of course could've done Davis before he left, but the timing is tricky. Plus the noise issue. Unless Dustin is involved. One the lookout, the other the shooter." She hooked a thumb on her belt. "We need to get into Dustin's cell phone and see if there's anything there. Any way we could get a warrant?"

Scoggins shrugged. "Maybe. I'll contact one of my friendly judges. I'm not optimistic though. We really have nothing solid to connect him to the shooting."

"He was one of the last people to see Carl alive," Pancake said.

"True, but most judges shy away from things that could be mere coincidence. Let me see what I can do."

"Might not be wise to let Dustin know he's being investigated," Pancake said. "He might destroy other evidence, or even bolt. I have another way."

Scoggins perked up. "What? How?"

"Best you don't know."

Scoggins gave a half smile, nodded.

Back in Pancake's truck, Peters asked, "What's the plan?"

"Have another friendly chat with Savannah and Dustin. Bring them up to date on Mitch's interview." He smiled. "That'll be the cover."

"Cover for what?"

He told her. She liked it.

Brooke phoned Savannah, saying they wanted to drop by to update her and Dustin on a couple of things. She agreed, adding that Dustin was home. He had a couple of appointments later in the day but right now was a good time.

Pancake called Jake. "What are you guys doing?"

"Having ice cream. Butter brickle."

"I'd say bring me some, but it'd melt before I got to it. Meet us at Savannah's."

"Why?" Jake asked.

Pancake went over the plan.

CHAPTER 53

IT WAS NEARING eleven by the time we pulled up to Savannah Davis' home. Pancake had called, saying he and Brooke were two minutes out, so we waited for them to arrive.

"That was a smart move," I said.

"The ice cream?"

"Yeah. It always pays dividends to feed Pancake."

Nicole had asked the server at the ice cream shop if they had dry ice. They did. Their daily shipments arrived packed in the smoky chunks and they had bags of it in their walk-in freezer. A pint of butter brickle, another of chocolate chip, and several chunks of dry ice now rested in a plastic bag on the floorboard.

Pancake pulled up behind us, and he and Brooke stepped out. Nicole handed him the bag. "A little something for you."

He looked inside. "Kind of small containers. Were they running low?"

Nicole laughed. "No. It's on dry ice so it'll keep."

"What if I want some now?"

"Men," Nicole said, glancing at Brooke. "Driven by instant gratification."

Brooke smiled. "Not always bad."

"True." Nicole looked at Pancake. "Wouldn't be polite to eat ice cream during an interview. Unless you share it with them."

Pancake gave her his best you've-got-to-be-kidding look and deposited the bag in his truck.

Savannah greeted us at the front door and led us to the rear flagstone deck, where Dustin sat at a rectangular teak table, sipping a glass of tea. His cell phone rested nearby.

"How about some sweet tea?" Savannah asked.

"That would be great," Pancake said.

"Coming up," Savannah said. She headed inside.

"I'll help you." Nicole followed her.

"So you have some news?" Dustin asked.

"We do," Brooke said. "When Savannah gets back, we'll get into that. One thing though, I noticed I don't have your contact info. Your cell number."

"I thought you did."

"Me, too. But I discovered that I don't."

Dustin recited his number and both Peters and Pancake added it to their contacts.

"Is that the new iPhone?" Pancake asked.

"Yeah," Dustin said. "Just got each of us one a few weeks ago."

"Mine's older," Pancake said. "You like the new one?"

"Oh yeah. Faster, longer life, and a great camera."

Pancake held out his hand. "Can I see it?"

"Sure."

Dustin passed the device to Pancake. The lit screen indicated the phone remained active, no password or fingerprint needed.

I watched the entire dance unfold. Pancake's plan working better than I would've guessed.

Brooke distracted Dustin while Pancake worked his magic. She asked Dustin how work was going. Chaotic without Carl, but overall okay. Any real issues? Not really. A couple of employees might leave but most remained loyal and will stay on. Things we already knew, but the questions served their purpose.

While the conversation proceeded, Pancake finished his inputs and placed Dustin's phone on the table, his nearby. I knew he had set up AirDrop and was now transferring Dustin's data to his own iPhone. Everything in the background with no visible evidence. Smooth and easy. Keep moving. Nothing to see here. Impressive.

Savannah and Nicole returned with the tea.

"So, what's up?" Savannah asked.

"A couple of things," Brooke said. She thumbed her phone, scrolled through several images, and turned it Savannah's way. "Have you ever seen this guy?"

Savannah examined the pic. "I don't think so. Who is he?"

"Tucker Moss. Denise's ex."

Now she studied the image. "Not what I imagined. He's not bad-looking. But has a dark and dangerous edge about him."

"Because he is," Brooke said. She angled the phone toward Dustin. "Ever seen him around?"

Dustin took his time inspecting the image. I watched him without watching him, looking for signs of recognition, or discomfort, or guilt. It crossed my mind that one possibility we never considered was that Dustin could've met Tucker, though I couldn't imagine when or how. But, if so, they could've formed a mutually beneficial alliance. Dustin gets the company, Tucker the girl. Far-fetched for sure. Too many coincidences involved. Besides, I saw nothing in his face or body language that hinted at that.

Dustin shook his head. "No. Never seen him."

"Is he the one?" Savannah asked. "The guy that killed my father?"

"We don't know," Pancake said. "It's possible."

"I hoped that was why you were here," Savannah said. "To tell me you had the guy."

"Not yet."

"We had another talk with Mitch Littlefield," Brooke said. "We confronted him about the missing funds and his offshore accounts."

"Offshore accounts?" Dustin asked.

"Caymans," Pancake said. "Three accounts. One legit, the other two for his stolen funds."

"I never knew that," Dustin said. "I don't think Carl did either."

"He kept them secret. Which, of course, makes sense."

"I take it the funds are still there?" Dustin asked.

Pancake nodded. "Seems so. I haven't excavated that deeply yet. This is new information. Overall, it appears the totals match."

"What did Mitch say?" Savannah asked.

"He confessed," Brooke said.

"So he stole from my father?" She looked at Dustin. "I still find it hard to believe."

"Unfortunately, it's true," Brooke said. "And your father learned he had done so."

"Did you arrest Mitch?" Savannah asked.

"No. It's more civil than criminal. Though with banks involved, it could be federal. But where it goes from here depends on what you want to do."

Savannah appeared confused. "You mean file a lawsuit? Something like that?"

"Yes," Pancake said. "Remember that if you sue him for breach of contract and for theft and you prevail, which you definitely will, the company passes completely into your hands, and the funds in the Caymans would return to the company accounts."

"And Mitch?"

"Again, up to you," Brooke said. "If you want to file theft and embezzlement charges against him, then we would be involved. If not, he likely just goes away."

"I see." She looked at Dustin. "I wish I knew what to do. What do you think?"

"I like Mitch. He's an asset to the company. Which I guess is obvious since he helped build it. But, that said, can we ever trust him again? What's to keep him from doing this in a more clever way? One that might be less trackable."

"You're saying he needs to go, then?" Savannah's eyes glistened.

"That's up to you." Dustin reached over and clasped her hand. "But maybe that's the best plan."

"It's up to you, too." Savannah looked at Brooke, then Pancake. "We're getting married next week."

"That soon?" Pancake asked.

She nodded. "With all this going on, I need something stable in my life. So does Dustin." She squeezed his hand. "We're getting married anyway, so why not just do it and get it behind us? Plus, I know nothing about running a real estate business. Dustin does."

CHAPTER 54

FOR PANCAKE, a typical Sunday varied little from any other day of the week. Except, rather than Ray's place, the Longly Investigations de facto office, he opted to work from home. Still, he worked. A habit he couldn't break. Never big on unproductive time. Unlike Jake, who could while away hours doing nothing. It was a gift, and on some levels, he envied that. The ability to take things as they came and not sweat the details.

The last twenty-four hours had been downtime, and that always made him antsy.

Yesterday, after leaving Savannah's home, he and Brooke decided that moving the investigation forward hinged on the firearm investigators' assessment of the recovered weapon. That wouldn't happen until Monday at the earliest. Peters had rushed it, but over the weekend, limited staff meant that little would be done.

Since they had nothing to do, Brooke suggested they enjoy the day and each other. Pancake didn't argue.

They drove out to Mobile Point and visited Fort Morgan. The pentangular structure, built after the War of 1812 and used during the Civil War, was a popular tourist destination. Today, the bright sun, clear blue sky, and warm breeze made for a perfect beach day, making the crowd sparse. They navigated the ramparts, explored the arched interior tunnels, and investigated the various cannons that littered the park.

They ventured down to the shoreline, sat on the sand, and watched the sailboats glide in and out of Mobile Bay through the gap between Mobile Point and Dauphin Island. Work not even a consideration, both content to enjoy the day.

Late afternoon, they drove back into Gulf Shores and to the Flora-Bama for drinks and blues. As the sun set, they rolled over to Brooke's condo, ordered pizza, watched a movie, and fell into bed.

A perfect Saturday.

This morning, after a stop at Captain Rocky's for free breakfast, they drove to Pancake's place. Brooke donned a skimpy bathing suit and stretched out on a deck lounge chair, soaking in the sun. Pancake sat next to her, working his laptop.

"I like your place better than mine," Brooke said. "Better views."

"I bought it when beachfront places around here were affordable."

"You made a good choice."

"A few sketchy neighbors though."

"Oh?" Brooke turned her head his way, lowered her sunglasses to peer over them.

"Jake lives a couple of hundred yards that way." He pointed west. "Drags down the property values."

"You pick on him too much."

"Nothing the boy doesn't deserve. He's a target-rich environment."

"Boys and their antics."

"Boy? Did you forget last night?"

She rolled to her side and looked at him. "Not for a minute. Doesn't mean you two aren't sophomoric." She smiled. "Not that I'm complaining."

"You need some more sunscreen?" Pancake asked.

"You just did that."

He bounced an eyebrow. "Might need a little extra rubbing in. Don't want you to burn."

"Ha. You're just trying to get me back in bed."

"So?"

Thirty minutes later, they rolled out of bed and back to the deck. Suntan lotion reapplied, Peters lay on her stomach and soon dozed. Pancake kept at it. His rummaging through the information he had downloaded from Dustin's phone became progressively interesting.

"Bingo," he said. Brooke stirred. He nudged her shoulder. "You need to see this."

She swung to a sitting position. "What is it?"

Pancake stood, his laptop in hand. "Let's go inside, out of the sunlight, so you can see it better."

They sat next to each other at the kitchen table.

"One thing that's bothered me," said Pancake, "is the timing. We established that the security camera at Carl's office and the one at the grocery store were accurate. Within a minute, anyway. The call Dustin made to Savannah matches the time the video showed him leaving the office parking lot."

Brooke nodded. "Okay."

"From the office to the store is a five-minute drive. Ten at the most. It took Dustin twenty-five minutes."

"You sure?"

"I am. The time stamps are reliable."

"Why did it take so long?" Brooke asked.

"Why do you think?"

She squared her shoulders. "He backtracked."

"Exactly. Look at this." He pointed to the computer screen, which displayed a map of the area around Carl's office. "This is what took so long. Getting into his GPS data isn't as easy as his phone records. See these red dots?"

"Yeah."

"Each represents one minute of time. Dustin left the office, turned that way." His finger traced the route. "He turned here, maneuvered around the block, and then looped back to the office. He stopped here in that sandy area behind the building. He remained there for eight minutes."

"You're amazing."

Pancake bounced an eyebrow. "I am. Anyway, he then headed back up Perdido Beach Boulevard and to the store."

"Dustin killed Carl."

"Looks that way. He at least returned to the office."

"Which he said he didn't. A lie is a lie and is often as good as a confession." Peters leaned back in her chair. "Do you think Savannah was involved?"

Pancake shrugged. "I hope not, but it's possible."

"They stand to gain the entire company. If we put this together, they learned of Mitch's thefts, knew that the agreement would lead to a forfeiture of his holdings in the company. I know they denied that, but again, a lie is a lie. Now Savannah, and Dustin, after next week's wedding, will own the place lock, stock, and barrel."

"That's how I see it."

"I need to call Scoggins," Peters said.

"Let's wait on the firearms report. If the gun we pulled from the bayou is the murder weapon, and if by some miracle we can place it in Dustin's hand, you'll have a tight case."

CHAPTER 55

NICOLE AND I had had a great weekend. Creatures of habit, we were up late Saturday night with dinner at Captain Rocky's, followed by tequila, the hot tub, and bed at Nicole's. Repetitive? Sure. Perfect? You bet.

Sunday we drove up to Fairhope and had lunch at Stella's Bistro before strolling down to Mullins Bakery to see the owner Allison Mullins. The reason for our visit twofold: to see how Allison was doing and to pick up a box of her latest creations for Pancake. Croissants, blueberry muffins, Danishes, and bear claws.

Back in Gulf Shores, we stopped by Captain Rocky's for a couple of drinks and dinner, followed by the fun part: tequila, hot tub, and Nicole. Did I say creatures of habit? Not that I'm complaining. It was a good conditioning program. Hot tubbing and bedsheet surfing with Nicole rivaled most Olympic events.

Monday came too early. Didn't it always? Not that my Mondays differed from any other day of the week. But today, Nicole and I slept in and didn't roll out of bed until after eight. We would've slept longer, but Pancake called asking if we were bringing him burritos today. He, too, a creature of habit. After assuring him we had something special for him, he grunted, and said hurry. We clamored out of bed and into the shower. Together. But Nicole wouldn't let me play, saying we needed to get a move on as an impatient and hypoglycemic Pancake was too much to handle on a Monday morning.

She had a point.

At Ray's, I tossed the bag of goodies on the table near Pancake. "Something from one of your fans."

"Which one? I have a lot." He opened the bag. "Oh, Allison. She's the best woman on the planet." He tugged a bear claw out and took a massive bite.

"What's new?" I asked as Nicole and I sat.

"Lots," Pancake said. Another bite of bear claw. "Dustin Hobson worked his way to the top of the suspect list."

"What?" Nicole said. "How?"

Pancake went over his GPS findings.

"I can't believe it," I said. "He backtracked and killed Carl?"

"Looks that way," Ray said.

"Please tell me Savannah's not involved," Nicole said.

Pancake finished the bear claw and grabbed a muffin, taking a bite. "Don't know."

That lowered a curtain of silence that lingered.

Savannah? I didn't want to see that. Sure, she stood to gain the most, but killing her father? I couldn't grasp it. Everything pointed to this being financially driven with Mitch Littlefield the triggerman. The truth? Savannah and Dustin had even more to gain than Mitch. Once they wrenched the other half of the company and the monies stashed in the Caymans from Mitch's hands.

Nicole broke the silence. "What about the gun? Anything on that?"

"Not yet," Pancake said, muffin gone, Danish in hand. "Brooke's over with the firearms techs. She seemed to think they had something, but she wasn't sure what. She'll be along soon."

While we waited, I made a pot of coffee. Everybody had some except Ray, who opted for another Mountain Dew. Thirty minutes later, Brooke called. Said she was on the way and that she had news.

Did she ever.

I poured her a cup of coffee and Pancake shared his goodies, allowing her to take a blueberry muffin. That's true love for Pancake. She sat, took a bite, a sip, and began.

"The gun is the murder weapon. One hundred percent. The test matched the bullet extracted from Carl at autopsy."

"Tossed where Dustin returned and parked for several minutes," I said.

Brooke nodded. "Even better, the guys found several prints. Most were smeared, but a few are usable."

"Really?" Ray asked. "That's surprising."

"Not on the gun itself." Brooke took a bite, chasing a crumb that tried to escape. "The magazine and three of the bullets inside."

"TV," Pancake said. "Too much TV. Killers wipe down the gun like they do on those cop shows. But they forget they handled the magazine and the ammo."

"So now we need Dustin's prints to compare," Brooke said.

"I assumed you printed everyone at the realty company," Ray said.

"We did, but a couple of folks were away, vacation, that kind of thing. Another few haven't come in for printing yet. Including Dustin."

"Really?" I asked.

Brooke shrugged. "It wasn't a top priority since we had nothing to compare the prints with. Except for that rear door handle. We found a pair of matches. The two office smokers. Everyone agreed they were the only ones who used that door."

"They were cleared?" Ray asked.

"They were. One was at a nursing home tending to her mother and the other finishing up an open house in Pensacola at the time of the murder."

"So, you need Dustin's prints?" I said.

"Savannah's too."

"But she was at home when it happened," Nicole said.

Brooke nodded. "That's what they both said. Doesn't mean it's true, though." She shrugged. "Maybe she loaded the gun for Dustin."

I looked at Pancake. "I thought you said the call was in his cell phone call log."

"It was. And someone answered. We just don't know who. Savannah or an answering machine. It lasted forty-three seconds. Enough time for her to tell him what she needed from the store. Or enough for him to leave a message. Or create an alibi for her."

That made sense. No way to know who answered, only that a connection occurred.

"They probably talked and Savannah was probably home," Brooke said. "If so, that'd be the end of that story. Still, I'd like to have Savannah's prints. To be complete." She shrugged. "But what if Dustin's the shooter, and Savannah loaded the gun for him?"

"She'd be an accessory," Pancake said.

"Can't you simply ask them?" Nicole said.

"I could," Brooke said. "It might spook them and they might refuse, which would generate a subpoena. They might lawyer up and fight tooth and nail."

"So we trick them into giving up their prints," Pancake said.

"You got it. I guess it means following them around."

"What about the gun?" Ray asked. "Any idea where and by who it was purchased?"

"You remember Ed Moran and Carlos Rivera? You met them at the crime scene."

"Sure."

"They did a hell of a job. The gun was originally purchased by a local farmer in Tallahassee. Two years ago. He sold it to his cousin in Macon, Georgia, who then sold it at a gun show in Waycross. It moved into obscurity after that. So, it's likely Dustin, or whoever, got it at a gun show."

"A dead end," Ray said.

Peters nodded. "Seriously dead."

"Back to the fingerprints," I said. "I have an idea."

CHAPTER 56

MY PLAN, simple but with a few moving parts that needed choreography. Good thing I had an ensemble cast: Nicole, Pancake, Brooke, my manager Carla, and employee Libby Sagstrom. I figured we had scammed Dustin once with Pancake grabbing his cell phone data, so why not again?

The first, and most crucial, step—getting Savannah and Dustin onboard. Lunch at Captain Rocky's to go over the case and plan the next steps. Decisions needed to be made. No problem for Savannah, but Dustin balked, saying he had a full plate. Thus, lunch. A time he would be away from his desk anyway, so why not meet and get an update and a free meal? He agreed. Major hurdle crossed.

Nicole and I arrived early. So did Pancake and Brooke. Carla and Libby prepped six smooth-surfaced water glasses wiped clean of residual prints, as were the plastic menu covers. They set my table for six, arrayed the glasses, plates, and utensils, and placed the menus over the folded napkins that lay on each plate.

All set.

We took our seats, leaving two with the best view for Savannah and Dustin. Savannah appeared first.

"Dustin called," Savannah said. "He just left the office, so he'll be another fifteen minutes."

"No problem," Pancake said. "I ordered some nachos and a platter of fried calamari."

Savannah sat. "Sounds good. I'm starving."

Carla appeared. "What can I get you to drink?"

Savannah nodded toward Nicole's margarita. "One of those would be good." She picked up her menu, scanned it, turned it over, and then extended it toward Carla. "I don't think I'll need this. I'm having those wonderful fish tacos."

Carla grasped the right upper corner of the menu between her thumb and forefinger. Smooth and natural. "Back in a sec."

"So, what's new?" Savannah asked.

"Let's wait for Dustin," Brooke said.

Savannah gulped half of her water. "I went for a run this morning. I'm dehydrated."

"Drink up," I said. "We have plenty more."

"I would hope so." She drained her glass.

Libby appeared, a fresh glass of water on a small tray. Savannah took it, then placed her empty on the tray.

Okay, so far, so good. Savannah's menu and glass collected. But the main event was yet to come. I glanced at my watch. Time for Dustin to show.

Five minutes later, he did. Just as Libby placed the nachos and calamari on the table.

"Perfect timing," I said.

"Sorry," Dustin said. "A talkative client showed up as I was getting ready to leave. Took a while to get away."

"What can I get you to drink?" Libby asked Dustin.

"I'm good with water." He took a sip. "I have a few meetings this afternoon and need to be clearheaded." Another sip of water.

"Oh," Libby said. "That glass has a chip."

It did indeed. A small one along the lip. Libby's idea. Gave her an excuse to take away the glass. Clever.

Dustin examined it. "It's small."

Libby picked it up with her fingers just touching the rim. "I'll get a fresh one."

We dug into the calamari and nachos and sipped our margaritas and waters. Libby returned with a fresh glass for Dustin.

"Here you go," she said. "How is everything?"

"Marvelous," Savannah said.

"Ready to order lunch?"

"The fish tacos for me," Savannah said.

The rest of us ordered while Dustin examined the menu, flipping it back and forth. Excellent. Lots of prints. He settled on fried catfish and cole slaw. He passed his menu to Libby, who like Carla, grasped its right upper edge. She headed toward the kitchen.

Brooke excused herself, saying she needed to call her office. I stood, saying I needed to talk to the kitchen staff. We walked to the kitchen, where Carla stood guard over the menus and glasses. We emptied the glasses and inserted them into the evidence bags Brooke had brought. Each getting its own. Brooke labeled them.

Mission accomplished.

For the next forty-five minutes, we enjoyed lunch, while Brooke brought Savannah and Dustin up to date. Mitch still occupied the top spot on the suspect list, but Tucker Moss also made the cut.

"I thought he had an alibi," Savannah said.

"Someone who works for him," Peters said. "Patrick McCall's a meth user who might be under Tucker's thumb, might even be afraid of him, and might lie for him"

I watched Dustin while Brooke spoke. He seemed calm. Relieved? Confident that he wasn't a suspect. Only the tapping of his index finger on the tabletop suggested any anxiety.

He didn't look like a killer. Not angry or aggressive. He looked younger than his age, and innocent. Did that facade hide someone clever enough to engineer this entire thing? My gaze shifted to Savannah. She hung on everything Brooke said. Was she part of the conspiracy?

"Let me ask you," Brooke said to Dustin. "Have you seen anything in Mitch's behavior since we confronted him about the missing funds? Anything that's off color? Any change in his activities or conversations or alterations in his work habits?"

"Some," Dustin said. "He's quieter and more subdued. He still does his job but maybe with a little less enthusiasm." He took a sip of water. "My read is that's due to him knowing that I, and even more so Savannah, know what he did. He came into my office yesterday and apologized. Profusely. Said he wasn't sure why he did it. That it wasn't who he was." He glanced at Savannah. "He asked if he should talk with Savannah and apologize to her. I said that he might want to give it a little more time. He, of course, asked if I knew what Savannah was going to do. As far as invoking the contract and ousting him."

"What did you say?" I asked.

"That she hadn't decided. That it was still up in the air."

"Is it?" Brooke asked Savannah.

"I'm not sure what to do." Savannah dropped her gaze to her lap. "I wish I could ask my father. He'd know how to handle it." She looked up, her eyes now glassy. "God, I miss him so much."

Dustin draped an arm around her shoulder. "It'll take time."

Lunch completed, Nicole and I walked Savannah and Dustin out to their cars. We said our goodbyes, and each drove away.

Pancake and Brooke then came out, carrying four evidence bags.

"We're off to the lab," Brooke said.

"Mind if we tag along?" I asked.

"Sure." She smiled. "Just don't touch anything."

CHAPTER 57

SO, WE WERE BACK at the Orange Beach Police Department. Seemed like a daily event. Brooke delivered the evidence bags to the lab and then joined us in the conference room.

"This won't take long," Brooke said. "I got our best print guy on it. Maybe half an hour tops."

Scoggins came in and grabbed a seat. "Where do we stand?"

Brooke ran through everything. The prints on the magazine and shell casings. How we engineered grabbing Dustin's and Savannah's prints at lunch. Now waiting on the lab to do their thing.

"Clever move inviting them to lunch," Scoggins said. "Better than following them around. Or spooking them with a subpoena."

"Jake's idea," Nicole said.

He nodded to me. "Good move."

"He has a few of those." Nicole mussed my hair. "Sometimes he's too clever for his own good, but this time I think he did well."

Yes, I did. That's me, Jake the Clever P.I.

Scoggins glanced at his watch, stood. "I have a meeting. Keep me in the loop."

"Will do," Brooke said as she also stood. "I'll run down to the lab and see where they stand."

For the next half hour, we waited. Nicole fidgety, Pancake hungry, me bored.

Brooke returned, a smile on her face. "We have a match. No doubt."

"So Dustin killed his future father-in-law?" I asked.

"He did."

"A diabolical SOB," Pancake said. "Kills Carl, gets Mitch tossed out on a morals clause, marries Savannah, gets the entire company."

"That puts Savannah in danger," Nicole said. "I mean, if he went this far, planned all of this, wouldn't it make sense to get rid of Savannah and take complete control of the estate and the business?"

"Unless she's involved," Brooke said.

Nicole shook her head. "I don't think so."

Brooke shrugged. "I hope you're right, but we won't know until we know."

"What's the plan?" Pancake asked.

"I called the DA. He's working on an arrest warrant right now. Should be a slam dunk, but you never know."

"How long will that take?" Nicole asked.

"He's rushing it. He's already sent the probable cause affidavit to the judge and is waiting for a call back. He said it'll be a few minutes, a half hour max."

"If the judge agrees," Pancake said.

"With what we have, he will."

"Then what?" I asked.

"We arrest Dustin."

"What about Savannah?" Nicole asked.

"If you mean are we going to arrest her too, the answer is no. We have nothing on her. But we need to make sure she's safe before we go for Dustin."

Brooke's cell buzzed. She answered, listened, and then thanked the caller. "The warrant's granted so we're good to go."

"It's just four o'clock," Nicole said. "Savannah's probably at home and I suspect Dustin's still in his office."

Pancake nodded toward Nicole and me. "You guys go over and make sure Savannah's safe. We'll head over to the office and grab Dustin."

"If he's in his office," Brooke said.

"One way to find out." I pulled out my iPhone. "I'll call."

"And say what?" Brooke said. "We don't want to spook him."

"I'll ask him if Mitch is there. Tell him to play it cool, but that you have a warrant for Mitch's arrest. That way, when you guys show up, he won't freak out and do something stupid."

Peters smiled, nodded. "Another good idea. You're on a roll today."

"My clever little boy," Nicole said.

As with most barbs Nicole flung my way, I had no response. In the past, I might've tried, but I learned that firing back only made things worse. Better to take the hit and move on. I called the realty company.

What I learned was that Dustin wasn't in the office. He had a four-thirty appointment in Destin and would then head home. I assured the receptionist that it wasn't urgent, that I didn't need to leave a message, and that I'd call him tomorrow.

That changed things. Brooke decided we would all go to Savannah's house, isolate and protect her, and wait for Dustin to show.

Seemed like a solid plan. Clean and easy. Yet, this was Ray's world. Fingers of unease crept up my spine.

CHAPTER 58

THE PLAN WAS SOLID, and simple.

The plan fell apart before it started.

I blamed it on Ray. Pancake called him and with perfect timing, he drove up the street along with the rest of the armada. Nicole and I in her car, Pancake and Brooke in his massive truck, Ray in his '66 Camaro, and Ed Moran and Carlos Rivera in a marked squad car.

An intimidating force. Which didn't work well in this situation.

We hoped to get Savannah out, Nicole and I take her to safety, and then everyone would scatter. Except for Brooke and her officers, who would remain inside and wait for Dustin. After they parked the patrol car around the corner and out of sight. Dustin would have no clue what awaited him, making the takedown less risky. I mean, Dustin had already used a weapon on Carl, and though he tossed it, he might have another. I flashed on the nickel-plated .38 revolver we had seen in Carl's desk drawer. Did Dustin know it was there?

What we hadn't counted on was Dustin being home. We rolled up to an open garage door, Dustin climbing from his car. When he saw us, particularly the patrol car, surprise erupted on his face.

What was he doing here? Did he stop by before his appointment? Was his meeting canceled?

This was not going well.

Without hesitation, Dustin raced to the door between the garage and the house, punched the button, and the garage door descended.

Have you ever seen an eight-hundred-pound grizzly bear run? Maybe on the National Geographic Channel? Hard to believe that half a ton of muscle and teeth and claws could move like that.

Same with Pancake. He flew from his truck and sprinted toward the descending door before I even knew what was happening. He hooked a foot beneath it, stopping and reversing its direction.

Dustin was gone.

Inside.

With Savannah.

Brooke called for backup but with the same breath said, "We aren't waiting."

"There's a gun in there," I said.

"It's in the top left drawer of Carl's desk," Nicole added.

"Great," Brooke said. "That changes things." She looked at Moran. "Let's do this by the book."

Moran and Rivera entered the garage, guns drawn. They reached the door that I knew entered the kitchen.

Moran took the lead. He cracked open the door, standing to one side. "Police. Dustin Hobson, we have a warrant for your arrest. Come out now. Keep your hands where we can see them."

Nothing.

Not that I expected Dustin would walk out and wait to be cuffed.

No doubt he knew the gig was up. Why else would all of us be there? It hadn't taken him long to do the math and react. Now, Moran had announced the warrant, erasing any remaining doubts.

But what would he do? He had no place to run so was this the hill where he would make his stand? Did he know where Carl kept his gun? Did he have it? Was he waiting for someone to come through the door?

Where was Savannah? In the line of fire? Would Dustin go quietly or duke it out in a gun battle that might take Savannah with him?

This smelled like every Ray situation I'd ever seen.

Brooke and Pancake approached the front door. She held her service weapon, Pancake the Glock he kept beneath his truck's seat.

Brooke went through the "come out, hands up" stuff, and she too got no response. She and Pancake flanked the door. She grasped the handle and pushed it open with one foot. Brooke peered around the jamb, gun extended ahead of her. They disappeared inside. Moran and Rivera did the same through the door to the kitchen.

"Wait here," Ray said. He jogged to his right and disappeared around the corner of the house.

"Let's go," Nicole said. She took off after Ray.

What happened to wait here? Wasn't that the smart thing to do? So many armed people running around, trying to take down an armed killer. Staying here, right here, shielded by Pancake's truck, seemed a reasonable option to me.

Nicole raced around the corner.

I followed.

A pea gravel pathway extended between the side of the house and a ten-foot wall of privacy shrubs toward the rear of the property. Lemon-sized stones lined the gravel. I scooped up two of them and moved up beside Nicole. Angled sunlight bathed the flagstone deck. The living room sliders stood open. Ray knelt behind the cook center near the edge of the deck, his gun leveled toward the house.

Staying low, we moved to his side.

"I told you to stay out front," Ray said.

"Tell her," I said.

"Here to help, boss," she said.

"Then stay down, and say nothing."

This vantage point gave us a view inside. Dustin stood with his back to us, Savannah's hair wadded in one fist, her body pulled against his, a gun muzzle pressed against her neck. Pancake and Brooke faced the couple. Behind them stood Moran and Rivera. Guns wagged in every direction.

"Put it down, Dustin." Brooke's voice.

"Let Savannah go." Pancake talking now.

"Then what?" Dustin said. "We sit down and have coffee?"

"If you want," Brooke said.

"Fuck that." Dustin's voice tight. "You leave. I'll get an attorney and then we can talk."

"We can't do that until you let Savannah go," Brooke said.

"Please, Dustin," Savannah pleaded. "Don't make things worse."

Dustin released an explosive laugh. "I don't think things can get much worse."

"They can," Pancake said. "There's no need for anyone else to get hurt."

"Listen to them," Savannah said. "Please do what they say."

"I'm not going to jail," Dustin said. "No way that's happening."

Savannah sobbed. "Why? Why are you doing this?"

"For us."

"What? For us? Are you insane?"

"I had to do it," Dustin said. "Carl was old and backward-thinking. He couldn't see the real future. The one that would make us millions."

"Don't tell me you killed my father for money," Savannah said. She tried to twist away, but he yanked her hair, pulling her even tighter against him.

"What else is there?"

"My father. My family."

"I'm your family. Your only family."

This was unraveling. Dustin's voice seemed strained to the snapping point. His brain too. Like a trapped animal. Unpredictable, scared, and angry.

Dustin walked backwards, dragging Savannah with him. "Leave this house," he said. He moved through the open sliders and onto the deck. I wasn't sure where he thought he was going. He had no escape route.

Pancake and Peters shuffled forward.

Dustin put the gun to his own head. "I'll kill her and then myself," he screamed. His hand shook as he returned the muzzle to Savannah's neck. "I swear I will. Now get the fuck out of here. Now." The last word a screech.

Something needed to be done. Peters and Pancake exchanged a look. Ray steadied his weapon on top of the grill cover.

Dustin didn't know we were behind him. Not sure how much of an advantage that was, but it was something.

"Or maybe I'll start with you," Dustin said. He pointed the gun at Pancake and Peters.

Neither flinched.

Dustin seemed confused by their lack of reaction. He waved the gun back and forth. "I'm going to count to five and then I'll kill everyone."

Ray leveled his weapon. The muscles of his forearm tightened.

"One," Dustin said. "Two. I mean it. Three."

I stood and tossed the rock in my left hand into the pool. It hit with a splash. Startled, Dustin whirled that way.

Things happened fast.

Savannah jerked free, staggered. Dustin reached for her.

Nicole bolted toward them, head lowered. She literally tackled Savannah, taking her down hard.

I launched the other rock I held at Dustin's head. A little low, it struck his throat with a thud. His back arched, a wheezing breath escaped. He recovered, saw me, and swung his weapon my way.

Uh-oh.

The concussive explosion to my right was more palpable than audible. Savannah screamed. A black hole appeared in Dustin's forehead. He froze in suspended animation, before crumpling into a wadded mass. His gun clattered on the flagstone deck.

CHAPTER 59

A HELL OF A DAY. No other way to put it. Gunfire, hurled stones, Nicole tackling Savannah, a gun pointed at my face, Dustin dead. Unnerving but a typical day with Ray.

To unwind, Nicole and I downed a pitcher of margaritas at Captain Rocky's. Where else? We needed familiar, comfortable. We then drove to my place rather than motoring out to The Point. A barefoot walk on the beach, the warm Gulf waters swirling around our feet, the night sky filled with stars. A quick shower before we nestled beneath the covers. Nicole lay against me, her head on my chest.

"Dustin planned this for a while," I said.

"You think?"

"He didn't dream this scheme up over the weekend. Too many moving parts. He had to get the gun, pick the date, make sure everything would point to Mitch."

"Which means he knew more about Mitch's embezzling than he admitted."

"The partnership agreement, too."

She looked up at me. "That makes sense."

"Carl was preparing him to be more involved in the company and to eventually take over his responsibilities. He probably discussed the partnership contract with him and showed where he would fit in. What changes would have to be made if Dustin became a full partner."

"Which means that Dustin would know about the morals clause and that Savannah, and him, would take over the entire company if Mitch went down."

"I think Carl brought him into the whole Mitch mess early on. Not just a couple of days and not just superficially. With Dustin's financial and accounting background, Carl probably wanted his take on things long before he hired Ray. So, Dustin saw Mitch as the perfect scapegoat. He stole money, had everything to lose, and if Carl ended up dead, Mitch became the perfect fall guy."

"All he needed was the perfect time to pull it off."

"Last Monday fit that. Dustin even set up Mitch to be his alibi. Them leaving together was clever."

She gave a nod. "Before, we wondered why Mitch would've left behind the information that implicated him. Why wouldn't he take it with him after killing Carl? Then try to erase all evidence of his activities."

"But Dustin would want all the evidence found since it would strengthen the case against Mitch," I said.

"He also knew Mitch would go straight home, and since he lived alone, he'd have no alibi."

"That's irony for you. Mitch makes a good alibi for Dustin, while not having one for himself."

She raised up on one elbow, looked at me. "Was killing Savannah part of his plan?"

"I don't know. If he believed that gave him total control, then maybe. But if he figured her death would be too suspicious to chance, maybe not. Probably not necessary anyway. Once they got married, he would control the entire company, and Carl's estate."

"He is one diabolical SOB," Nicole said.

"But not as clever as he thought."

She sighed. "It gives me a headache to think about it."

I smiled. "I can fix that."

She rolled on top of me. "Why don't you?"

CHAPTER 60

FOUR WEEKS LATER, Nicole and I sat in Savannah's living room. It was nearing six p.m. and she had opened a bottle of merlot to go with the tray of cheeses and salamis that sat before us on the coffee table.

"I wanted to thank you for everything," Savannah said.

"I think Pancake and Brooke Peters did most of the work," I said.

"But your support through all of this has been amazing and oh so comforting. It hasn't been an easy month."

File that under understatement.

Savannah continued. "The first few days I spent in a knot on my bed. Trying to make sense of things. Losing my father and my fiancé in one week was a bit much. But then I pulled myself together. I realized I had a business to run. Learn to run anyway. I didn't have time for self-pity."

Definitely a chip off Carl's block. He would be proud.

"How's that going?" I asked.

"It's going. A process for sure."

"You'll do fine," Nicole added.

"I hope. What I still can't believe is how badly I misjudged Dustin. I was stupid. I've racked my brain for some clue as to his true makeup." She sighed. "I came up with nothing."

"Some people hide things well," Nicole said. "It's like they're two people in one. My take on you is that you see the good in everyone. Not the dark edges."

"Trust me, this has been a reality check." She looked at Nicole. "I can't thank you enough for introducing me to Denise Scholander. We've gotten together a few times and are becoming fast friends."

"I hoped that would be the case."

"We are so much alike. Plus, we both loved my dad." She looked at me. "And you? Hitting Dustin with that rock? Amazing!" She smiled. "I guess you never lose your major league skills."

"I was aiming for his head."

"Your father took care of that." She shrugged. "I included a thank-you note with the check I sent." She took a sip of wine. "The best money I ever spent."

"What are you going to do now?" Nicole asked.

"Become a career woman." She laughed. "Hopefully. I guess we'll see. Right now, I'm a fish out of water." She brushed a wayward strand of hair from her forehead. "It's something I resisted for years. My father wanted me to be involved in the business, but I never could warm to the idea." She shrugged. "I wish I had. Then I'd know what I was doing. Plus, I could've worked with my father. I'll forever regret that."

"Don't look back," Nicole said. "Old choices are simply old choices. They can't be changed."

"That's exactly what I'm trying to do. I've already begun the classes I need to get a broker's license, and exploring options for getting an MBA degree."

"What about Mitch?" I asked.

"I invoked the morals clause. He didn't contest it at all. I now own the entire company. Signed, sealed, and delivered. He also returned the company's stolen funds."

"Do you plan to file any charges against him?" Nicole asked.

She shook her head. "The opposite. I hired him to manage the agency. At least until I get up to speed. And maybe beyond."

Not what I expected. "Really?"

"No one knows the company better than him."

"Can you trust him?"

"I think so. He was so broken up by what he did. Remorseful and then some. I don't see him ever doing anything like that again. That said, I've hired an outside accounting firm to take care of the books and the cash flow monitoring and all that money stuff."

"Smart move," I said.

This coming from me who possessed no clue how my restaurant worked or how much money it made or really anything about it. I had Carla to take care of that. Maybe Mitch could be Savannah's Carla. To a point.

"I'm also hiring Denise," Savannah said. "She knows nothing about real estate, but she knows people and marketing. I'm arranging for her to get her license and become part of Orange Coast Realty."

"You're amazing," Nicole said. "To take on all of this."

"You know what they say, adversity brings out either the best or the worst in everyone."

"I'd go with best in your case," I said.

NOTE FROM THE PUBLISHER

We trust that you enjoyed *Unbalanced*, the seventh novel in the Jake Longly Thriller Series. While the other six novels stand on their own and can be read in any order, the publication sequence is as follows:

Deep Six

Jake Longly and Nicole Jamison explode onto the thriller scene in *Deep Six* when their quiet Alabama shore town takes on corruption, vendettas and cartels—complete with murders and lavish yachts.

"Corruption, vendettas, cartel killers, oh my! *Deep Six* puts the fun back into late-night reading with this fast-paced romp through murder and mayhem. Prepare to flip the pages."

—Lisa Gardner,
New York Times best-selling author

A-List

Reluctant P.I. Jake Longly and his girlfriend, Nicole Jamison, head to New Orleans and an A-list actor who woke up on location with a dead girl in his bed.

"D. P. Lyle hits it over the fence with *A-List*. This mystery, featuring former Major League pitcher and reluctant P.I. Jake Longly, is fast-paced, slick, and funny. Bad times in the Big Easy mean a great time for readers. Head to New Orleans with Jake, and enjoy the trip."

—Meg Gardiner,
best-selling author

Sunshine State

Sunshine State throws Jake and Nicole into the bizarre case of a convicted serial killer who now claims: Two of those seven murders I confessed to are not mine—but I won't tell you which two.

"*Sunshine State* sizzles with just the right mix of action and mystery, a rollicking roller-coaster ride on a track lined with thrills and spills."

—Jon Land,
USA Today best-selling author

Rigged

Rigged finds Jake and Nicole trying to sort out the murder of Jake's best friend Tommy "Pancake" Jeffers' first love from back in the sixth grade.

"Snappy dialogue, fun characters, smart writing, a juicy mystery—all had me flipping pages until I reached The End. Jake and Nicole remind me of my favorite mystery duo, Nick and Nora Charles, with a modern twist. The Jake Longly series never fails to entertain."

—Allison Brennan,
New York Times best-selling author

The OC

Jake's and Nicole's fun in *The OC* is rudely interrupted when Nicole's girlfriend triggers a desperate search for a deadly stalker.

"*The OC* is a poignant and wickedly funny tale. Lyle's prose is stylish, smart, and compelling. Another grand slam in an immensely entertaining series."

—Sheldon Siegel,
New York Times best-selling author

Cultured

Jake Longly is dragged into a private investigation he wants no part of when a girl goes missing from a cultlike resort—is she the only one?

"Starts innocently with whimsical humor, but turns dark. The dark side of *Cultured* seems to tear a page from Jeffrey Epstein and Ghislane Maxwell's rap sheet."

—*Bookreporter*

We hope that you will read the entire Jake Longly Thriller Series and will look forward to more to come.

If you liked *Unbalanced*, we would be very appreciative if you would consider leaving a review. As you probably already know, book reviews are important to authors and they are very grateful when a reader makes the special effort to write a review, however brief.

For more information, please visit the author's website.
www.dplylemd.com

Happy Reading,
Oceanview Publishing
Your Home for Mystery, Thriller, and Suspense